The Cost of the Impossible

Harry A Minter

First published in 2025 by Blossom Spring Publishing
The Cost of the Impossible Copyright © 2025 Harry A Minter
ISBN 978-1-0684329-9-6
E: admin@blossomspringpublishing.com
W: www.blossomspringpublishing.com

Chapter One

John sat slumped in the cold, hard chair of the hospital room, his gaze fixed on the small still form lying on the sterile white bed. The square tiled ceiling lights above cast a harsh, unforgiving glow, illuminating every inch of the room with an almost surgical precision. Their relentless brightness felt invasive, exposing his raw grief to the indifferent walls. The quiet hum of medical equipment was a cruel mockery, their beeps and whirs continuing their rhythm even as Ethan's heartbeat had ceased. The broken silence filled the air, a constant, unnerving reminder of the fragility of life. John had been in this room for so long, he had lost track of time—time that seemed to stretch endlessly, looping back on itself in a never-ending spiral of grief and despair.

To John, time had lost all meaning, in fact everything had. Minutes bled into hours, hours into an abyss where past and present intertwined. John's mind drifted, unbidden, to the day Ethan was born. The tiny infant had gripped his finger with surprising strength, his newborn eyes blinking up as if trying to memorize his father's face. That memory was so vivid, so real, that for a fleeting moment, John half-expected Ethan to stir, to open his eyes and end this waking nightmare.

The doctors had come and gone, their faces grim, their words hushed and careful. They had done all they could, they said. But John knew better. There was nothing they could say now to bring back what he had lost. Ethan, his beautiful baby boy, lay there, his tiny chest no longer rising and falling with the breath of life. Reality was unforgiving. Ethan lay motionless, his cherubic face devoid of the mischief that had once danced in his eyes.

1

John reached out, his hand trembling, to brush a stray lock of hair from Ethan's forehead. The skin was cold, a stark contrast to the warmth that had once radiated from his lively son. A strangled sob escaped John's lips, the weight of his loss pressing down like a physical force.

John's mind again drifted back to happier times, memories that seemed to belong to another life, to another man. He saw Ethan's first smile, heard his joyous giggles, felt the warmth of his small, feeble breaths from those early, sleepy cuddles. Those moments felt like distant echoes now, faint and fading, swallowed by the overwhelming weight of the present. He wanted to scream, to rage against the unfairness of it all, but he couldn't find the strength. Instead, he sat in silence, his grief a heavy, suffocating blanket that smothered any semblance of hope.

The nurses moved skittishly around him, their expressions a mixture of sympathy and detachment. They had seen this before, countless times, and would see it again. But for John, this was singular, unique—a wound that would never heal. One nurse, a kind-faced woman with tired eyes, had placed a gentle hand on his shoulder, offering words of comfort that he couldn't remember. Her touch had been warm, but it had done little to penetrate the cold numbness that enveloped him.

John's eyes were drawn to the clock on the wall, its hands ticking away the seconds with a cruel, indifferent regularity. How many hours had passed? How many more would he have to endure? The room felt like a cage, the walls closing in around him, the air growing thin and oppressive. He stood up, his legs weak and unsteady, and walked back over to the bed. He reached out and touched Ethan's cheek once more, the skin cool and pale under his fingertips.

A tear traced a slow path down John's face, falling silently onto the sheet. He wanted to say something, to find the right words, but his throat was tight with emotion, and all that came out was a choked sob. He sank to his knees beside the bed, his head bowed, his shoulders shaking with the force of his sorrow.

In the corridor outside and beyond, life went on. Doctors and nurses moved with purpose, patients were wheeled from one place to another, and the world continued to turn. But inside that room, time stood still. John's world had come to a screeching halt. It had crashed entirely, and he was left to grapple with the unthinkable reality of his loss.

Hours had passed, unnoticed and uncounted. The light outside the window began to fade, the shadows lengthening and deepening as the day gave way to night. John stayed by Ethan's side, unwilling to leave, unable to let go. The hospital room, with its sterile walls and antiseptic smell, became a mausoleum, a place where the living clung to the dead, and where hope had no place.

As the darkness settled in, John knew he would never be the same. The man who had walked into the hospital with his baby boy was gone, replaced by someone hollowed out by grief, scarred by the cruel hand of fate. He would carry this night with him forever, a ghost that would haunt his every step, a reminder of all that he had lost.

He stood there solemnly, holding his once breathing baby in his arms. The hospital room echoed with the occasional beep of a machine or conversations outside the now open doorway, but John's world had plunged into a heavy silence. Utter sadness filled his insides as he looked at the lifeless form of his infant son, a tiny bundle of dreams now cold and still.

Tears rolled down John's cheek as he cradled the small body. "I can't let you go," he whispered, his voice breaking. "I just can't let go."

A soft knock interrupted his reverie. Nurse Clara, identifiable by her name tag and the gentle lines etched by years of empathising with grieving families, stepped in. Her eyes, a deep shade of hazel, reflected profound sorrow.

"Mr Morrison," she began softly, her voice barely above a whisper, "I ... I can't begin to express how sorry I am."

John didn't respond, his eyes still locked onto Ethan.

Clara hesitated before continuing, "Would you like some more time?"

He finally looked up, eyes red-rimmed and hollow. "Time," he echoed bitterly. "What good is time now?"

Clara took a tentative step forward. "Sometimes," she said, choosing her words carefully, "saying goodbye helps. Holding onto the good memories ..."

An unnatural flicker passed through the room, the lights dimming momentarily. John felt a sudden chill, as though a cold breeze had swept through, though the air remained still. He shuddered, dismissing it as a product of his exhaustion.

Clara, a woman in her early thirties with a calm, composed demeanour, wore the standard hospital uniform, designed for both functionality and comfort. She had on a pair of light blue scrubs made from a soft, breathable fabric, allowing her to move easily during her shift. The scrubs were well-fitted but not tight, with practical pockets at the top and sides of the trousers, containing a pen, a small notepad, and a pair of gloves. She approached John gently, her eyes heavy with sympathy.

"I think it's time to let go, sir. I'm sorry," she said, her words carrying the weight of the inevitable.

Anger surged within him, a volcanic eruption of frustration and despair. "I can't let him go!" he snapped, his voice laced with desperation.

Clara, alarmed, called for security, her voice trembling. Within moments, two large men entered the room, their stern expressions signalling the grim duty that lay ahead. Tom Reynolds and Mike Sanchez had arrived swiftly, their faces set with determination. They exchanged a brief, knowing glance before Tom took the lead. Both men wore navy-blue shirts with the hospital's security emblem on the left chest and a name tag stitched above the right pocket. Their shirts were tucked neatly into black cargo trousers. As they advanced, John's grief transformed into a blazing rage.

"I won't let you take him!" he shouted, clutching the baby tighter, his knuckles turning white.

"Mr Morrison," Tom said in a calm but authoritative voice, "we're here to help. We need to take Ethan now."

John's grip tightened around Ethan's tiny body. "No!" he shouted, his voice cracking. "You can't take him from me!"

Tom and Mike stepped closer, their hands raised in a placating gesture. "John," Mike said softly, "please let us help you. We can get you the support you need."

John's eyes darted between the two men, his breath coming in quick, shallow gasps. The pain and rage in his eyes were palpable. He felt cornered, like a wild animal ready to strike. "Stay back!" he warned, his voice a mix of desperation and fury.

Ignoring the warning, Tom moved in to gently take Ethan from John's arms. In a flash, John shifted his grip, clutching Ethan to his chest with one arm while pushing Tom away with surprising strength. Tom stumbled but quickly regained his footing.

"John, we don't want this to turn into something it doesn't need to be," Tom said, his voice firmer now.

Mike positioned himself to the side, ready to assist. "Just put Ethan down, and we can talk this through," he urged.

Seeing no other way out, John erupted. He lunged at Tom, using his free hand to shove him hard in the chest. Tom staggered back, but John's momentum carried him forward. John swung his elbow, catching Tom in the ribs. Tom grunted in pain but managed to stay upright.

Mike reacted instantly, stepping in to grab John's arm in an attempt to restrain him. John twisted violently, freeing himself from Mike's grip. He pivoted, bringing his knee up sharply into Mike's stomach. Mike doubled over, gasping for breath, but didn't go down.

Tom, recovering from the initial attack, tried to subdue John from behind. He wrapped his arms around John's chest, attempting to pin his arms. John thrashed wildly, Ethan still cradled protectively in his arm. The struggle was intense, with John's raw emotion fuelling his strength.

In the ensuing struggle, the baby slipped from John's arms, plummeting to the floor. A sound, like wood splitting in a bonfire, echoed through the room, freezing everyone in place. The room became a tableau of tragedy, with the shattered silence only broken by John's guttural cry.

An immediate, steely rage burned in John's eyes. Without a second thought, he lunged at the security guard with a savage intensity, punching him square in the jaw. Tom reeled, blood trickling from his split lip. John followed up with a flurry of blows, his fists a blur of desperate rage. Tom, dazed and bleeding, tried to block the punches, but John's assault was relentless.

Mike, recovering from the knee to his gut, saw his partner in trouble. He tackled John from the side, sending both of them crashing into the hospital bed. The metal frame rattled, and medical equipment clattered to the ground.

On the floor, John and Mike grappled fiercely. John used his elbows to strike Mike's sides, and Mike responded by trying to pin John's arms to the floor. They rolled, each struggling for dominance. John, driven by sheer desperation, managed to get his knee under Mike's ribcage and shoved him off with all his might.

Mike crashed into a nearby cabinet, the impact knocking him momentarily senseless. Tom, bruised and bleeding, tried to stand but wavered on his feet, his vision blurred.

Seizing the moment, John scrambled to his feet, and without uttering a word, he gathered his now cold, once beautiful child from the floor. His eyes were wild, a mixture of sorrow and madness. He glared at the two guards, who were struggling to recover, and then bolted for the door.

Tom, through the pain, called after him, "John, stop! Think about what you're doing!"

But John was beyond reason. He burst out of the hospital room, cradling Ethan, his mind set on his desperate mission to get out of there. The echoes of the struggle lingered in the room, a haunting reminder of the depths of a father's grief.

As the sun began to set, the wide, clinical corridors of Hull Royal Infirmary were bathed in a cold, artificial light that contrasted sharply with the darkening world outside. John stood at the end of one such corridor, holding Ethan's lifeless body in his arms. His mind was a whirlwind of emotions—grief, anger, desperation—but he moved with a singular purpose. He had to escape.

The corridor walls blurred as John, still holding onto Ethan's lifeless form, moved with a haste that defied the weight of grief. The dimly lit corridors, usually a maze of hope and healing, became a labyrinth fraught with the echoes of tragedy. Nurses and doctors moved with urgency, their faces etched with concern, but John's singular focus rendered their existence irrelevant. His eyes, burning with determination, saw only the path ahead.

John burst down a thin corridor, its walls an off-white colour with a blue border running along its entirety at hip height. The bright white lights overhead flickered ominously, casting unsettling shadows that seemed to chase him as he ran. His breath came in ragged gasps, the sound echoing off the hard surfaces, amplifying his sense of urgency. He didn't have time to think, to second-guess his actions. All he knew was that he had to keep moving, had to get away.

The door at the far end of the corridor loomed closer with every step. John didn't slow down as he reached it, instead raising a booted foot and kicking it open with a resounding crash. The door swung back with a groan, revealing a small platform. On his left, two escalators descended lazily, their mechanical hum at odds with his pounding heart. On his right, a winding staircase beckoned, its steps disappearing into the levels below.

John opted for the stairs, taking them two at a time, his hand skimming the cold metal railing to keep his balance. The walls here were the same clinical white, but the air felt different, heavier somehow, as if it was thick with the weight of unseen eyes. He tried to push the feeling away, focusing only on the rhythm of his feet hitting the steps and the pounding of his heart.

Three flights down, he finally reached the first floor. He didn't pause to catch his breath; he couldn't afford to. Ahead, the final staircase stretched out before him—a long, straight, automatic escalator with a descent that led to the heart of the atrium. Beyond it, he could see the automatic doors of the exit, their glass panes reflecting the harsh interior light.

John bolted down the stairs, not waiting for them to take him automatically, his eyes fixed on the doors. His legs burned with the effort, but he forced himself to keep going, driven by a need that was primal and all-consuming. As he neared the bottom, he prepared to weave his way through the crowd. The atrium was bustling, a sea of faces and bodies moving in every direction. He would have to blend in, disappear among them like a ghost.

His shoes slapped against the polished floor as he hit the last step. He slipped into the crowd, his movements swift and deliberate. People jostled him, their voices a dull roar in his ears, but he paid them no mind. Every step brought him closer to the exit, to freedom. He could see the doors now, so close he could almost taste the cool night air beyond them.

But then, something caught his eye—a reflection in

the glass of the doors. A figure, standing still amidst the chaos, watching him with a cold, calculated gaze. John's heart skipped a beat. He turned his head slightly, just enough to see the man in the reflection.

Tall and imposing, with a face that seemed carved from stone, the man was dressed in a dark suit that contrasted sharply with the bright surroundings. His eyes were hidden behind reflective sunglasses, but John could feel their intensity, the weight of their scrutiny. The man didn't move, didn't react, but John knew that he was there, and even amidst the chaos, John knew his presence was out of place.

A surge of adrenaline shot through John, sharpening his senses and quickening his pace. He ducked his head, trying to make himself smaller, less noticeable. The crowd became his shield, a living barrier between him and the man. He pushed forward, slipping past people, his eyes still fixed on the doors.

A nurse, her eyes scanning the crowd, approached him with a mix of concern and recognition. "Sir, you can't leave without proper discharge—"

"I can't let go!" John's voice, laced with desperation, cut through the nurse's words. His glare, a reflection of the rage within, met hers in a chilling confrontation.

Security guards alerted by the commotion converged on the scene. Two large men, their expressions stern, entered the atrium, locking in on the problem they were duty bound to respond to. As they advanced, John's grief transformed into a blazing rage.

"I won't let you take him!" he shouted, clutching Ethan tighter, his knuckles grinding as they turned white.

A burly security guard, now alarmed and closing in, became an obstacle in John's desperate escape. His large hand, fuelled by primal ferocity, clasped the oncoming guard's throat. The hospital atrium, once a sanctuary of healing, now bore witness to a struggle between grief-stricken determination and the forces seeking to uphold order.

"I won't let you take him from me!" John's voice, a fierce roar, reverberated through the atrium.

The atrium became a stage for chaos, the ordinary transformed into a scene from a nightmare.

The hospital's exit, a set of automatic doors, stood like a gateway to the unknown. John, carrying the weight of loss in his arms, approached with a haste accompanied by the heaviness of grief. The entryway flashed as he passed through, the world outside the hospital beckoning him with an unknown purpose.

However, the hospital's alarm had been raised, and the night air became charged with tension. Hospital staff, now aware of the disturbance, emerged from the building with a mix of shock and concern. Among them, a security detail, armed with determination and the mandate to restore order, fanned out to intercept John.

"Stop! You can't just leave!" one of the security guards called out, his voice echoing in the damp night air.

John, ignoring the plea, moved with a desperate swiftness. The crowd outside, a mix of patients and curious onlookers, became unwitting witnesses to the unfolding drama. The city streets, still damp from the earlier rain, served as the battleground for John's escape.

"Sir, please, we can help you," a nurse pleaded, her voice carrying genuine concern.

But John, now in the throes of an unholy purpose, paid no heed. He crossed the threshold between the hospital and the city, a man marked by tragedy, holding a precious burden that defied the natural order.

The chase intensified, the security detail determined to bring an end to the chaos. John, guided by a single-minded mission, moved through the crowds like a phantom. The city lights, reflecting in his eyes, seemed to fuel the fire that burned within him.

As John navigated the city's labyrinth of commercial and residential streets, the sounds of pursuit and distant sirens blended with the symphony of urban life. The night became witness to a man's descent into darkness, driven by a culmination of the loss of everything that would lead him into the shadows of morality.

"I will find a way to bring you back," he whispered to his son, as if the wind itself could carry the promise to the departed.

Chapter Two

The rain fell in a fine mist at first, a cold whisper on John's skin, but soon it grew heavier, each drop striking like a pinprick, soaking through his clothes and chilling him to the bone. The dampness clung to him, a reminder of the weight he carried—not just Ethan, but the crushing burden of his own failure. Every step forward felt like a penance, each drop a bitter accusation. Each step was an act of will, his legs trembling beneath him as the adrenaline began to wear off. The harsh glow of the streetlights reflected off the wet pavement, casting the world in shades of sickly yellow and black. His breath came in short, ragged bursts, his heart pounding a frantic rhythm in his chest.

He hadn't planned for this, hadn't thought it would end up like this. His mind replayed the scene in Ethan's hospital room on an endless loop—the sterile white sheets, the steady beeping of the heart monitor, and then … nothing, as if Ethan had been swallowed whole by the hospital itself. The memory felt like a splinter lodged deep in his brain, impossible to dislodge. And underneath it all, the gnawing, insistent thought: they took him.

John shook his head, trying to clear the fog that had settled there. He darted across the main road, not even bothering to check for oncoming cars, trusting that the night would cover his desperate escape. A horn blared in the distance, the sound muted by the rain, but he didn't look back. He couldn't.

The estate rose before him, a land mass of narrow streets and suffocating alleys that twisted like the veins of a diseased heart. The buildings, once proud, were now crumbling relics of neglect, their facades pocked and scarred by time. Darkened windows stared down at him like empty, accusing eyes, reflecting the desolation that chewed at his soul. The air was thick with the smell of rot and damp, mingling with the sharp, acrid tang of burning rubbish from an unseen fire, as if the very city was decaying around him, swallowing him into its ruin.

His feet splashed through puddles, the cold water seeping into his shoes, but he didn't slow down. He turned onto Linnaeus Street, his mind racing, trying to calculate the quickest route to his car. Every step brought new doubts, new fears. What if they're watching me? What if they know where I'm going?

John turned the corner, his heart racing as his eyes darted down the deserted street. Every shadow seemed to stretch towards him, every flicker of movement at the edge of his vision setting his nerves on edge. The estate was unnervingly silent, as if the night itself was holding its breath, waiting to strike. But was it truly silent? He couldn't shake the feeling that something—or someone— was watching him, tracking his every step. The distant rumble of the city felt like the low growl of a predator, unseen but always close, and John's pulse quickened with the terrifying thought that he was no longer alone.

He cut through the grounds of the Living Hope Christian Church, the towering silhouette of the building looming over him like a dark omen. The modern looking church's window was lost in the shadows, but he could almost feel it staring down at him, judging him. For a moment, he hesitated. The gap in the fence that led deeper into the housing estate seemed impossibly narrow, and for a brief second, he was paralyzed by the thought that he wouldn't fit, that he would be trapped here, exposed. But then he pushed forward, squeezing through the opening, the rough wood scraping against his skin.

The housing estate mirrored the hospital grounds, but here, everything felt different—oppressive, claustrophobic. The rain-soaked streets were deserted, the houses hunched together, their walls closing in. He ran along the roads at the back of the houses, garage doors and worn looking fences surrounding him wherever he looked. The shadows were deeper here, the darkness more complete, as if the estate itself was trying to swallow him whole.

John kept moving, his thoughts a whirlwind of fear and anger. His mind flashed back to the happy moments with Sarah and Ethan—their laughter, their warmth, the life they had before it all went to hell. Those memories now felt like a cruel joke, a taunt from a life he could never have back. He tried to push them aside, focusing on what needed to be done, but they clung to him, dragging him down like an anchor.

As he turned onto another street, he could hear the faint sound of a television through a half-open window— a sitcom, the canned laughter jarring in the stillness. It struck him how alien that sound was now, how out of place it felt. Once, it would have been a comfort, a reminder that life went on, that normality existed somewhere. But now it was just noise, a grating reminder of everything he'd lost.

Finally, running through a narrow alleyway that connected roads unreachable by car, he reached Lyric Close, the narrow street where his own car waited. The rain was coming down harder now, the drops heavier, colder, each one a tiny needle pricking his skin. The street was lined with parked cars, their windshields reflecting the dim light of the streetlamps in fractured, watery patterns. The houses here were slightly better kept, but there was still a sense of abandonment, of lives lived behind closed doors, out of sight.

John spotted his car—a nondescript Volkswagen Passat—tucked away in the shadows, barely visible from the road. It was his sanctuary, the one place where he felt he had any control left. He approached it cautiously, his eyes scanning the street for any sign of movement. Every rustle of the wind, every creak of the houses, set his nerves on edge. He was so close now, but the fear that something would go wrong at the last second crept into him.

He reached the car, his hand trembling as he fumbled for the keys in his pocket. His breath fogged the window as he leaned against the door, his thoughts swirling with what he had to do next. He didn't have a plan, not really, just a desperate need to keep moving, to stay one step ahead of whatever nightmare was closing in on him.

He opened the back door of the car gently, careful not to make any noise. The car seat was still in place from the days when Ethan was alive, a poignant reminder of the life that had been so cruelly taken from him. John cradled Ethan's small unmoving body as he placed him gently into the car seat, his hands shaking as he fumbled with the straps. The ritual of securing Ethan as if he were just napping tore at his heart, each click of the buckle a cruel mockery of the normality they had once known. He couldn't bring himself to look directly at Ethan's face— he feared that if he did, the finality of it all would crush him completely. But even in his peripheral vision, the sight of his son, so still and silent, was a dagger to his soul. The weight of Ethan's absence hung heavy in the air, a suffocating reminder that the world had irrevocably changed.

John slid into the driver's seat, his hands gripping the wheel tightly as he took a deep breath. He whispered a promise to Ethan, his voice breaking with emotion. "I'll bring you back to me, I swear it." The words hung in the air, a solemn vow that drove him forward.

With a final, lingering glance at the upper floors of the hospital in the rearview mirror, John started the car. The engine roared to life, breaking the silence of the night. He pulled out of Lyric Close, merging into the sparse traffic, his mind already racing with the plans he had formed. The streets of Hull blurred past him, the city lights reflecting off the wet road, guiding him towards an uncertain and dark future. He turned left at the roundabout to merge onto the Clive Sullivan way, a route that would take him east and towards the less built-up half of the city.

John gripped the steering wheel, knuckles tight as he navigated the narrow streets leading away from the hospital. His mind was a tempest of fear and desperation, but his hands moved with a grim efficiency, guiding the car through the roads and streets he had driven along many times before. The rain, which had started as a fine mist, now came down in earnest, the rhythmic drumming on the windshield a grating soundtrack to his flight.

As he approached Humber Street, the road dipped slightly, revealing the small harbour ahead. The water lay dark and still, a black mirror reflecting the overcast sky. The boats moored along the dock rocked gently, their ropes creaking in the damp air. The scent of saltwater mixed with the tang of fish and diesel fuel was a pungent reminder of the city's industrial heart. John barely noticed the few figures moving along the quayside, their silhouettes blurred by the rain and distance. They were fishermen, mostly, hunched against the weather, their movements slow and methodical as they secured their boats for the night.

He pressed on, the car tires splashing through shallow puddles as he made his way towards the bridge that spanned the River Hull. The bridge loomed ahead, a hulking mass of steel and concrete, its girders stretching into the gloom. As John drove over it, he glanced to his right and caught sight of The Deep, its angular structure jutting out over the water like the prow of a great ship. The aquarium's blue lights shimmered in the rain, casting an eerie glow over the surrounding area. For a brief moment, John's thoughts wandered, recalling a day long ago when he had taken Ethan there and the boy's wide-eyed wonder at the sights within. But that memory was a knife twisted in his gut, and he forced himself to look away, focusing instead on the road ahead.

The traffic thinned as he moved deeper into the city's outskirts, the buildings becoming more spaced out, more derelict. He passed HMP Hull, the prison's high walls and watchtowers standing like sentinels in the night. The place always gave him an uneasy feeling; even now, as he drove by, the thought of being trapped within those walls, with no way out, sent a shiver down his spine. The rain had pooled in the dips and cracks in the road, creating small lakes that his car splashed through, sending up sheets of water that smacked against the undercarriage. The streetlights here were fewer and farther between, casting long shadows that seemed to reach out for him as he drove by.

Roadworks appeared ahead, a line of orange cones and blinking lights signalling the obstruction. The road narrowed to one lane, and John slowed, weaving between the barriers. A couple of workmen in high-visibility jackets stood under a makeshift shelter, huddled against the rain, their cigarettes glowing like tiny beacons in the dark. They barely glanced at him as he passed, too absorbed in their conversation to pay much attention to a lone car creeping through the night.

Finally, the Falcon Hotel came into view, a nondescript building crouched along Hedon Road like a forgotten relic. The neon sign above the entrance flickered fitfully, the blue letters spelling out "FALC N" in a sickly glow. The bulbs had been damaged previously but never replaced, adding to the neglect of the area. The hotel was flanked by a closed laundrette, its windows covered in grime, and a petrol station that had been repurposed as a car wash, its once-bright paint now peeling and faded. A lone car sat under the station's awning, its tyres slashed and its windows smashed, a grim testament to the area's decay.

John pulled into the hotel's car park, choosing a spot in the far corner, away from the prying eyes of the few pedestrians still out at this hour. The car park was nearly empty, save for a couple of cars that looked as though they hadn't moved in weeks. The rain drummed on the roof of his car, the sound merging with the distant hum of the motorway beyond.

He sat there for a moment, the engine idling, the warmth from the heater doing little to chase away the chill that had settled in his bones. Ethan lay in the back seat, still and silent. John's hands trembled on the steering wheel, and for a moment, he considered just driving, driving until the car ran out of petrol, and then walking until he could walk no more. But there was no escaping this.

With a deep breath, John killed the engine and stepped out of the car. The cold night air hit him like a slap, the rain soaking through his clothes in an instant. He carefully lifted Ethan from the car, cradling him close as he hunched his shoulders against the downpour and made his way to the hotel entrance, the neon sign casting his shadow long and distorted across the cracked pavement.

The Falcon Hotel stood as a modest yet notable establishment on Hedon Road, Hull. The building, a relic from the early 20th century, featured a facade of weathered red brick and white stone accents. The hotel rose three stories high, its architecture a blend of Edwardian and early modernist styles. Large bay windows with wrought iron balconies punctuated the front, giving it a somewhat stately appearance despite its age. Another neon sign inside the main entrance window flickered intermittently, casting a pale blue light that spelled out "The Falcon Hotel."

The entrance was marked by a heavy wooden door darkened by years of exposure and flanked by two stone pillars. Above the door, an ornate stone arch had the hotel's name etched into it. Topiary in large, weathered planters sat on either side of the entrance, giving a touch of greenery to the otherwise urban setting. The brass handle on the door was polished but showed signs of wear from the countless hands that had turned it over the decades.

John pushed the door open with his shoulder, the bell above the door jangling loudly in the stillness. Inside, the reception area was dimly lit, with a faded carpet and peeling wallpaper that might have once been a cheerful floral pattern. A television mounted in the corner played an old black-and-white movie, its sound barely audible over the hum of a buzzing tube light above.

The reception desk, a grand piece of mahogany furniture, stood directly opposite the entrance. To the right of the desk, a small seating area featured a cluster of leather armchairs and a low coffee table. A few magazines and local newspapers were scattered across the table, and the walls were adorned with old photographs of Hull, capturing moments of its history and the hotel's own past.

The receptionist was an older man with thinning hair and a haggard expression, sitting behind the scratched wooden counter. He barely looked up as John approached, his attention focused on a dog-eared paperback novel. His weathered face was a map of deep lines and creases, each one telling a tale of years gone by. His hair, once a rich brown, was now a wispy white, thin and combed back neatly. A pair of thick, horn-rimmed glasses rested on the bridge of his nose, magnifying his watery blue eyes, which had seen countless faces come and go over the decades.

His skin was pale and marked with age spots, giving a sense of fragility, yet his posture remained upright and dignified. He wore a faded plaid shirt buttoned up to the neck and a pair of brown corduroy trousers held up by suspenders. Over this, he had donned a woollen cardigan frayed at the cuffs and elbows, hinting at its long service. His hands were gnarled and veined, with large knuckles and a slight tremor that became noticeable when he reached out to place his book down.

John approached the counter, his heart pounding in his chest. "I need a room," he said, his voice barely above a whisper.

The receptionist, Ted, finally looked up, his eyes

flickering with mild curiosity. He had no interest in niceties or even suspicion; all Ted wanted was to clock out and grab a pint at the Sportsman's Arms before heading home to be chastised by his overbearing wife of more time than he cared to remember.

"We charge by the hour," he said flatly, his voice raspy from years of smoking.

John nodded, shifting Ethan's weight slightly in his arms. "That's fine. I'll pay for the night."

The receptionist raised an eyebrow but didn't ask any questions. He reached under the counter and pulled out a ledger, flipping it open to a fresh page. "Name?" he asked, pen poised.

"John Morrison," John replied, glancing around nervously.

The receptionist scribbled the name down, then slid a key across the counter. "Room 14, up the stairs and to the left," he said. "Payment up front."

John fumbled for his wallet, pulling out a few crumpled notes and handing them over. The receptionist took the money without comment, his eyes already returning to his book.

"Thank you," John muttered, gripping the key tightly as he headed towards the staircase.

The stairwell was narrow and steep, the carpet worn thin from years of use. Each step creaked ominously under John's weight as he ascended, the sound echoing in the confined space. He reached the top and turned left, finding room 14 at the end of a cosily lit hallway.

The door was painted a dull green, the number barely visible. John unlocked it and pushed it open, the hinges squealing in protest. Inside, the room was small and sparsely furnished. A single bed with a threadbare blanket, a rickety bedside table with a flickering lamp, and a battered wooden chair and desk were the only pieces of furniture. The wallpaper, once white, had yellowed with age and was peeling in several places.

A small window overlooked the carpark, its glass streaked with dirt and grime. The air inside the room was musty, carrying the faint scent of mildew and old cigarettes. John gently laid Ethan on the bed, his heart aching at the sight of his son's lifeless form against the dingy surroundings.

Exhaustion weighed heavily on John as he sat on the edge of the bed, his mind racing with grief and desperation. He kicked off his shoes and lay down next to Ethan, pulling the blanket over both of them.

As he lay next to Ethan, the thin blanket barely offering warmth, the dim light from the flickering lamp painted the walls with long, ghostly shadows. John's thoughts spiralled, a relentless storm of grief, guilt, and desperate hope. The memories of Ethan's laughter, once a balm to his soul, now cut like razors, mingling with the grim reality of his present. He whispered a prayer—a plea to a god he no longer believed in—that he might find a way to undo the horrors of the day. But even as his body ached for rest, his mind refused to quiet, haunted by the gnawing fear that this night, like so many before, would offer no peace. And just as sleep began to claim him, a faint noise—a creak in the hallway, or perhaps just the wind—jolted him awake, his heart pounding with the dread that his flight was far from over.

Chapter Three

Sleep crept over John like a thick fog, enveloping him in its cold, oppressive embrace. His breathing slowed, and the world around him faded away, replaced by the vivid clarity of a dream.

In his dream, he was back in the hospital, but this time it was starkly different from reality. It was bright and full of life. The sterile walls seemed warmer, pristine white, gleaming under the bright overhead lights. The atmosphere was one of hope and new beginnings. The hospital room was spacious, filled with the soft hum of medical equipment and the gentle rustling of linens. Sarah stood by the bed, cradling a newborn Ethan. Her long auburn hair cascaded over her shoulders, her face glowing with health and happiness. She wore a simple white gown, and her smile was radiating pure joy.

The nurse, a woman in her mid-fifties with kind eyes and soft features, stood in the room with them, camera in hand. Her hair, streaked with grey, was tied back in a neat bun. She wore a traditional nurse's uniform: a crisp white dress with a matching cap, black shoes, and a small silver watch pinned to her chest. She snapped a picture of them, capturing the pure joy of that moment. John felt an overwhelming sense of peace and happiness, a stark contrast to his waking life, which had become a relentless nightmare.

The light in the room was soft, almost ethereal, casting a gentle glow over everything. The walls, painted a calming shade of blue, seemed to breathe with a life of their own. The room smelled faintly of lavender, a scent that brought back memories of simpler, happier times. John looked down at his baby son, Ethan, cradled in his arms. The child's tiny fingers curled around his thumb, and for a moment, everything felt perfect.

"He's beautiful," the nurse said, her voice a soothing melody that wrapped around John's heart. "You must be so proud."

John nodded, tears welling up in his eyes. "I am," he whispered, his voice choked with emotion. "He's everything to me."

The nurse smiled, her eyes crinkling at the corners. "Would you like another photo? It's important to capture these moments."

John looked at his son, then back at the nurse. "Yes, please," he said, his voice trembling. "I want to remember this forever."

The nurse raised the camera again, and John turned his gaze back to Ethan. The baby looked up at him, his eyes wide and curious. John's heart swelled with love and pride. He leaned down and kissed Ethan's forehead, feeling the softness of his skin against his lips.

"Perfect," the nurse said, lowering the camera. "Absolutely perfect."

John looked up, a smile spreading across his face. "Thank you," he said, his voice filled with gratitude.

The nurse nodded, her expression gentle. "It's my pleasure," she said. "Moments like these are why I do what I do."

John felt a deep sense of peace settle over him. In this room, in this moment, everything was right. The horrors of his waking life seemed distant and unimportant. Here, he was just a father holding his son, surrounded by love and kindness.

But then, a shadow passed over the nurse's face, and the room grew colder. John shivered, a sense of unease creeping into his heart. He looked around, and the soft glow began to fade, replaced by a harsh, flickering light.

"What's happening?" John asked, his voice filled with fear.

The nurse's kind eyes turned dark, and her features twisted into a cruel smile. "You can't stay here forever, John," she said, her voice now a chilling whisper. "Reality is waiting for you."

John's heart pounded in his chest. "No," he pleaded. "Please let me stay. I need to stay with Ethan."

The nurse shook her head, her smile widening. "You have to go back," she said, her voice echoing in the room.

John clutched Ethan tighter, tears streaming down his face. "I can't," he sobbed. "I can't go back."

The room began to dissolve around him, the walls crumbling into darkness. The nurse's laughter filled his ears, a haunting sound that followed him as he fell into the void.

John woke with a start, his heart racing. The room was dark and cold, in sharp contrast to the warmth of his dream. He sat up, his breath coming in ragged gasps. He looked around, but there was no sign of the nurse, no sign of Ethan.

The dream shifted seamlessly, and he found himself in Ethan's nursery. The room was a sanctuary of love and hope. The walls were painted a soft pastel blue, adorned with white clouds that seem to float gently across the ceiling. A wooden crib, painted white, stood against one wall, filled with plush toys and soft blankets. A changing table was set up nearby, stocked with nappies and baby supplies. The room was bathed in natural light from a large window, its curtains drawn back to let in the sunshine.

John stood in the nursery, a place that seemed almost sacred to him. He dipped the roller into the paint tray, coating it with a fresh layer of blue, and started to apply it to the walls with slow, deliberate strokes. The rhythmic motion of his arm, back and forth, was a soothing routine, a labour of love. His old, paint-splattered Guns N' Roses t-shirt hung loosely on his frame, the fabric soft from years of wear. His tatty jeans, worn and frayed at the hems, completed his work ensemble, a testament to the many projects he had tackled over the years.

Sarah stood nearby, cradling Ethan in her arms. Her laughter filled the room, a melodious sound that seemed to emanate warmth and light. She wore a light blue sundress that flowed around her legs, her hair cascading in loose waves over her shoulders. She looked radiant, the very embodiment of happiness and contentment. Her flat sandals clicked softly against the wooden floor as she gently rocked Ethan, swaddled in a soft white blanket. His tiny face peeked out, eyes wide with curiosity as he took in the colours and shapes around him.

"You're doing a great job, babe," Sarah said, her voice filled with admiration. "I can't wait to see it all done and dusted."

John paused and looked over his shoulder, a smile tugging at the corners of his mouth. "Thanks, love. I'm just trying to make it perfect for our little guy."

Ethan gurgled in response, his small fingers reaching out towards the roller. Sarah laughed again, the sound like music to John's ears. "I think he approves," she said, kissing Ethan's forehead.

John's heart swelled with joy, the love for his family almost overwhelming. He turned back to his work, but just as he was about to dip the roller into the paint again, the scene began to shift. The vibrant colours of the nursery walls started to fade, the blue turning to a dull, lifeless grey. Sarah's laughter was abruptly cut off, replaced by a harsh, persistent cough.

John spun around to see Sarah doubled over, one hand clutching her chest, the other braced on her knee for support. "Sarah!" he cried, rushing to her side. He placed a hand on her back, feeling the tremors of her coughing fit.

She tried to wave him off, a weak smile on her face. "It's ... it's nothing, John. Just a little tickle in my throat," she gasped, struggling to catch her breath.

But John knew better. The light in the room dimmed, the warmth replaced by an icy chill. The walls seemed to close in around them, the air heavy with an oppressive silence. As Sarah's coughing fit subsided, she straightened up, but the vibrant life that had once filled her eyes was now replaced by a weary, haunted look.

The scene shifted again, the nursery dissolving into a graveyard shrouded in fog. John found himself standing alone, a cold wind biting at his skin. The air was thick with the scent of damp earth and decaying leaves. He looked down and saw a coffin draped in a black cloth, resting on a bed of wilting flowers. The name etched into the stone beside it made his blood run cold: Sarah.

The day was overcast, the clouds heavy with impending rain, the sky a dismal reflection of his grief. The cemetery was a vast expanse of grey tombstones, their inscriptions weathered and worn. John stood by Sarah's grave wearing a black suit, impeccably tailored, but it could not hide the deep lines of grief etched into his face. The coffin was lowered into the earth. Ethan's tiny hand clutched his, the little boy's eyes wide with confusion, not fully understanding the gravity of the situation. John's other hand clutched a white handkerchief, his knuckles white and aching with the effort of holding back tears. The cold wind bit at his cheeks, a cruel reminder of the warmth he had lost. The memory was raw, a wound that refused to heal seared into his soul.

The dream shifted again, taking him to the park. The park was a striking contrast to the funeral. The sun was shining, children were playing, and birds sang from the treetops. He pushed Ethan in a pram, the wheels crunching softly on the gravel path. The park was lush with greenery, the trees swaying gently in the breeze. John was dressed casually in a light jacket and jeans, trying to maintain a semblance of normality.

Ethan, in the pram, was wearing a light blue onesie, his small hands reaching out to the world. The air was filled with the sounds of laughter, the gentle rustle of leaves in the breeze, and the distant hum of life. But then Ethan began to cough, a violent, rasping sound that echoed Sarah's final moments. John watched helplessly as his son's face contorted in pain, mirroring Sarah's last agonizing days, his hands trembling on the pram's handle. The sound tore at his heart, each cough a dagger to his soul and the joy of the moment slipping away like sand through his fingers.

All of a sudden, the dream plunged him into darkness. He was engulfed in a void. The dream had dragged John into an abyss. He was engulfed in a void so thick it seemed to suffocate him. The darkness was vast and impenetrable, stretching infinitely in all directions. John stood alone, the profound silence pressing in on him, making the beat of his heart sound like a drum in his ears.

Disoriented and desperate, he stumbled forward, his footsteps echoing in the nothingness, each one a hollow reminder of his isolation.

"Ethan!" he called out, his voice swallowed by the void. The only response was the frantic pounding of his own heart. Panic clawed at his insides as he strained to hear, to see anything in the oppressive blackness.

Suddenly, Ethan's cries pierced the silence, distant and haunting. John's pulse quickened, his breath coming in ragged gasps. He stumbled forward, his hands reaching out, grasping at nothing but the cold emptiness around him. His fingers clawed at the air, desperate to touch, to hold, to save.

"Ethan! Where are you?" John's voice was hoarse, raw with desperation. The cries grew louder, more frantic, mingling with Sarah's voice. Her tone was filled with an agony that cut through him, a desperate plea from beyond.

"John, help us!" Sarah's voice echoed, a ghostly whisper that seemed to come from everywhere and nowhere at once.

The cacophony of their voices grew, swelling into a haunting symphony of his failures and fears. Ethan's cries were sharp, each one a dagger to his heart, while Sarah's voice was a mournful wail, the sound of a soul in torment. John's mind reeled, overwhelmed by the noise, the darkness, the suffocating weight of his guilt and sorrow.

He stumbled and fell, the impact jarring him to the core. The floor was cold and unyielding, a stark contrast to the void above. He lay there, gasping for breath, the darkness pressing down on him like a physical force.

Suddenly, a flicker of light appeared in the distance, a

tiny pinprick in the sea of black. John's heart leapt, hope surging through him like a lifeline. He scrambled to his feet, his legs trembling, and began to move towards it. The light grew brighter, and he could make out shapes, shadows that danced and flickered.

"Ethan! Sarah!" he cried, the light guiding his steps.

As he drew closer, he saw Ethan, his tiny form huddled on the ground, tears streaming down his face. Beside him, Sarah knelt, her eyes wide with fear and pain. The sight of them, so fragile and lost, tore at John's soul.

"I'm here!" he shouted, reaching out.

But as his fingers brushed against Ethan's, the light flickered and dimmed. The darkness surged back, swallowing them up. John screamed, a guttural sound of pure anguish, as the suffocating weight of the void closed in once more.

"No! Please, no!" he begged, his voice breaking.

The darkness continued to press in on him, a shroud that blotted out everything. The cries faded, replaced by a cold, dead silence. John was alone again, the weight of his failures and fears a crushing burden.

And then, with a jolt, he was pulled from the void, this part of his dream shattering into a thousand fragments.

John sat up in a bed, his own bed, his heart pounding, sweat clinging to his skin. The room was dark and silent, the shadows of his dream lingering in the corners. The reality of his situation crashed down on him once more. He was in their house, a place once filled with love and laughter, now a mausoleum of broken dreams. The wallpaper in Ethan's room was peeling, toys lay abandoned on the floor, and the crib, once a symbol of hope, was now a cruel reminder of what he had lost.

Ethan lay beside him, still and silent, his tiny body cold and lifeless. John reached out, his hand trembling, touching Ethan's soft hair. His son was a painful reminder of the lengths he was willing to go to defy the natural order and bring him back. John's heart ached with a grief that was almost unbearable. He closed his eyes, fighting back tears, and whispered into the darkness, "I'm so sorry, my little man. I need you."

The house around him felt empty and hollow, every room a reminder of the life they had lost. Sarah's presence lingered in the photographs on the walls, her smile forever frozen in happier times. The furniture was old and worn, each piece carrying the weight of their shared memories. The air was thick with the scent of decay and abandonment, a stark contrast to the vibrant life that had once filled the space. John buried his face in his hands, his sobs breaking the silence. He had lost everything, and the weight of his actions crushed him with relentless despair.

Then everything faded and an empty black sleep took over.

Chapter Four

As John awoke, the pale light of dawn was filtering through the grimy window, casting long shadows across the room. Dust particles hung in the air, suspended like the heavy weight of John's grief. His eyes, bloodshot and sunken, bore the evidence of countless sleepless nights. Each breath he took felt shallow, as though the oppressive air in the room had thinned to the point where it could no longer sustain life. The sour taste of despair lingered in his mouth, a constant reminder of the darkness that had consumed him.

His movements were sluggish, burdened by the relentless ache in his chest. The room itself seemed to mirror his inner turmoil—the peeling wallpaper like the fragments of his shattered soul, the worn chair and desk the remnants of a life that had once held promise. The walls felt like they were closing in, the space growing smaller with each passing second, as if trying to suffocate the life out of him, just as death had done to his family.

The bed was unmade, its thin, stained sheets tangled from a restless night's sleep. Next to the bed lay Ethan's lifeless form, covered with a blanket that did little to hide the painful truth.

The carpet of his hotel room, once a vibrant hue, was now a faded, patchy expanse, its fibres worn thin from years of neglect. A small, bare lightbulb hung from the ceiling, its dim glow adding to the room's oppressive atmosphere. The air was heavy with the scent of must and decay, mingling with the faint aroma of antiseptic from the hospital.

John stirred in the uncomfortable chair, his neck aching from the awkward position he had slept in. His eyes felt gritty from the lack of sleep, and his mind was a foggy swirl of grief and determination. As he stood up and stretched, the old building creaked around him, the sound a reminder of its dilapidated state. He looked over at the bed where Ethan lay, his heart clenching with renewed grief and desperation. The sight of his son's lifeless form was a brutal jolt, bringing him back to the grim reality of his situation. One that, even though seemingly impossible, he was determined to alter.

John had once been a successful computer technician specializing in cybersecurity. He had a natural talent for understanding complex systems and had made a name for himself by uncovering vulnerabilities in some of the most secure networks. His expertise lay in navigating the intricacies of the digital world, finding loopholes, and understanding the hidden pathways that most people couldn't even imagine existed.

He had worked for several high-profile firms, ensuring their data remained secure from the ever-present threat of hackers. His work required a meticulous mind, an ability to think several steps ahead, and a deep understanding of the dark web, where he often had to trace and counteract the illicit activities of cybercriminals.

John's skills as a computer technician were not just confined to cybersecurity; they extended to the darker recesses of the internet. He knew how to navigate the dark web, a hidden layer of the internet where anonymity was prized and forbidden knowledge exchanged hands. This shadowy realm was home to forums and marketplaces dealing in all manner of illicit activities, including the arcane and the occult.

A company called Bio-Rad had recruited John not merely for his technical prowess, but for his expertise in the darker recesses of the internet. They needed someone who could understand and control the flow of information, someone who could keep their sinister activities hidden from the prying eyes of law enforcement and rival corporations. At first, the job had seemed like just another high-stakes assignment. John was tasked with securing Bio-Rad's networks and fortifying their defences against any potential cyber threats. He implemented encryption protocols, firewalls, and intrusion detection systems with the precision of a master craftsman. But eventually, it became a place he didn't want to be. One good thing came from his time there, though: he had met Sarah. He would now, however, use the skills developed over his career to do something that seemed entirely illogical.

Determined to bring Ethan back, John set up his laptop on the small desk. He connected to the Tor network, the gateway to the dark web, his fingers moving deftly over the keyboard. The familiar hum of his laptop was a comforting sound amidst the chaos of his life. He knew that within this hidden part of the internet, there were whispers from individuals who claimed to possess knowledge that defied the natural order.

As he delved deeper into the dark web, he felt a mix of fear and hope. The information he sought was dangerous and elusive, hidden behind layers of encryption and anonymity. Yet his skills gave him an edge. He knew how to bypass security measures, trace hidden pathways, and decode cryptic messages.

John's obsession had begun with a simple question, one that had gnawed at the back of his mind ever since Sarah's death: What if there was a way to bring her back? It was a thought that terrified him as much as it enticed him, a whisper from the darkest corners of his grief. He knew it was madness, but madness was all he had left. The living room of his small, suffocating house had become his sanctuary for this forbidden knowledge.

A single hard wooden chair was pulled close to a rickety desk, its legs wobbling with every movement. The desk was cluttered with remnants of John's previous desperate attempts at illogical research after Sarah died—old leather-bound books, yellowed with age and filled with archaic symbols that seemed to dance in the flickering light of a single lamp.

He had found them in dusty, forgotten corners of second-hand bookshops, places where the shop assistants looked at him with a mix of pity and suspicion as he paid cash for titles like *The Grimoire of the Dead* and *The Book of Shadows*. They were not mainstream literature; they were tomes that had passed through countless hands, each one a little more desperate than the last. His trusty laptop sat among the mess, its screen glowing faintly, the search history littered with enquiries that would send shivers down the spine of any rational person—keywords like 'necromancy', 'resurrection rituals', 'soul binding'. The internet had been his first gateway, a vast, sprawling web of information where the line between myth and reality blurred. He started with the basics, threads on paranormal forums and poorly edited videos on YouTube of supposed resurrections, most of which would have been laughable if not so pathetically tragic.

But there were nuggets of truth, too, or at least enough to keep him digging. He learned about the ritualistic practices of ancient civilizations, how the Egyptians believed in the power of preserving the body to anchor the soul or how the Aztecs performed sacrifices to appease gods that might grant life after death. He took notes, filling pages and pages of a worn notebook with his feverish scrawl, his handwriting growing more erratic as the nights wore on. He learned about the 'Rules of Three': the necessity of something personal to the deceased, the importance of timing—when the veil between worlds was thinnest, during the witching hour, or on specific days when the stars aligned just so.

Yet it wasn't enough. None of it brought him closer to Sarah. None of it offered the key to reversing what had been taken from him. As time went on and the ache in his heart deepened, his search took a darker turn. After Ethan's death, that faint glimmer of hope he'd held onto shattered, replaced by something far more dangerous—an all-consuming rage and despair that drove him deeper into the shadows of the internet. The dark web became his new playground, a place where he could delve into the truly forbidden and where the line between morality and atrocity vanished altogether.

He discovered forums hidden behind layers of encryption, where anonymity was a currency and the topics discussed were ones that could damn a soul for eternity. The things he read there were not merely occult; they were obscene, blasphemous, the kind of knowledge that felt like it could taint a man's very soul just by understanding it. There were detailed instructions on how to craft necromantic circles, where to find the necessary materials—often harvested from the dead themselves— and how to bind a spirit to a corpse, though the results were said to be ... unpredictable.

John read and read, his mind absorbing the darkness like a sponge. He knew what he was doing was wrong, that it defied every law of nature and God, but he didn't care anymore. The world had taken everything from him, and he would bend or break any rule to get it back. He found himself scouring the deepest, most twisted corners of the web, his hands trembling as he clicked on links that promised to reveal the secrets of eternal life, of resurrection, of undoing death itself.

John's heart raced as he sifted through countless forums and chat rooms, each filled with cryptic conversations and coded messages. He searched for any mention of necromancy, resurrection, and ancient rituals that could offer a glimmer of hope. His mind was a whirlwind of thoughts and emotions, driven by the desperate need to undo the tragedy that had befallen his family.

John managed to download several PDFs of the texts he found, their pages filled with incomprehensible symbols, archaic languages, and intricate illustrations of dark rituals. Titles like *The Necronomicon*, *The Book of the Dead*, and *De Vermis Mysteriis* appeared on his screen. He pored over these manuscripts, slowly deciphering their contents with the help of online translators and occult glossaries.

Every click, every keystroke brought him closer to a potential solution. The room around him blurred into the background as he became engrossed in his search. The faded wallpaper, the creaky floorboards, and the musty smell all became distant concerns as he focused on his mission. The pain of losing Sarah and Ethan fuelled his determination, pushing him to explore avenues he had never considered before.

John's world had been shattered, but his skills as a computer technician provided a sliver of hope. In the dim, oppressive hotel room, amidst the clutter of books and notes, he worked tirelessly, navigating the darkest corners of the internet in search of a way to bring his son back. His journey was fraught with danger and uncertainty, but he pressed on, driven by the unwavering love for his son and the desperate need to restore his family.

In the twisted labyrinth of the dark web, there existed a forum known only to the most desperate and the most depraved. It was a place where the boundaries of morality had long since crumbled into dust, where the line between the living and the dead was nothing more than a faint, frayed thread. The forum was called *The Black*, and it was here that John Morrison found himself drawn, as if by some unseen force, in the days following Ethan's death.

The Black wasn't just a website; it was a void, a digital abyss that seemed to suck in all the light and hope from anyone who ventured too deep. Its interface was crude, almost archaic, with a black background and blood-red text that flickered as if written in a liquid that was still warm. There were no ads, no banners, no avatars—just thread after thread of pure, undiluted horror. Users communicated in whispers, their usernames more like incantations than monikers: 'DeathDealer', 'SoulBinder', 'NecroPriest', and 'thevoiceofthehand'.

It was thevoiceofthehand that first caught John's attention. This user seemed different from the others. While most posts on *The Black* were filled with the ramblings of the deranged or the vague promises of dark power, thevoiceofthehand spoke with a quiet, assured authority. Their posts were not frequent, but when they appeared, they were treated with a reverence that bordered on worship. Others on the forum would respond with a fearful respect, their replies laden with gratitude and awe. Whoever thevoiceofthehand was, they were a figure of significance, a master of the dark arts, a guide through the murky waters of necromancy.

It wasn't long before John found himself combing through every post, every word this mysterious user had ever written. thevoiceofthehand was not just an occult enthusiast; they were a gatekeeper, a curator of ancient, forbidden knowledge. They spoke of 'The Five' with a familiarity that was unsettling, as if they were recounting tales of old friends rather than malevolent spirits. The Five, according to thevoiceofthehand, were not just spirits but entities that had once been human and had transcended, through acts of unimaginable cruelty, into something far worse. They were bound by blood and death, and they walked the earth not as ghosts, but as harbingers of doom.

The Five, as detailed in these cryptic posts, had existed for centuries, a group of individuals who had each committed an act so heinous that it had granted them power beyond death. They were necromancers, murderers, and worse, bound together in a pact that defied time and reason. The Five did not die in the conventional sense; they shed their mortal coils but retained their influence and their essence. Over the centuries, they had been worshipped by cults, feared by villagers, and hunted by those who dared to believe they could end their reign. But The Five always returned, reborn through the darkest of rituals.

thevoiceofthehand hinted at having encountered The Five, or at least their lingering influence. Their posts were filled with obscure references to rituals, ancient texts, and locations where The Five had once walked. There was talk of a book, something called *The*

Manuscript of Shadows, a text that was said to contain the secrets of The Five and the knowledge needed to summon or banish them. But the book was lost, or hidden, and those who sought it often met grisly ends.

John was captivated, and as he read more, a terrible realisation began to take root in his mind. The more he understood, the more he saw parallels between what thevoiceofthehand described and what he had experienced. It was as if everything he had gone through—the loss, the grief, the madness—was connected to something much larger, something he was only beginning to comprehend.

The Black became John's new obsession, his new haunt where he devoured every piece of information thevoiceofthehand provided. He found himself slipping further from reality, diving into a world where death was not an end but a doorway, a gateway to powers he could barely fathom. And with each passing hour, the name thevoiceofthehand etched itself deeper into his mind, a beacon in the darkness, guiding him toward something he was not sure he wanted to find.

For thevoiceofthehand was not just a user on a forum. They were part of something bigger, something ancient, something that had been whispering to John long before he ever logged onto *The Black*. They were connected to The Five in ways he could not yet understand, and they were watching him, guiding him, waiting for him to take the final step.

And deep down, John knew that whatever step he took next, there would be no turning back.

The conversation started innocuously enough, with John probing the depths of the digital abyss for any clues about necromancy, his heart a leaden weight in his chest. He typed his questions with trembling fingers, the glow of the laptop screen casting eerie shadows on the peeling wallpaper of the dingy room. Each keystroke echoed his desperation, a plea sent into the void.

"Is it possible to bring back a loved one from the dead?" John's question hung in the air, a whisper of hope amidst the silence.

The reply came swiftly, the username 'thevoiceofthehand' blinking to life on the screen. "Such things are not meant for the faint of heart. What you seek is forbidden, and the cost is high."

John's pulse quickened. "I have nothing left to lose. Tell me how to do it."

There was a pause, pregnant with dark possibilities. Then, the response came, laden with an unsettling authority. "There are rituals, ancient and dangerous, that can open the door between life and death. Are you prepared to pay the price?"

John felt a shiver run down his spine. The conversation was surreal, the reality of it all slipping through his grasp like sand. But his determination was a burning coal in his chest. "Yes. Tell me what I need to do."

John's hand shook as he scribbled down every detail, the words a macabre blueprint to his dark desire. The ritual sounded horrific, but the image of Ethan's lifeless body was a constant, gnawing agony. He was willing to endure any horror, any nightmare, to hold his son once more.

With the instructions in hand, a grim determination settled over him. He gathered the necessary items with a methodical detachment—Ethan's baby blanket, salt and ash from a nearby shop, and a sharp knife. The ancient texts lay open on the desk, their pages whispering of forbidden knowledge. His laptop screen flickered, the words blurring as exhaustion clawed at his consciousness.

As night fell, the room was swallowed by shadows, a creeping sense of dread thickening the air. John knew the risks, knew that what he was about to attempt was both dangerous and unnatural. But the thought of holding Ethan again, of hearing his laughter fill the house once more, propelled him forward.

He cleared a space on the floor, his hands moving with a mechanical precision as he drew the circle. Salt and ash mixed under his fingers, the symbols forming with disturbing ease. The knife felt cold and heavy in his grasp, a tangible promise of pain. As he stood over the circle, ready to begin the ritual, John glanced at Ethan's lifeless form on the bed, and a sob caught in his throat.

"I'm doing this for you, Ethan," he whispered, his voice breaking with the weight of his grief. "I will bring you back."

John had crossed a threshold from which there was no return, driven by a love that defied death, a grief that knew no bounds, and a desperation that pushed him to the edge of madness. He braced himself for whatever would come next, his heart a storm of fear and hope.

Chapter Five

Detective Inspector Jack Palace stood at the entrance of the police station on Clough Road, his tall, imposing frame casting a long shadow in the morning sun. At 6'3", he had the build of a former athlete, broad-shouldered and muscular, but his sharp, angular features and piercing blue eyes gave him an air of relentless intensity. His dark hair was flecked with early grey, and a perpetual five o'clock shadow lined his jaw, giving him a rugged, world-weary appearance that spoke of countless sleepless nights and hard-fought battles.

Jack's history was as complex as his appearance suggested. Born and raised in Hull, he had grown up in a rough neighbourhood, Orchard Park, where he quickly learned the value of toughness and street smarts. His father, a decorated police officer, had been killed in the line of duty when Jack was just sixteen, a loss that fuelled his determination to follow in his footsteps. After a stint in the military, where he honed his investigative skills and discipline, Jack returned to Hull and joined the police force. Over the years, he had earned a reputation as a tenacious detective, one who never shied away from the most challenging cases.

Clough Road Police Station stood as a beacon of modernity amidst the industrial landscape of Hull. The new, state-of-the-art facility gleamed under the grey, northern English sky, its sleek silver cladding catching and reflecting every stray beam of sunlight. The building was an architectural marvel, a testament to the city's commitment to progress and security. Massive floor-to-ceiling windows lined the exterior, distinguishing it from the utilitarian buildings that surrounded it.

Inside, the station was a hive of activity, bustling with officers and staff who moved with purpose and precision. The air was filled with the hum of technology—computers whirring, phones ringing—and the constant chatter of voices coordinating efforts to maintain law and order. The walls were adorned with digital displays, flashing updates on ongoing cases, and important announcements.

Jack felt a sense of both comfort and unease as he walked through the automatic sliding doors. The lobby was spacious and bright, the polished white tiles reflecting the natural light streaming in through the vast windows. A large, modern reception desk dominated the centre of the room, manned by a receptionist who greeted visitors with a practised smile.

To the left, a corridor led to a series of glass-walled offices where detectives and officers worked diligently, their focus unwavering despite the occasional distraction from the outside world. The open-plan design fostered a sense of transparency and collaboration, a far cry from the cramped, poorly lit stations of the past.

On the right, a staircase with stainless steel railings ascended to the upper levels, where more specialized units operated. The second floor housed the forensic labs and interrogation rooms, all equipped with the latest technology to aid in the pursuit of justice. The scent of freshly brewed coffee wafted through the air from the break room, a small oasis of comfort amidst the chaos of police work.

As Jack made his way to his office, he couldn't help but admire the efficiency and sophistication of the facility. A large window behind his desk offered a view of the city, a reminder of the world they were all working to protect.

Jack's office was a cluttered sanctuary amidst the modern chaos of simplicity. His desk was a battlefield of paperwork, case files, and personal mementos. Photographs of his father and his military unit were pinned to a corkboard on the wall, reminders of the life that had shaped him. A worn leather chair sat behind the desk, its surface cracked and faded from years of use. The walls were adorned with certificates and commendations, but they seemed to offer little comfort to the man who occupied the room.

He made his way to his desk, his eyes scanning the room with practised ease. The chief inspector's office, in contrast to Jack's cluttered workspace, was a pristine, almost sterile environment, with everything in its place. The chief himself was a stern, no-nonsense man in his late fifties, with thinning grey hair and a perpetual scowl etched into his features. His uniform was always impeccably pressed, and his piercing gaze could cut through any pretence.

"Palace, get in here," the chief's voice boomed from his office.

Jack nodded and made his way inside, the door closing behind him with a soft click.

Chief Inspector Harold Winters was a man whose presence commanded respect with an undercurrent of fear among his subordinates. Standing at a solid six feet two inches, his broad shoulders and barrel chest gave him an imposing silhouette that seemed to fill any room he entered. His hair, once a vibrant auburn, had now faded to a dignified silver, closely cropped to his scalp in a no-nonsense fashion. His face, though lined with the passage of time, bore the marks of a career spent in the trenches of law enforcement: a crooked nose from a long-ago altercation, a jagged scar above his right eyebrow from a knife fight with a desperate criminal, and deep-set blue eyes that had seen too much.

On this particular day, he wore a dark charcoal suit, impeccably tailored to his muscular frame, with a crisp white shirt and a navy-blue tie that bore the faintest pattern of stripes, the only hint of whimsy in his otherwise stern appearance. Three silver pips on his epaulettes, catching the light with every movement, were a constant reminder of his authority. His shoes, polished to a mirror shine, clicked sharply against the polished tiles of Clough Road Police Station as he moved through the halls.

Winters had been a fixture in the force for over three decades, rising through the ranks with a combination of brute strength, sharp intellect, and an unyielding sense of justice. His career had begun in the gritty streets of London, where he had quickly made a name for himself as a fearless and relentless officer. Stories of his exploits were whispered in the corridors—how he single-handedly took down a gang of armed robbers, or the time he saved a child from a burning building. These tales, half legend and half truth, added to the aura of invincibility that surrounded him.

Despite his tough exterior, those who knew him well understood there was a depth to Winters that went beyond the warrant card and the uniform. His office was a testament to this complexity, adorned with framed photographs of his family—his late wife, Julie, who had succumbed to cancer five years prior, and his two grown children, both of whom had followed in their father's footsteps and joined the force. A small collection of worn detective novels lined a shelf behind his desk, the only indulgence in an otherwise austere space.

Jack had always admired Winters, seeing him as the embodiment of what a police officer should be. As Jack entered the chief's office, he couldn't help but notice the weight of responsibility that seemed to hang in the air, mingling with the faint scent of old leather and aftershave. Winters looked up from his desk, where he had been reviewing a stack of reports, and fixed Jack with a piercing gaze.

Jack's hands trembled slightly as he took the case file from Chief Winters. The weight of it felt like an anchor pulling him deeper into a sea of chaos. He flipped it open, his eyes scanning the details—John Morrison's photograph, hospital reports, and witness statements. Each piece of paper seemed to scream a warning, a portent of the darkness he was about to dive into.

"This one's going to be tough, Jack," Chief Winters said, his voice carrying a gravity that matched the situation. "John Morrison fled the hospital with his deceased son, Ethan. We need to recover the child's body and bring John in. He's already assaulted hospital staff, and we don't know what he's capable of next."

Jack's expression grew even grimmer as he read through the notes. John Morrison wasn't just a distraught father; he was a man on the edge, pushed to the brink by grief and desperation. "I'll get on it right away," Jack replied, his voice steady but his mind already racing through possible scenarios.

The chief nodded, his eyes hardening with resolve. "I know you will. Just be careful. This guy's desperate, and desperate people do dangerous things."

Jack met Winters' gaze, the unspoken understanding

between them heavy in the air. "What do we know about his movements after he left the hospital?"

Winters leaned back in his chair, his face etched with lines of worry. "Not much. He was last seen heading towards the outskirts of town. We've got roadblocks set up, but he's slippery. He knows how to avoid detection."

Jack nodded, closing the file and tucking it under his arm. "I'll start with the places he knows. Maybe he's gone to ground somewhere familiar."

"Good idea," Winters said, rubbing his temples as if trying to stave off an impending headache. "And Jack, don't underestimate him. The man's been through hell. He's lost everything. That kind of pain can make a man unpredictable."

Jack swallowed hard, the image of his own father flashing briefly in his mind. He understood the kind of torment that could twist a person, could drive them to the brink. "I won't," he promised. "I'll bring him in, Chief. And I'll bring Ethan back."

As Jack turned to leave, Winters called out to him once more. "Jack, one more thing. Morrison's not a bad man. He's just broken. If there's a way to bring him in without violence, take it. We don't need any bloodshed."

Jack paused at the door, nodding solemnly. "I understand."

Jack left the office, the gravity of the task ahead settling on his shoulders. The station around him buzzed with activity, but he felt a cold, solitary resolve. As he headed back to his desk, the noise of the station faded into the background. He had a job to do, and nothing would stand in his way.

Back at his desk, Jack opened the file on John. He started with the basics: John Morrison, 35 years old, a cyber security technician. Married to Sarah Morrison, now deceased, with one child, Ethan, now deceased. Jack began digging deeper into John's background, pulling up medical records, employment history, and personal information.

As Jack sifted through the family's medical records, a pattern emerged. Sarah Morrison had died six months prior, and her death certificate listed a rare and aggressive respiratory illness as the cause. Further investigation into hospital records revealed that Ethan had been diagnosed with the same illness shortly after his birth. The parallels were chilling, and Jack could see the timeline of John's descent into despair.

John had been a devoted husband and father, but Sarah's illness had taken a toll on the entire family. Jack found photos on social media accounts of a once happy couple, Sarah's smile radiant even as her health deteriorated, and John's expression growing more strained with each passing month. Ethan's medical records showed numerous hospital visits, treatments, and ultimately, the failure to save him from the same fate that had claimed his mother.

Jack then turned his attention to John's professional life. As a cyber security technician, John had a reputation for being meticulous and highly skilled. He worked for a prominent global tech firm based in London, where his job involved protecting sensitive information from cyber threats. This background made Jack uneasy; John's expertise in cyber security meant he knew how to cover his tracks, making the detective's job significantly harder.

Jack pulled up John's employment records and performance reviews, which painted a picture of a man who had once been highly respected in his field.

Colleagues described John as dedicated and brilliant, but also noted a change in his behaviour following Sarah's death. He had become withdrawn, his work performance declining as he struggled to cope with his grief.

As Jack delved deeper into John Morrison's background, a nagging sense of unease settled over him. On the surface, Morrison was the epitome of a model citizen—no criminal record, steady employment, a loving father and husband. But the more Jack looked, the more he realized that it was all too perfect. There were no slip-ups, no moments of weakness, no signs of the strain that should have accompanied the trials Morrison had faced. It was as if someone had gone to great lengths to present an immaculate image, to cover up the cracks that Jack was certain had to be there. A closer look at Morrison's work history revealed odd gaps, periods where he seemed to disappear off the radar, only to reappear with no explanation. The hospital records were another red flag—entries missing, treatments that didn't match up with the symptoms Ethan was supposedly exhibiting. Jack's instincts screamed that something was off, that there was more to this case than met the eye. He could feel the pieces starting to come together, forming a picture that was still out of focus but undeniably odd. Jack had been a police officer long enough to know that monsters rarely looked like monsters. They wore cardigans and mowed their lawns. They picked up their kids from school and remembered birthdays. Jack had seen it before—the guy who seemed too clean, the woman whose smile never quite reached her eyes. It was never the ones who looked like trouble; it was the ones who bent over backward to seem normal, like they were reading from a script titled *How to Be a Good Person*. And John Morrison? Jack's gut told him that no one lived through the kind of grief Morrison had without some sign of wear and tear. No anger, no despair, not even a bad day at the office? It didn't add up. It made Jack wonder if Morrison's clean-cut life was a mask, and if so, what kind of face lay underneath. Maybe it was nothing. Maybe the guy was just the rare breed who handled tragedy with grace. But if there was one thing Jack Palace knew, it was that "maybe" had a way of getting people killed.

Jack knew the key to finding John lay in understanding his state of mind. He started by contacting Hull Royal Infirmary and asking to review the CCTV footage from the night John had fled. His request was promptly granted, but since he knew John was not at the hospital, Jack thought it a priority to get to know more about the man he was seeking, and a visit to his home might bear fruit and help Jack understand the frame of mind John was in.

Palace navigated the congested streets of Hull, his mind a whirl of thoughts as he drove his beat-up old Ford Mustang. The car was a relic from another time, a symbol of both nostalgia and stubborn resilience, much like Jack himself. The engine growled loudly as he turned onto the main road, heading towards Cottingham. The route was familiar, a maze of narrow lanes and busy junctions, each turn etching deeper into the landscape of his mind.

The police station on Clough Road faded into the rearview mirror, its grim facade replaced by the more suburban sprawl of Cottingham, a village that formed an eastern boundary to the city. St Margaret's Avenue was a quiet, tree-lined street, the kind of place where children played in the front gardens and neighbours exchanged pleasantries over neatly trimmed hedges or whilst walking the dog. Yet today, there was an air of unease hanging over it, a disquiet that matched the storm clouds gathering on the horizon.

Jack's car rumbled to a stop in front of John Morrison's home. The house was an unassuming two-story structure, its exterior a weathered shade of white with dark green shutters. The garden was overgrown, the lawn untamed, as if the house itself had given up on trying to maintain any semblance of normality.

He stepped out of the car, the gravel crunching under his boots, and made his way up the cracked path to the front door. The air was thick with the scent of impending rain and the whispers of forgotten laughter. Jack knocked on the door, his knuckles rapping against the chipped paint, but there was no answer. He tried the handle, finding it unlocked, and stepped inside.

The interior was a snapshot of happier times now lost. The living room was cluttered with the detritus of a life once lived fully: toys scattered across the floor, a coffee cup left half-drunk on the table, and photographs lining the walls. Each image was a portal to a moment of joy, now tinged with a sorrow that was almost palpable. Jack's eyes lingered on a family portrait—John, his wife Sarah, and baby Ethan—all smiles and promise.

Jack Palace hadn't always been a detective. He hadn't always been the grim-faced, sleep-deprived shell of a man who haunted crime scenes like a ghost desperate for closure. Once upon a time, he was just Jack—a young copper in his mid-twenties with a spring in his step and hope in his heart and a belief that justice was not just a word but a tangible force in the world. But that was before *it* happened. Before the case that carved a hole in his soul so deep, nothing had ever managed to fill it.

It had been a rainy afternoon in March, the kind of day when the clouds hung low and heavy, casting a dull, oppressive pall over the city. Jack had been assigned to routine patrol duty in a part of town where crime had a way of creeping into every corner—a crumbling old neighbourhood that had seen better days, back when the factories still churned out goods and the streets buzzed with life. Now the factories were long silent, and the only sound that echoed through the narrow alleys was the occasional scuffle or the distant wail of a siren.

Jack was partnered with Tom Everett, an older officer with a gut that hinted at too many doughnuts and a disposition that was as sour as the coffee in the station break room. Tom had a way of looking at things—at people, at the city, at life—that was jaded and cynical, as if he'd seen the worst the world had to offer and didn't expect anything better. Jack had always been the opposite—hopeful, optimistic, eager to make a difference.

They were cruising down an empty street, the window wipers beating a monotonous rhythm against the glass, when the call came in: a domestic disturbance, potential child endangerment. The address was a dilapidated block of flats on the far side of town, a place notorious for its tenant troubles. Jack's heart skipped a beat. Domestic disturbances were always tricky, and when a child was involved … it was the kind of call that made your stomach knot up.

"Great," Tom muttered, flicking his cigarette out the window. "Another bloody mess."

Jack didn't reply, but he felt a tightness in his chest, a sense of impending doom that he couldn't quite shake. They arrived at the building, a monolith of decaying brick and peeling paint, and made their way up the narrow, graffiti-splattered staircase to the third floor. The air was thick with the smell of dampness, rot, and something else—something acrid, metallic.

They could hear the shouting before they reached the door. A man's voice, low and menacing, punctuated by the shrill cries of a child. Jack felt the hairs on the back of his neck stand on end. Tom raised his hand to knock, but before he could, the door flew open and a man stood there, wild-eyed, a broken beer bottle clutched in his fist.

"What the hell do you want?" the man snarled, his breath reeking of alcohol.

"We got a call about a disturbance," Tom said, his voice steady, but Jack could hear the tension in it. "We just want to make sure everyone's okay."

"Everything's fine," the man snapped, his eyes darting nervously. "Just … get the fuck out of here."

Jack glanced past the man and caught sight of a woman huddled in the corner, her face bruised and tear-streaked, clutching a little girl no more than five years old. The girl's eyes were wide with terror, her small frame shaking uncontrollably. Jack felt something inside him snap.

"Sir, we need to see the child," Jack said, stepping forward, his hands hovering, ready for conflict. "Now."

The man's eyes narrowed, and for a split second, Jack saw the decision form in his mind. It was like watching a train wreck in slow motion—inevitable, unstoppable. The man lunged, the bottle swinging wildly, and in that instant, everything blurred. Jack deflected the attack with the bottle and shoved the drunken man back. The man tripped on the unsteadily laid carpet and rolled to his side, reaching for something from underneath the tatty, stained sofa next to him.

He grinned menacingly as he pulled out a small black pistol and looked towards Jack as he began to get to his feet. Without hesitation, Jack leapt forward, diving onto the now armed, abusive man.

There was a struggle, a shout, the shattering of glass, and then … a gunshot.

The man crumpled to the floor, a dark red stain blossoming on his chest. Jack stood there, the gun now in his hand, his breath coming in short, ragged gasps. Tom was yelling something, but Jack couldn't hear him. All he could see was the little girl, her face pale, her eyes wide and unblinking, staring at the man who had been her father.

The aftermath was a blur. The woman was hysterical, the little girl silent, and Jack … Jack was broken. The shooting was ruled justified—self-defence, they called it—but it didn't matter. Something inside him died that day, along with the man on the floor.

From that moment on, Jack wasn't the same. The bright-eyed optimism that had once defined him was gone, replaced by a cold, unyielding determination. He threw himself into his work, driven by a need to save others from the darkness that had consumed that little girl's life. Every case became personal, every victim a reflection of the one he couldn't save.

Years passed, and Jack climbed the ranks, his reputation as a relentless, tireless detective growing with each case he solved. But the darkness never left him. It lingered, a constant shadow, a reminder of his failure.

And now, standing in the hallway, staring at the door to Ethan's room, that same darkness gnawed at him. Jack had seen too much, lost too much, to let another child slip through his fingers. Ethan wasn't just a case—he was a lifeline, a chance for redemption. The stakes were higher than ever, and Jack knew he couldn't afford to fail.

As he stood there, the house lights flickering overhead, Jack thought of that little girl, her haunted eyes, her father's blood on the linoleum floor. He thought of all the times he'd come close to breaking, to giving up, but had pushed through because he had to—because there was no other choice.

And then, with a deep breath, Jack turned the doorknob and stepped into the nursery, ready to face whatever horrors awaited him. Because if there was one thing he had learned in all his years as a detective, it was this: the past never stays buried. It claws its way to the surface, dragging you down with it if you let it. But Jack had never let it—not then and not now.

The nursery was a place of profound sadness. Once painted a cheerful pastel blue, with clouds dancing across the ceiling, it now stood as a mausoleum of shattered dreams. The crib was neatly made, a blanket folded at its foot, and a layer of dust coated everything, muting the once vibrant colours. Ethan's belongings were meticulously packed away, each item a testament to John's desperate attempt to hold onto his son.

Jack's heart ached at the sight. He could feel the weight of John's grief in every corner of the room. He made his way back to the living room, his thoughts heavy, when a movement outside caught his eye. A woman was peering over the fence, her curiosity and concern evident. Jack stepped outside to meet her.

"Morning, madam," Jack said, his voice gentle but authoritative.

"Oh, good morning," she replied, her eyes darting nervously between Jack and the house. "Is everything alright?"

Jack studied her for a moment. She was in her mid-sixties, with greying hair pulled into a neat bun, wearing a floral print dress that seemed to belong to a different era. Her face was lined with worry.

"Detective Inspector Jack Palace," he introduced himself, flashing his warrant card. "I'm looking for Mr John Morrison. I don't suppose you have seen him recently?"

The woman's eyes widened slightly. "I'm Mrs Peterson. I've lived next door for years. John's a good man, but ... well, after his wife passed, he hasn't been the same. I saw him leave with Ethan the other day, but I thought it was strange. The boy ... he didn't look well."

Jack nodded, absorbing the information. "Anything else you've noticed? Any visitors, perhaps?"

Mrs Peterson shook her head. "No, just John. He's been so reclusive lately. I'm worried about him, Detective Inspector. He loves that boy so much. There have been a few cars parked on the road recently that I haven't seen before, though. I would know if they belonged to anyone on the street. But not John, since he left with Ethan."

Jack offered a reassuring smile and handed her his card. "Thank you, Mrs Peterson. If you think of anything else, please give me a call."

As he walked back to his car, Jack felt the weight of the task ahead. The house, the nursery, the grief that hung in the air—it all pointed to a man pushed beyond his limits. Jack knew he had to find John, not just to solve the case, but to prevent further tragedy. The storm clouds overhead mirrored the turmoil in his heart, and he resolved to bring some semblance of peace to this fractured family, no matter the cost. Jack made his way back to the station.

The detective sat in his cluttered office, the harsh fluorescent lights casting long shadows across the room. The air was thick with the scent of stale coffee and old paper. He leaned back in his creaky chair, the wheels squeaking in protest, and dialled the number for Bio-Rad, John Morrison's most recent employer.

Bio-Rad was a cutting-edge biotech firm with a new centre located on the outskirts of Hull, a gleaming edifice of steel and glass that stood in stark contrast to the industrial grime that surrounded it. The company was known for its work in medical diagnostics and life science research, a beacon of innovation in a city that often felt stuck in the past.

The phone rang twice before a brisk, no-nonsense voice answered. "Bio-Rad. This is Mr Allen. How can I help you?"

Jack cleared his throat. "Mr Allen, this is Detective Inspector Jack Palace with the Humberside Police Force. I need to ask you a few questions about a former employee of yours, John Morrison."

There was a pause on the other end, and Jack could almost hear the man straightening up in his chair. "Of course, Detective Inspector. How can I assist you?"

"John Morrison worked for you as a computer technician in your cyber security division. Can you tell me what he was like on the job, especially after his wife passed away?"

Mr Allen sighed, a sound that conveyed a world of weariness. "John was one of our best, a brilliant mind when it came to network security. He was meticulous, dedicated, always the first to arrive and the last to leave. But after Sarah died ... well, he changed."

Jack leaned forward, scribbling notes on a yellow legal

pad. "How so?"

"There was a noticeable shift in his demeanour. He became withdrawn, almost obsessive about his work. He started taking on more projects than he could handle, as if trying to drown himself in tasks to keep his mind off his grief. He'd spend hours staring at his computer screen, barely speaking to anyone. It was like he was a ghost just going through the motions."

Jack could picture it clearly—John hunched over his desk in the sterile, high-tech environment of Bio-Rad, the glow of the monitor reflecting off his tired eyes. "Did he ever mention anything unusual? Any talk about ... unconventional interests?"

Mr Allen hesitated. "Not directly. But there were rumours. Some of the staff mentioned seeing him on the dark web, researching strange topics late at night. At the time, I dismissed it as gossip. Now I'm not so sure."

Jack's pen paused mid-sentence. "What kind of topics?"

"I don't know exactly, but the gist of it were things that had no place in a biotech firm. I confronted him about it once, and he denied everything, said it was just idle curiosity. But I could see the desperation in his eyes. He was a man searching for something."

Jack felt a chill run down his spine. "Did he ever mention his son, Ethan?"

There was a long silence before Mr Allen spoke again, his voice softer, almost regretful. "He talked about Ethan constantly before Sarah died. Afterward, not so much. But you could tell he was doing everything for that boy. He loved him more than anything. I think losing Sarah broke him, and losing Ethan ... well, I can't even imagine."

Jack's mind raced as he processed the information. John Morrison wasn't just a grieving father; he was a man on the edge, willing to cross any boundary to reclaim what he had lost. "Thank you, Mr Allen. You've been very helpful."

"If you find him, DI Palace, please ... try to help him. He's a good man."

Jack hung up the phone, the weight of Mr Allen's words pressing down on him. How did he know that Ethan was dead? Maybe he had guessed, Jack thought, and put it to the back of his mind. He looked around his office, the walls lined with case files and unsolved mysteries. John Morrison was more than a case now; he was a desperate soul, teetering on the brink of something dark and dangerous. And Jack knew he had to find him before it was too late.

Chapter Six

As Jack paced the cafeteria, the memory of a case from years ago clawed at the edges of his mind. The press had turned a simple investigation into a witch hunt, and an innocent man had paid the price. The headlines had been just as lurid, the public just as frenzied. Jack had sworn then that he'd never let it happen again. But here he was, facing the same storm, and the old wounds burned like fresh cuts

The cafeteria at the police station was a drab, lifeless space, its walls stained with the remnants of long-forgotten meals and the weariness of countless officers. The air was thick with the scent of stale coffee and overcooked eggs, the kind of institutional food that did little to nourish and even less to comfort. Around him, the low mumbling of conversation blended with the mechanical whir of a vending machine, a discordant symphony that only heightened the tension gnawing at his nerves.

Jack sat at a roughly polished steel table, absently stirring a cup of the sludge-like brew in front of him, his eyes fixed on the newspaper spread open on the table. The headline screamed at him in bold, black letters:

Rampage at Local Hospital: Grieving Father Turns Violent, Escapes with Dead Son!

His stomach churned as he read the first few lines of the article. The words felt like acid burning through his veins:

In a shocking turn of events, John Morrison, a previously unremarkable man from the village of

Cottingham, has unleashed a wave of terror upon our quiet community. After assaulting an elderly woman in her own home and escaping from security guards at Hull Royal Infirmary, Morrison, in an act of sheer madness, abducted the corpse of his deceased son, Ethan Morrison, from the hospital. Eyewitnesses describe the scene as something out of a horror film, with Morrison ranting about dark forces and demonic influences. Authorities believe he is armed, dangerous, and utterly unhinged.

Jack's grip tightened on the edge of the newspaper, his knuckles going white. He could almost feel the words crawling off the page, twisting around his neck like a noose. The image the article painted of John Morrison was grotesque, a caricature of a broken man turned monster. It wasn't the John he knew—or rather, the John he thought he knew.

The article continued, each sentence more sensationalized than the last:

Sources inside the hospital, who have asked to remain anonymous, claim that Morrison had been acting erratically for weeks. While there is no concrete evidence linking Morrison to any occult practices, his behaviour suggests a deep mental instability, perhaps even possession.

Possession. Jack could hardly believe what he was reading. The media had jumped from a man's grief-stricken breakdown to supernatural nonsense, and people would eat it up, gobbling down every lurid detail like it was gospel truth. The more he read, the deeper his irritation grew. The article was riddled with inaccuracies, half-truths, and outright lies.

Morrison's wife, Sarah, was reportedly a devout member of a fringe religious group, further fuelling speculation that the family was involved in something sinister. The police have yet to release an official statement, but sources suggest that Morrison may have had accomplices, and that his son's death was not the result of natural causes as initially believed.

Jack slapped the newspaper shut, unable to stomach any more. The mention of Sarah, dragged through the mud like that, twisted the knife in his gut. She had been a devoted mother, loving and kind. Whatever had happened to John—and by extension, to Ethan—had nothing to do with cults or rituals. This was grief, pure and simple, twisted by forces Jack still couldn't fully understand.

His frustration bubbled over as he thought about the damage this article would do. The public would latch onto these sensationalized details and it would make his job nearly impossible. Every tip from the public would be tainted with the paranoia and hysteria this article would fuel. And then there was John himself—if he saw this, if he read these lies about his wife and his son, it might push him even further over the edge.

Jack's phone buzzed on the table, the sound sharp against the backdrop of his brooding thoughts. He snatched it up, recognizing Sergeant Williams' number on the screen.

"Palace," he answered, his voice taut with irritation.

"Palace, you see the paper this morning?" Williams' voice was gruff, laced with the same frustration Jack felt.

"Yeah, I saw it," Jack replied, his jaw clenched. "Can't

believe they're allowed to print this rubbish. It's only going to make things worse."

"There's more," Williams said, his tone darkening. "The article's not just in the paper. It's online, on every major news site, and it's spreading like wildfire. And get this—Cassandra Lane's the one behind it. She's been digging, pulling in every bit of speculation and half-baked theory she can find, and now it's out there, poisoning the well."

Jack swore under his breath. Lane was relentless, a bloodhound for sensational stories, and she had a reputation for bending the truth to fit her narrative. She wasn't interested in justice or the truth; she was interested in headlines, in clicks, in making her name by any means necessary.

Cassandra Lane wasn't just any journalist—she was a predator, feeding on fear and scandal like a vulture on carrion. Jack had crossed paths with her before, during a high-profile case that had ended in tragedy. She'd twisted every fact and sensationalized every detail until the truth was unrecognizable, buried beneath layers of lies and speculation. And now she was at it again, exploiting the pain of a grieving father for a few more clicks and a splashy headline.

"What the hell is she thinking, putting this out there?" Jack snapped, pacing the small space of the cafeteria. "She's got no idea what she's stirring up. If John sees this—shit, if anyone close to this case sees it—it could blow everything up. And now she's got the whole town convinced he's some kind of demon-possessed psychopath."

"There's more," Williams continued, his voice grave. "I've just got word from the brass. They're getting pressure from higher up—because of the article. They want this wrapped up fast and clean. No more delays, no more excuses. And they don't care how we do it."

Jack rubbed his temples, feeling the weight of the situation pressing down on him from all sides. "So now we've got the media spinning fairy tales, the public in a panic, and the brass breathing down our necks. This just keeps getting better."

Williams let out a heavy sigh. "Yeah. And if you think it's bad now, wait until Lane gets wind of any more details. She's like a dog with a bone, and she won't stop until she's chewed it to pieces."

Jack knew he had to act, and fast. The longer this dragged on, the more damage it would do—not just to the case, but to everyone involved. He had to find John before anyone else did, before the situation escalated into something far worse than it already was. But with the media fanning the flames and the pressure from above mounting, it felt like a race against time, with the odds stacked firmly against him.

"Keep me posted on anything else that comes up," Jack said, his voice firm with resolve. "I'm going to see what I can do to shut this down before it gets even more out of hand."

"Roger that," Williams replied. "And Palace—watch your back. This whole thing's turning into a shit storm."

Jack ended the call and stared at the closed newspaper in front of him. The story wasn't just in print—it was everywhere, like a virus spreading through the veins of the city, turning fear into hysteria and truth into fiction. And somewhere out there, John Morrison was running, driven by grief, hunted by the very people who were supposed to protect him.

Jack grabbed his coat and headed for the door. There was no time to waste. The hunt was on, and if he didn't find John first, he wasn't sure anyone would.

As Jack pushed through the heavy glass doors of the station, a chill wind swept across his face, carrying with it the scent of rain and something else—something foreboding. The streets were quiet now, but there was a tension in the air, a feeling that something was about to break. Jack couldn't shake the sense that this was just the beginning, that the storm was far from over and that when it hit, it would tear through the town like a blade through flesh.

Chapter Seven

The morning light filtered through the thick, dusty blinds of Cassandra Lane's flat, casting long, slanted shadows over the clutter that dominated the small space. The flat, located in a newly developed building in the heart of Hull, was more of a command centre than a home. Stacks of newspapers, each one meticulously folded and marked with scrawled notes, covered the floors. The walls were a chaotic mosaic of corkboards pinned with photographs, police sketches, and handwritten timelines. Coffee mugs, some half-empty, others tipped over and forgotten, added to the general sense of disarray.

Cassandra herself stood in the centre of the room, a striking figure amidst the chaos. She was in her mid-thirties, with dark brown hair that she wore in a no-nonsense bun at the nape of her neck. Loose strands framed her face, which was sharp, angular, and deceptively beautiful. Her green eyes were hard and calculating and seemed to miss nothing, and they could cut through the veneer of any falsehood. Today she wore a tailored black blazer over a simple white blouse, paired with sleek, dark trousers. The outfit was businesslike, but there was an edge to it, something that hinted at the relentless drive and ambition simmering beneath her polished exterior.

Her flat was a testament to her obsession. Every surface was a battleground where she waged her personal war on secrets and lies. The desk was strewn with printouts and notebooks, each filled with the details of her latest investigation: John Morrison. The case had landed in her lap like a gift from some twisted god, ripe for the kind of sensationalist reporting that had made her a household name.

Cassandra's rise at the *Hull Daily Mail* had been nothing short of meteoric. She'd started at the bottom, fresh out of a journalism course, taking any assignment they threw at her—reporting on local fairs, writing obituaries, covering city council meetings that put most people to sleep. But it didn't take long for her to realize that the real money, the real power, was in the big stories, the ones that made the front page and had everyone talking. She'd clawed her way up, earning a reputation for tenacity and a willingness to do whatever it took to get the story, even if it meant bending the truth a little to fit the narrative she wanted to tell.

She leaned over the cluttered desk, picking up a newspaper that had just been delivered, the ink still fresh. The headline blared:

John Morrison's Terror Continues: The Untold Horror Behind the Man on the Run.

She smirked, her lips curling in satisfaction. The article beneath the headline was hers—a mix of fact, speculation, and just enough fiction to make it irresistible to the public. The truth, as far as Cassandra was concerned, was less important than the story itself. And the story of John Morrison was pure gold.

As she read through her own words, a sense of pride swelled in her chest, but it was quickly followed by a pang of something else—something that had been gnawing at her since she first broke the news of Morrison's escape. Despite her public persona, despite the hard, cynical exterior she showed the world, Cassandra had once been a true believer in the power of journalism to make a difference.

Cassandra Lane had always been haunted by the past,

by the whispers of a world that seemed so much larger and more terrifying than the one she'd known. She had grown up in the small Yorkshire village of Wroghton, a place that seemed to exist outside of time. The village was nestled between rolling green hills and dense forests, a patchwork of ancient stone cottages and narrow winding lanes that twisted through the landscape like veins. It was the kind of place where the fog clung to the ground like a living thing, and the wind carried the echoes of old secrets.

Wroghton was a village of stories, of things that had happened so long ago that no one could remember when or why. But Cassandra's grandmother, Edith Lane, remembered. She remembered everything. Edith was the village's unofficial historian, the keeper of tales that had been passed down through generations. She was a stout woman with a face carved by time and a voice that could command attention with a single word. Her cottage was a fortress of memories, filled with books and trinkets from a life lived on the edge of history. The walls were lined with shelves that sagged under the weight of leather-bound volumes, and the air was thick with the scent of old paper and pipe tobacco.

Cassandra had spent her childhood in that cottage, sitting at her grandmother's feet as she spun tales of a world that was both wondrous and terrifying. There was one story in particular that had lodged itself deep in Cassandra's mind, a story that had shaped her in ways she couldn't fully understand until much later.

It was a cold autumn evening, the kind where the wind howled through the village like a banshee and the trees whispered secrets to one another. Cassandra was eight years old, her wide green eyes reflecting the flickering light of the fire as she sat cross-legged on the rug. Edith had just finished her tea and leaned back in her chair, her eyes glinting with a mixture of mischief and gravitas.

"Cassy, love, have I ever told you about the Night of the Thirteen Bells?" Edith's voice was low and full of portent, a tone that meant the story was one of the darker ones.

Cassandra shook her head, her small hands clutching a woollen blanket as she leaned forward, eager for the tale.

"It was many years ago, before even my time," Edith began, her voice carrying the weight of countless retellings. "The villagers back then were a superstitious lot, and they believed that at certain times of the year, the veil between our world and the next grew thin. One such time was All Hallows' Eve, a night when the dead could walk among the living. But the Night of the Thirteen Bells was different. It only happened once every century, when the moon was full and the wind blew from the east."

Cassandra shivered as Edith continued, her voice weaving a tapestry of dread.

"The legend goes that on this night, the church bells would ring thirteen times—an impossible thing, since our church has only twelve bells. But on that night, the thirteenth bell would toll, a bell that didn't exist in our world. Those who heard it were said to be marked by death, cursed to die before the year was out unless they could solve the riddle of the thirteenth bell."

Edith paused, her eyes narrowing as she peered into the fire, as if seeing the events unfold in the dancing flames. "That year, it happened. The bells rang out across the village, thirteen clear, mournful chimes that sent a chill through every heart. The people were terrified, knowing the old legend. They searched the village high and low for the source of the thirteenth bell, but they found nothing. As the days passed, people began to die, one by one, in the most terrible ways."

Cassandra was rapt, her breath coming in shallow gasps as the story reached its climax.

"Finally, there was only one man left—a blacksmith named Thomas. He was a clever man, and he figured out that the thirteenth bell was not of this world. It was a bell from the other side, calling the dead to claim their own. Thomas knew he had to act fast. He made his way to the old church, where the bells were kept, and there he did something extraordinary. He forged a new bell, a thirteenth bell, to match the one from the other world. When he hung it in the tower and struck it, the curse was broken. The dead were appeased, and the killings stopped. But Thomas was never seen again. Some say he was taken by the spirits as payment, others say he went mad and wandered off into the moors."

Edith's voice trailed off, leaving a heavy silence in the room. Cassandra's mind raced, the story embedding itself in her young psyche. It was a story of danger, of mystery, of the thin line between life and death. But more than that, it was a story of truth—a truth that was hidden, buried under layers of legend and fear, waiting to be uncovered.

As Cassandra grew older, the stories of Wroghton and the mystery of the thirteenth bell stayed with her. They were a part of her, as much as the green hills and the foggy mornings. But they also sparked something deeper—a burning desire to uncover the truths that lay hidden beneath the surface of the world. She wanted to be like her grandmother, a keeper of stories, but she wanted more than that. She wanted to dig deeper, to find the truths that others were too afraid to see.

When the time came, Cassandra left Wroghton for university, a move that felt like stepping into another world. She attended the University of Leeds, a sprawling, bustling campus that seemed a universe away from the quiet, insular village she had known. She enrolled in the journalism course, drawn by the idea of storytelling as a profession, of uncovering the hidden truths of the world.

University was a revelation for Cassandra. It was a place where she could sharpen her mind, where she could immerse herself in the art of investigation and writing. But it was also a place of challenges. The first semester was tough; the academic pressure was relentless and the competition fierce. But Cassandra thrived on it, driven by the stories her grandmother had told her and by the memory of Wroghton's secrets.

It was during her second year that something happened which solidified her path in journalism. Cassandra was taking a course in investigative reporting, a class that delved into the darker side of the profession— the part where you had to dig through layers of lies and deception to find the truth. The professor, a grizzled veteran of the industry, tasked them with a project: uncover a story on campus that no one else had reported.

Cassandra threw herself into the assignment, combing through student records, interviewing people in hushed tones, and piecing together clues. She discovered a scandal involving a well-respected professor who had been falsifying research to secure funding for years. The story was explosive, and when she presented it, the reaction was immediate. The professor was dismissed, and the scandal rocked the university.

The rush Cassandra felt was indescribable. It was the same thrill she'd felt listening to her grandmother's stories—the feeling of holding the truth in her hands, of revealing something that had been hidden. From that moment on, she knew that journalism wasn't just a job; it was a calling. She would be a storyteller, but more than that, she would be a truth-seeker, no matter the cost.

And so, Cassandra Lane's path was set. She would leave Wroghton behind, but the village would never leave her. The stories, the secrets, the dark tales of the thirteenth bell—they were all a part of her, shaping her into the relentless, driven woman she would become. The truth was out there, buried beneath layers of lies and fear, and Cassandra Lane was determined to uncover it, no matter what darkness she had to wade through to find it.

But somewhere along the way, the idealism had faded, eroded by the harsh realities of the industry. The truth had become secondary, an inconvenience to be shaped and manipulated to fit the story that would sell the most papers and get the most clicks. Now, as she prepared to dig even deeper into the Morrison case, Cassandra couldn't help but feel a flicker of the old guilt, the same guilt that had haunted her after every story where she'd pushed the boundaries too far.

She shook off the thought, forcing her focus back to the task at hand. She couldn't afford to dwell on the past, not when there was work to be done. The phone on her desk buzzed, pulling her attention away from the article. She snatched it up, already knowing who it would be—her editor, pushing her for more, always more.

"Lane," she answered, her voice clipped and professional.

"Cassandra, I need something bigger on Morrison,"

her editor barked. "We're getting traction, but we need to keep the momentum going. Dig deeper. Find something no one else has. I don't care how you do it, just get it done."

"I'm on it," she replied, her voice smooth and confident. She hung up and tossed the phone onto the desk, her mind already spinning with possibilities. She knew there was more to the Morrison story than what had been reported, something much darker, something that went beyond the usual tragedies she covered. And, if there wasn't, she would tell it as she wanted to.

The thrill of the chase was intoxicating, the promise of uncovering something truly sensational. But there was also a part of her, buried deep under layers of cynicism and ambition, that still longed for the truth. As Cassandra gathered her notepad, camera, and voice recorder, she meticulously checked her equipment. The notepad was filled with scribbled ideas and leads, some more promising than others. She reviewed her list of contacts, considering which ones might yield the most information. Her camera was set to capture high-resolution images, ready to document any evidence she might uncover. Each item was a tool in her arsenal, a means to further her relentless pursuit of the next big story.

She stepped out of her flat, locking the door behind her, and headed down the narrow stairwell into the chilly morning air. The streets were just beginning to wake, the hum of traffic a distant roar. Cassandra's mind was already on the next step, the next clue, the next interview that would bring her closer to the heart of the story. She was ready to dive into the darkness, to wade through the murky waters of John Morrison's life and pull out the truth—or something close enough to it.

As she walked towards her car, her thoughts turned to Morrison himself. What kind of man could do what he'd done? What kind of desperation, what kind of madness drove someone to steal the body of their dead child and go on the run? She knew there was more to the story, and she was determined to find it. But deep down, she also knew that some truths were better left buried.

She just wasn't sure if she cared enough to leave them there.

Chapter Eight

John spent hours meticulously setting up the room for the ritual. The dim light of the single bulb cast long shadows on the peeling wallpaper. The air was thick with a sense of foreboding. He referred to the instructions given by thevoiceofthehand, scribbled hastily in his notebook.

John's heart pounded like a war drum as he stood in the dim light of the decrepit hotel room. The air was thick with the scent of mildew and a stale, suffocating musk that clung to the back of his throat. In the centre of the circle John had drawn on the floor, Ethan's lifeless body lay on a black cloth, his small, pale form almost ethereal in the flickering candlelight. Ethan's skin was an alabaster white, and his little face, serene in death, was a haunting contrast to the turbulent emotions raging within his father.

John's hands trembled as he arranged the items for the ritual. Five supermarket-bought candles stood at the points of a pentagram he had meticulously sketched with chalk, each flame flickering like the hesitant hope in his heart. He had lit them one by one, the flames casting dancing shadows that seemed to mock his desperation.

As John gathered the ritual items, his hands trembled, not just from fatigue but from the enormity of what he was about to do. Each item he picked up—Ethan's baby blanket, now frayed and faded from use, the salt and ash, stark reminders of mortality—carried with it a piece of his broken heart. The sharp knife, gleaming with a cold, merciless light, was a symbol of the irreversible path he had chosen.

The ritual required precise movements and unwavering focus, but John's mind was a tempest of conflicting emotions. As he drew the symbols on the floor, his thoughts wandered back to memories of Ethan, of the sound of his laughter, the warmth of his small hand in John's own. Every line he traced, every word he whispered in the ancient tongue, felt like a betrayal of the natural order, a defiance of the very laws that had governed his life until now.

He retrieved the knife, its cold weight a stark reminder of the grim task ahead. He glanced down at Ethan, his heart aching with a sorrow that threatened to shatter his resolve. His fingers brushed against the cold metal, and he recoiled slightly, as if the blade had shocked him. The weight of what he was about to do pressed down on him, a leaden burden that made his legs weak and his head spin. He took a step back, staring at the arrangement before him, and for the first time in days, a crack appeared in his resolve.

"What am I doing?" he muttered to the empty room, his voice sounding foreign in the oppressive silence. His eyes locked onto the altar, the grotesque items he had so carefully laid out, and a wave of nausea rolled through him. "This isn't real … This can't bring him back."

The words echoed in his mind, reverberating like a gong, each repetition louder and more insistent than the last. The absurdity of it all hit him like a sledgehammer. He was a man, a father, reduced to this. He was an educated man, a man of logic and reason, and yet here he was, grasping at the thin, brittle straws of hope in the form of ancient symbols and forbidden knowledge. It all felt so utterly foolish, so completely insane.

He stumbled back, clutching at the sides of his head as if to keep his mind from splitting apart. For a moment, he could see himself as an outsider might: a grieving father driven mad by the loss of his child, desperately clinging to anything that offered even the faintest glimmer of hope, no matter how irrational. The rituals, the promises of bringing Ethan back—were they anything more than the fevered delusions of a broken mind?

His gaze flicked to the symbols on the walls, the flickering candles, the knife—objects that had once seemed to hold so much power, so much promise. Now they looked like nothing more than props in a twisted play, meaningless and empty. A part of him wanted to tear it all down, to rip the symbols from the walls and throw the knife out the window, to let go of this insane quest and accept the truth he had been running from.

But the thought of Ethan's face, that innocent smile that had been snatched away too soon, stopped him. The image of his son, lying cold and still in a small coffin, flashed through his mind like a bolt of lightning, searing his brain with its intensity. The grief, the pain—it was too much to bear. He had to believe there was another way, that this wasn't the end.

John shook his head violently, as if trying to dislodge the doubts that clung to him like leeches. No, he couldn't give up now. Not when he was so close. Maybe it was madness, maybe he was teetering on the brink of insanity, but if there was even the slightest chance that this ritual could bring Ethan back, he had to take it. He had to see it through.

He forced his hands to steady as he reached for the knife once more, setting it back in its place with a grim determination. The doubt still lingered, a shadow at the edge of his mind, but he pushed it down, burying it deep within himself where it couldn't interfere.

The line between reality and madness was razor-thin,

and John knew he was dancing dangerously close to the edge. But if that was the price he had to pay, then so be it. He would walk that line, he would cross it if he had to, because there was nothing he wouldn't do for his son.

His determination burned brighter. He had come too far to turn back now. He made a small cut on his palm, the sting a mere whisper compared to the agony of his grief. Blood welled up and dripped into a small vial, each drop a symbol of his sacrifice.

John mixed the blood with dried herbs, their scent sharp and pungent, and poured the mixture into a glass bowl. He held the bowl over Ethan's body, his breath coming in ragged gasps. The room seemed to close in around him, the walls pressing in with a malevolent sentience.

Night descended, and the room grew colder, the temperature plummeting as if the very essence of life was being drained from the space. Shadows danced on the walls, and the silence became suffocating, broken only by the sound of John's ragged breathing. His heart pounded in his chest, each beat a drum signalling the approach of something unknown, something terrifying.

He hesitated before beginning the ritual, the enormity of his actions crashing down on him like a tidal wave. What if this went wrong? What if, in his desperation to bring Ethan back, he unleashed something far worse? The thought clawed at his mind, but the alternative—living without his son—was a fate he couldn't accept.

As John began the incantations, the words felt foreign on his tongue, their meaning lost to time but their power undeniable. The air grew thick with a malevolent energy, a force that pressed against his skin, threatening to crush him under its weight. The symbols on the floor began to glow faintly, a sickly green light that pulsed in time with his racing heart.

The knife in his hand felt heavier with each passing second, as if it was absorbing the weight of his sorrow, his fear, his desperation. When the time came to make the sacrifice—to spill his own blood as an offering—John hesitated for the briefest of moments. But then his gaze fell upon Ethan's lifeless body, and the grief surged anew, pushing him forward. The blade bit into his palm, and as the blood dripped onto the circle, the room seemed to exhale, a cold breath that sent shivers down his spine.

As he continued to chant, his voice was low and steady, the ancient words now rolling off his tongue with a familiarity born of desperation. The air grew colder with each syllable, the temperature plummeting until his breath came out in visible puffs. The candle flames flickered violently, as if agitated by an unseen force, casting grotesque shadows that writhed and twisted on the walls.

John's voice grew louder, more urgent, his chants rising and falling in a rhythm that echoed the frantic beating of his heart. The brass bowl in his hands grew warm, the mixture inside beginning to bubble and hiss. A chill ran down his spine as the air around him seemed to thrum with an otherworldly energy.

He focused on Ethan, his eyes burning with a mix of hope and fear. "Come back to me, Ethan," he whispered, his voice breaking. "Please, come back."

The room was filled with a cacophony of sounds— whispered voices that seemed to come from the very walls, the soft rustle of unseen movements, and the distant, mournful cry of something ancient and sorrowful. The scent of burning herbs mingled with the metallic tang of blood, creating an acrid, heady aroma that made John's head swim.

As the final words of the chant left his lips, a sudden silence fell over the room, heavy and oppressive. The candle flames stood still, frozen in time. The air was thick with anticipation, every molecule charged with a palpable tension.

John's heart raced as he stared at Ethan; his breath caught in his throat. For a moment, there was nothing—just the body of his son lying still and cold. Then, a faint ripple seemed to pass through the air, a disturbance that sent a shiver down his spine. The candles flickered again, their flames dancing wildly as if caught in an invisible wind.

In that moment, time seemed to stretch, elongating into an endless abyss where the past, present, and future blurred together. John's senses were overwhelmed—the smell of blood and salt, the feel of cold air against his skin, the sight of the glowing symbols, and the sound of that terrible growl. But above all, he felt an overwhelming presence, something ancient and powerful, something that had been awakened by his actions.

He heard a series of knocks, starting from one corner of the room and moving rapidly to another, as if something unseen was pacing around him. The knocking grew louder, more insistent, and was soon accompanied by angry whispers.

John's heart pounded in his chest like a jackhammer, each beat reverberating through his ribcage as the voices grew louder, more insistent, filling the room with a sense of malevolence that made his skin crawl. The knocks, now more like pounding fists, hammered against the walls, the floor, the very air around him. It felt as though the building itself had come alive, a beast of wood and stone, breathing and snarling, eager to trap him within its jaws.

"They are coming for you, John," the voices hissed, a chorus of serpentine whispers that slithered through the shadows. "Leave now. Quickly!"

The words were like ice water in his veins, freezing his blood, numbing his thoughts. He could feel them, those unseen entities, closing in on him, pressing down on his mind with an unrelenting weight. He couldn't breathe, couldn't think. He was drowning in a sea of fear, a primal, animalistic terror that clawed at his sanity and urged him to run, to get the hell out of there before it was too late.

His hands trembled as he fumbled with the candles, extinguishing each one with a desperate swipe of his fingers. The room plunged into darkness, the shadows deepening and thickening as if the absence of light had given them new life. He could feel them watching him, their eyes burning with hatred, with hunger.

John forced himself to focus, to push down the rising tide of panic threatening to overwhelm him. He had to move, had to get out. There was no time to think, no time to waste. Every second was a heartbeat closer to whatever horror was coming for him.

His laptop was the first thing he grabbed, shoving it into his worn backpack with shaking hands. He could barely feel the weight of it, could barely feel anything beyond the cold sweat that slicked his skin and the raw, gnawing fear that twisted his gut. He moved to the small table in the centre of the room, where Ethan's body lay wrapped in the black velvet cloth. His son's face, pale and serene in death, was hidden from view, but John could still feel his presence, a cold, empty void that tore at his heart.

He lifted Ethan's body with a tenderness that seemed out of place amidst the chaos, cradling the bundle against his chest for a moment. His breath hitched, a sharp, painful sound, as he felt the weight of his son's lifeless form. The reality of what he had done—what he was trying to do—pressed down on him like a ton of bricks. But there was no time to mourn, no time for second thoughts. He gently placed Ethan into the duffle bag, his fingers lingering for just a moment before zipping it shut.

The knife, still sticky with blood, and the vial—so small, so innocuous—were next, hastily shoved into the bag alongside his son. They were tools, nothing more, but they felt like anchors dragging him down into the abyss of his own making. He tried not to think about the blood, about what it had cost him to obtain it. He tried not to think about the ritual, about the voices, about the things that now pursued him.

With everything packed, John slung the duffle bag over his shoulder, the weight of it pulling him down, and grabbed his car keys from the table. The metal was cold in his hand, grounding him, pulling him back from the brink of hysteria. He took a deep breath, his chest tight, his lungs burning, and turned toward the door.

The knocking was louder now, more frantic, as if something was trying to break through the walls, to tear its way into the room. The whispers had become a cacophony of voices, all screaming at him to run, to leave before it was too late. They filled his head, drowning out all other thought, pushing him forward on pure instinct.

He stepped out of the room, the door slamming shut behind him with a force that shook the walls. The air in the hallway was thick and oppressive, as though the building itself was pressing down on him, trying to trap him inside. He could feel the weight of it on his shoulders, the cold, clammy touch of unseen hands brushing against his skin.

John didn't look back. He couldn't. The urge to flee, to escape, was overwhelming, a primal drive that screamed at him to move faster. His steps were quick, almost frantic, as he made his way down the narrow hallway, his breath coming in ragged gasps. His vision tunnelled, the edges of his sight blurred with shadows that seemed to reach out for him, to pull him back.

The front door loomed ahead, a beacon of escape, of safety. But even as he reached for the handle, he felt the darkness closing in, pressing against his back, whispering threats of what would happen if he stayed a moment longer.

He yanked the door open and stumbled out into the night, the cold air hitting him like a slap to the face. It was refreshing, shocking, a jolt that cleared his mind just enough to keep him moving. The whispers were still there, just behind him, but they were fading, losing their power as he put distance between himself and the hotel.

John's car was parked at the edge of the carpark, a dark shape in the moonlight. His fingers fumbled with the keys, the metal slipping against his sweat-slicked skin, but he managed to unlock the door and throw his bags inside. His hands were shaking uncontrollably now, and it took him several tries to get the key into the ignition.

As the engine roared to life, John felt a brief surge of relief, but it was fleeting, swallowed up by the overwhelming need to get as far away as possible. He slammed the car into gear, the tires screeching as he peeled out of the driveway and onto the road. The night stretched out before him, an endless ribbon of black, but he didn't care where it led. He just needed to be gone.

As the hotel disappeared in the rearview mirror, John's breath began to slow, but the fear remained, a cold knot in his stomach. The voices, the knocks, the ritual—it was all behind him now, but it was far from over. Something had changed, something had been set in motion, and John knew, deep in his bones, that there was no going back. The darkness was still there, just out of sight, waiting for him to slip, to falter. And when it did, it would consume him whole.

John drove through the empty streets of Hull, the city's lights casting an eerie glow on the wet pavement. His hands were obsessively tapping the steering wheel, his eyes darting to the rearview mirror again and again. He couldn't shake the feeling that something was following him, something unseen and malevolent.

As John sped down the deserted roads, the night pressed in on him from all sides, the darkness thick and impenetrable. The headlights of his car cut through the black, illuminating the winding path ahead, but the light seemed feeble, barely holding the shadows at bay. The air outside was crisp, the chill seeping into the car despite the heat blasting from the vents. The radio was off, the silence broken only by the low noise of the engine and the distant echo of the voices that still lingered in his mind.

His hands gripped the steering wheel tightly, knuckles white, as if the pressure alone could keep the terror at bay. But no matter how hard he tried, he couldn't shake the feeling that something was still with him, that the ritual had left a door open, and something had followed him through.

He glanced in the rearview mirror, half-expecting to see a shadowy figure sitting in the back seat, but there was nothing—just the empty road stretching out behind him. Yet the feeling of being watched persisted, crawling along the back of his neck like a cold finger tracing his spine. He blinked, shaking his head as if he could dislodge the creeping dread, but it was no use.

The road ahead forked suddenly, and without thinking, John veered left, the tires skidding slightly on the loose gravel. The road narrowed, the trees closing in on either side, their gnarled branches twisting like skeletal hands reaching out to snatch him from the safety of his car. The headlights caught the glint of something up ahead, and John's heart skipped a beat as he saw a figure standing by the side of the road.

For a split second, he thought it was a trick of the light, a shadow cast by the swaying branches, but as he drew closer, the figure came into sharp focus—a man, tall and thin, his face obscured by the brim of a wide-brimmed hat. He stood perfectly still, his posture unnaturally rigid, as if he had been waiting there, just for John.

The hairs on the back of John's neck stood on end, and his foot instinctively pressed down harder on the gas pedal, the car lurching forward with a burst of speed. The figure didn't move, didn't react, but as John passed, he caught a glimpse of the man's face—or what should have been his face. Instead, there was nothing—just a dark, featureless void where eyes, nose, and mouth should have been.

John's breath caught in his throat, his heart hammering in his chest as he sped away, but he couldn't shake the image of that blank face. It was burned into his mind, a sight so unnatural, so wrong, that it defied explanation. He forced himself to keep his eyes on the road, but his mind was racing, his thoughts spiralling into a panicked frenzy.

What the hell was that? A ghost? A hallucination? Something left over from the ritual?

His rational mind fought to regain control, to find a logical explanation, but nothing made sense anymore. The world had twisted and warped, and John felt like he was losing his grip on reality, sliding down a slippery slope into madness.

The road seemed to stretch on forever, an endless tunnel of darkness, and John realized he had no idea where he was going. His only thought had been to get away, to put as much distance between himself and that house as possible, but now he was lost, the familiar roads and landmarks of his small town gone, replaced by this unfamiliar, foreboding landscape.

He knew he couldn't keep driving aimlessly, not with whatever was out there, lurking in the shadows. He needed to find a place to stop, to gather his thoughts, to figure out his next move. Up ahead, he saw the faint glow of lights through the trees—a petrol station, a tiny oasis of light in the vast ocean of darkness.

John slowed the car as he approached, the old neon sign weakly lit above the dilapidated building. The place looked like it hadn't seen a customer in years, the windows dirty and cracked, the pumps rusted and covered in grime. But it was a place to stop, to think.

He pulled up to the pump and turned off the engine, the sudden silence almost deafening. For a moment, he just sat there, hands still gripping the steering wheel, trying to steady his breathing, to calm the wild pounding of his heart. The lights from the petrol station cast long shadows across the cracked pavement, and John found himself scanning the darkness, half-expecting to see that faceless figure standing there, watching him.

He needed somewhere to go, somewhere to regroup and figure out just what the hell he planned to do. He had no family that he could rely upon, no one to help in his time of need. But he did have one thing … memories. Memories of Sarah and Ethan. And there was one place he now knew he needed to go to. A place, as a family, they all loved. He turned the ignition back on and pulled away.

John's destination was Whitby, a small coastal town known for its gothic charm and historic abbey. He needed to find another small, independent B&B where he could lay low and continue his desperate quest. The road stretched out before him, a black ribbon cutting through the desolate landscape.

He took the A165, a winding coastal road that would lead him north to Whitby. The journey was long and tense, the dark night adding to his anxiety. As he drove, the hum of the engine was the only sound that filled the silence, a low, constant drone that seemed to match the relentless pounding of his heart. The air inside the car was stale, tinged with the scent of his own fear and determination. The headlights cut through the darkness, revealing fleeting glimpses of the world outside.

As he passed through small villages, their quaint, picturesque houses, so peaceful, only served to amplify the turmoil in his mind. The smell of the sea mingled with the earthy scent of the countryside, creating a heady, almost intoxicating mix. Every so often, the road would twist and turn, his headlights revealing breathtaking views of the cliffs that loomed high above the crashing waves. The sight was both beautiful and haunting, a fitting backdrop for the storm raging within him.

John knew he had to get rid of his phone to avoid being tracked. Halfway to Whitby, he found the perfect spot. He pulled over on a deserted stretch of the road, near a motorway bridge that spanned a narrow valley. The location was remote, with no immediate signs of life. The bridge was old, its stonework weathered by time and the elements, a silent witness to the passage of countless travellers.

He took his phone, which had been a lifeline but was now a liability, and climbed out of the car. The night air was cold and biting, carrying the faint, salty tang of the sea. Standing on the bridge, he hesitated for a moment, staring at the device. It felt heavy in his hand, a physical manifestation of the ties he needed to sever. He took a deep breath, the chill filling his lungs, and hurled the phone over the edge.

He watched as it tumbled through the air, landing with a metallic thud on the roof of a passing lorry. The lorry was an old, battered vehicle, its trailer covered with grime and dust from countless miles on the road. The side of the trailer bore the faded logo of a long-forgotten company, its name obscured by years of wear and tear. It was carrying industrial equipment, the kind that could easily mask the sound and presence of the phone. The driver, an unsuspecting middle-aged man with a weary expression, continued on his route, unaware of the additional passenger on his roof.

Relieved to be rid of the phone, John climbed back into his car and continued his journey. The road ahead was dark and lonely, the only company being his thoughts and the occasional whisper that seemed to linger in his mind. Each mile brought him closer to Whitby but also deeper into his own personal hell.

As he neared Whitby, the landscape changed, becoming more rugged and dramatic. The cliffs loomed high above the sea, their jagged edges silhouetted against the night sky. The waves crashed against the rocks below with a relentless fury, a stark reminder of the power of nature and the insignificance of man. The sight was both beautiful and haunting, a fitting backdrop for the turmoil in John's soul.

His thoughts were a chaotic jumble of fear, hope, and determination. He couldn't shake the feeling that he was still being watched, that unseen eyes were tracking his every move. The whispers in his mind grew louder, more insistent, as if the very air around him was alive with unseen forces. He tightened his grip on the steering wheel, his knuckles white with tension.

Finally, the lights of Whitby appeared on the horizon, a small beacon of hope in the darkness. John drove into Whitby as the first hints of dawn crept over the horizon, the sky a bruised mixture of purple and grey. The narrow road twisted through the hills, and as he reached the crest of the last incline, the town unfurled before him like an ancient, slumbering beast. Whitby, nestled between the dark North Sea and the shadowy cliffs, was a place where the past clung to every stone, where history was so thick in the air you could practically taste it.

The town was waking up, though reluctantly, its streets still empty save for the occasional early riser or stray cat slinking through the alleys. The old houses, their bricks blackened by centuries of sea salt and coal smoke, huddled close together as if seeking comfort from one another. Whitby had the look of a place that had seen too much, survived too much, and had no choice but to carry on. The air was damp and carried with it the faint, briny scent of the sea, mixed with the earthy smell of wet stone and moss.

John felt a shiver run through him as he drove slowly down the narrow streets, his headlights sweeping over the cobblestones that had borne witness to countless footsteps over the years. He'd been here before, a lifetime ago it seemed, but Whitby had a way of making time blur, of folding it in on itself until past and present became indistinguishable. He could almost see the ghosts of the town's history lurking in the corners, waiting for the right moment to step out and remind him that in Whitby, the past was never really gone.

The town was famous, of course, for its connection to Bram Stoker's *Dracula*, and it was easy to see why the place had inspired such a dark tale. The ruins of Whitby Abbey loomed on the cliffs high above the town, their jagged remains stark against the sky like the bones of some ancient, long-dead creature. Below, the harbour was a labyrinth of narrow alleyways and steep staircases, the kind of place where one could easily imagine being followed by something unseen, something not quite human.

John's eyes were drawn to the abbey, its silhouette a black mass against the slowly lightening sky. The place had an almost magnetic pull, a dark gravity that seemed to draw all thoughts of the present away, leaving only the cold, hard grip of history. He felt a strange unease, a crawling sensation at the back of his mind, as if the town was watching him, waiting to see what he would do next.

He shook his head, trying to dispel the feeling, but it clung to him like a wet cloak.

John took a deep breath, steeling himself for the next step in his grim journey. The road ahead was uncertain, fraught with danger and despair, but he knew he had no choice. He had come too far to turn back now.

Chapter Nine

Jack Palace was at his desk, surrounded by stacks of case files and the constant hum of the police radio. His thoughts were consumed by the case of John and Ethan, a haunting mystery that seemed to defy reason. Just as he was reviewing witness statements from the hospital incident, his phone rang, the shrill sound cutting through the untidy office. He reached for it, his heart already starting to race with a mix of anticipation and concern. It had been a long day, and he hoped this call would bring some clarity to the chaos that had been swirling around him since morning.

"Palace," he answered, his voice rough from disuse.

"Jack, it's Constable Stevens," came the reply, the voice on the other end sounding breathless and urgent. Stevens was a rookie, fresh out onto the beat, but he had a sharp eye and a relentless drive that Jack admired. The young officer had been instrumental in gathering intel on the Morrison case, working tirelessly to follow up on leads.

"What's up, Stevens?" Jack asked, leaning back in his chair and closing his eyes, trying to focus.

"I just got a call from a hotel in Hull, not far from the hospital. A member of their staff spotted John Morrison. Said he looked frantic, like he was on the run. They recognized him from the news reports," Stevens explained, his words tumbling out in a rush.

Jack's eyes snapped open. "Which hotel?"

"The Falcon," Stevens replied. "The staff member who called in, a night manager named Lena, gave a pretty detailed description. Said John was dishevelled, wearing a grey hoodie and jeans. He had a wild look in his eyes, like he hadn't slept in days. She also mentioned he was carrying a bundle, something wrapped in a blanket. She thought it might be the baby."

Jack felt a cold knot form in his stomach. "Did she say anything else?"

"Yeah," Stevens continued, his voice dropping to a conspiratorial whisper. "She said he was muttering to himself, something about needing to find a safe place. He asked about the back exits, ways to leave without being seen. She got the impression he was trying to avoid the main entrances, probably to stay off the radar."

Jack stood up, grabbing his coat from the back of his chair. "Good work, Stevens. I'm heading over there now. Make sure backup is ready if we need it but keep it low-key. We don't want to spook him."

"Got it, sir," Stevens replied, the line clicking dead a moment later.

Jack hung up the phone, his mind racing. The Falcon was only a few miles from the hospital, close enough that John could have made his way there on foot. He tried to picture John's state of mind, the desperation that must have driven him to such lengths. His own heart ached with a mixture of sympathy and dread.

He threw on his coat, grabbed his keys, and headed out the door. As Palace exited the police station, the air was thick with the scent of rain, the kind that clings to the skin and seeps into your bones. His mind was already racing ahead, thinking of the hotel and the possible scenarios waiting for him. But before he could leave, he needed to make sure his team was ready.

He approached Sergeant Ellis, a grizzled veteran who'd seen more than his share of strange cases. Ellis looked up from his own pile of paperwork, sensing the urgency in Palace's stride.

"Ellis, we've got a lead on Morrison," Palace said, his tone clipped and direct. "He's holed up in The Falcon. I need you to coordinate backup but keep it low-key. We don't want to spook him."

Ellis nodded, already reaching for his radio. "How many men do you want?"

"Two cars, no lights. Keep them on the perimeter. We need to cover the exits. If Morrison's as desperate as he seems, he could bolt the moment he hears a siren."

Ellis raised an eyebrow. "You think he's dangerous?"

Palace hesitated, then shook his head. "Not to us, but he's unpredictable. He's got his kid with him, and that makes him twice as dangerous. We can't afford any mistakes."

"Understood." Ellis's voice was calm, but Palace could see the tension in the set of his jaw. "Anything else?"

Palace ran a hand over his stubble, his mind flipping through the possibilities. "Make sure the team knows what they're walking into. This isn't just a pickup. Morrison's in a bad place, mentally and emotionally. We need to be prepared for anything."

Ellis gave a curt nod, already moving to relay the instructions. Palace watched him for a moment, grateful for the man's steady presence. Everything was routine, yet the stakes felt higher than ever.

As Palace walked to his car, he pulled out his phone, quickly scanning the notes he'd compiled on Morrison. The man's descent into obsession was evident, a slow unravelling that had led them all to this point. Palace had seen this kind of desperation before, but never in someone who still had so much to lose.

He slid into the driver's seat, the leather creaking under his weight. As he started the engine, he couldn't shake the image of Morrison's face, wild-eyed and frantic, clutching that dark bundle like it was the only thing keeping him tethered to this world. With a deep breath, he set off towards the hotel, every nerve on edge. As he pulled out of the car park, he couldn't help but think about the report Stevens had relayed.

Lena, the night manager, had done everything right. She had noticed something off about John immediately, her instincts telling her that this was more than just a weary traveller. Her detailed observations and quick thinking had provided them with a crucial lead, one that might just bring them closer to finding Ethan.

Jack's thoughts drifted to the child, imagining him wrapped in a blanket, innocent and unaware of the turmoil surrounding him. He clenched the steering wheel tighter, his resolve hardening. He had to find them. He had to bring Ethan home quickly and stop John before things spiralled further out of control.

With utter haste, Palace and his team arrived at the hotel. The exterior was a rundown building on the outskirts of Hull. Rain had started to drizzle, casting a sombre atmosphere over the scene. As Palace entered the hotel lobby, he was greeted by the anxious faces of the staff and curious onlookers.

The receptionist was a young woman in her late twenties, with tired eyes that suggested many sleepless nights. Her hair was pulled back into a loose ponytail, and she wore a faded hotel uniform that looked two sizes too big. The nametag on her chest read 'Lena'. She had a soft, almost fragile appearance, with pale skin and dark circles under her eyes that told a story of their own. Her hands trembled slightly as she pointed towards the stairs leading up to the second floor.

"The man you're looking for," Lena said in a hushed voice, "he's in room 14. I saw him go up not long ago. He looked ... disturbed."

Palace nodded, offering her a reassuring smile, and led his team up the creaking staircase. Each step echoed in the empty hallway, a foreboding symphony that matched the tension in the air.

The hallway leading to room 14 was dimly lit, the old wallpaper peeling at the edges, giving the place an abandoned feel. The floorboards creaked beneath Palace's weight, each step echoing in the stillness, amplifying the tension that coiled tight in his chest. He could hear the faint hum of a television from a room further down, but otherwise, the place was eerily silent.

As he approached the door, a cold draft brushed past him, making the hairs on the back of his neck stand on end. He paused, listening, and for a moment, he thought he heard something—a soft whisper, barely audible, like the wind murmuring secrets through the cracks in the walls. He strained to hear, but the sound was gone as quickly as it came, leaving him with a deep sense of unease.

Palace reached for the door, his hand hovering over the handle. The door was slightly ajar, a thin sliver of light spilling out into the hallway. He hesitated, his instincts screaming that something was off, something beyond the ordinary tension of a high-stakes situation.

With a gentle push, he eased the door open. The room was dim, lit only by the glow of a single lamp on the bedside table. The air was thick with the scent of incense, but beneath it was something else, something metallic and sharp—blood, or the promise of it.

His eyes swept the room, taking in the details. The bed was unmade, sheets twisted and bunched as if someone had been thrashing in their sleep. The furniture was sparse, but on the floor near the window, he noticed something that sent a jolt of alarm through him—a child's drawing, hastily scrawled with crayons. It depicted a stick figure family: a man, a woman, and a small boy holding hands. But the figures were distorted, their faces scribbled out, and in the corner, a dark shape loomed, larger than the others, its form undefined.

Palace's heart pounded in his chest as he crouched to pick up the drawing. The paper was crumpled, stained with what looked like dried tears. He could almost feel the fear that had seeped into it, a fear so deep and consuming that it had left a mark on the very fabric of the room.

Suddenly, from the direction of the bed, came a low, anguished moan. Palace snapped his head up, adrenaline spiking. The sound was faint, almost imperceptible, but it was enough to send his pulse racing.

He rose slowly, his hands moving instinctively to fists. The moan came again, this time clearer, more defined. It was a sound of despair, raw and unfiltered, the kind that clawed at your soul.

Palace took a step forward, the creak of the floorboard loud in the silence. His mind raced with possibilities, each one more terrifying than the last. Was Morrison in there, on the edge of something unspeakable? Or had something else, something darker, taken root in his mind?

With one last deep breath, Palace moved towards the source of the sound, his senses hyper-alert. Whatever waited for him in that room, he knew it was more than just the remnants of a desperate man. There was something else here, something lurking just beneath the surface, ready to pull him under if he wasn't careful.

As he reached the bed, he steeled himself for what he might find, the tension in the air thick enough to choke on. But no matter what, he knew he had to face it— because if he didn't, he might never find his way back.

But there was nothing there, only the sound, which had gone now. Jack's eyes looked past the bed to the other side of the room. On the floor, remnants of what appeared to be a makeshift altar caught Palace's attention—a circle of chalk, scattered candle wax, and dried herbs. The atmosphere was charged with an unsettling energy.

Amidst the chaotic scene, Palace spotted a letter placed carefully on the edge of a small wooden table. It was addressed simply to "Whom It May Concern." The handwriting was hurried, frantic even, as if penned in haste. Palace picked up the letter with gloved hands, noting the trembling strokes of the pen.

As he read, Palace's expression softened. The letter detailed John's anguish, his desperate attempt to bring back his son, Ethan. It spoke of love and loss, of a father's broken heart and his willingness to defy the natural order for one last chance. Palace felt a pang of empathy for John, understanding the depths of grief that had driven him to such extremes.

To Whom It May Concern,

If you're reading this, then I'm already too far gone to be saved. Maybe I always was. There's a part of me that hopes you understand, though I'm not sure I even understand myself anymore. I've tried to write this a dozen times, and each time the words just seem to slip away from me, like sand through my fingers. But I need to try. I need you to know why I've done what I've done, and what I'm going to do.

I'm sorry. God, I'm so sorry for what happened at the hospital. I never wanted to hurt anyone. The staff there—they were just doing their jobs, trying to help. But they couldn't see what I see. They didn't understand that it wasn't just about letting go, it was about holding on to what matters most. They tried to tell me to move on, to accept that Ethan was gone. But I can't. I can't let go of my son. I won't.

I know what you're thinking. That I'm mad, delusional, caught up in some fever dream of grief. Maybe you're right. Hell, maybe I am mad. But if madness is the price I have to pay to bring Ethan back, then so be it. You see, I've learned things. Dark things. Things that no father should ever have to learn, things that twist your soul and make you question everything you once believed.

There's a way. A way to bring him back. But it's not easy, and it's not clean. It's like walking a razor's edge, where one wrong step could send you tumbling into the abyss. And maybe that's where I'm headed, into the darkness, where there's no coming back. But if that's what it takes to see my boy's face again, to hold him, to tell him that I love him one more time ... then what choice do I have?

May God have mercy on my soul.

John Morrison

Standing in the middle of the room, Palace took a moment to collect his thoughts. He knew John was not a criminal mastermind but a grieving father driven to the edge by loss. Despite the assault charges looming over him, Palace couldn't help but feel a sense of sympathy and determination to help.

He made a mental note to secure the room as a crime scene and to gather any evidence that could shed light on John's whereabouts. He knew time was of the essence, that every moment counted in the race to find John and, hopefully, to bring closure to this tragic chapter.

As he turned to leave, Palace glanced once more at the letter in his hand. It was a poignant reminder of the human side of policing, of the complexities that lurked beneath every investigation. With renewed resolve, he knew he had to find John and unravel the mystery that had brought them to this moment.

Chapter Ten

John drove into Whitby under the cover of night, his eyes darting nervously as he navigated the narrow, winding streets of the old coastal town. The B&B he had chosen, The Seafarer's Rest, was a small, unassuming building nestled between a fish and chip shop and an antique bookstore. The building's facade was weathered, its white paint peeling in places, and the sign creaked gently in the breeze. The smell of saltwater was pervasive, mingling with the faint aroma of frying fish. He parked the car around the corner on a quiet, rarely used street and carried Ethan, wrapped in a blanket, into the building.

The Seafarer's Rest was a relic of the past, a creaking, time-worn building that whispered of old maritime tales and seafaring adventures. The lobby was dimly lit, its walls adorned with sepia-toned photographs of rugged sailors and storm-battered ships. The scent of sea salt and aged wood permeated the air, mingling with the faint, lingering aroma of sea life from the nearby docks. Nautical memorabilia cluttered the shelves: miniature ship models, brass compasses, and coils of rope, all casting long shadows in the flickering light of ancient lanterns hanging from the ceiling.

John stepped inside, the heavy door closing behind him with a creak that echoed down the narrow hallway. The floorboards groaned underfoot, adding to the sense of entering another era. Behind the reception desk stood a woman in her early fifties, her presence both warm and weary. Her name tag read 'Margaret', and she wore a dark blue blazer with brass buttons, reminiscent of a naval uniform, paired with a crisp white blouse. Her hair, a shade of silver-grey, was pulled back into a neat bun, and her eyes, though tired, held a spark of kindness.

"Welcome to the Seafarer's Rest," she said, her voice a melodic lilt with a hint of Yorkshire accent. "How can I help you today?"

John, weary from his journey, managed a tired smile. "I need a room for a few nights," John replied, his voice hoarse from exhaustion and stress. "Just me and my ... son."

Margaret nodded, reaching for the heavy leather-bound registry book. She flipped through the pages with a practised hand, the sound of paper rustling filling the quiet lobby. "We have a room available on the third floor at fifty pounds a night. Will that be alright?"

"That's fine," John replied, his voice tinged with exhaustion.

John handed over the cash, grateful for the simplicity of the transaction. Margaret handed him an old-fashioned brass key attached to a heavy, worn leather fob. "Room 302. Follow the corridor to the end and take the stairs up. The room is on your right."

John thanked her and made his way down the dimly lit hallway, the air thick with the smell of aged wood and a hint of mustiness. He climbed the narrow, creaking staircase, the banister smooth from years of use. The walls of the stairwell were lined with more maritime artefacts: a rusted ship's wheel, a frayed map of the North Sea, and an old diving helmet that seemed to watch him with empty eyes.

Reaching the third floor, John found room 302 easily. The door, like the rest of the hotel, bore the marks of time – its paint chipped and the brass numbers dulled with age. He inserted the key and turned it with a satisfying click, pushing the door open to reveal his temporary sanctuary.

The room was small but cozy, pleasant after the dim hallways outside. A single window overlooked the churning sea, the sound of waves crashing against the cliffs below providing a constant, rhythmic backdrop. The bed, dressed in crisp white linens, stood close to one wall, flanked by wooden bedside tables holding antique lamps. A faded sea-green armchair sat in the corner, its upholstery worn but inviting. The walls were painted a soft, calming blue, adorned with framed sketches of tall ships and coastal scenes.

A small writing desk, cluttered with brochures of local attractions and a stack of yellowing stationery, stood near the window. The room's only concession to modernity was a small television mounted on the wall opposite the bed, its remote control resting on the neatly folded towels at the foot of the bed.

John set his bag down and crossed to the window, looking out at the dark, restless sea. He felt a momentary peace, the kind that came from being in a place so steeped in history and removed from the chaos of his recent days. He gently placed Ethan on the bed and collapsed into the worn armchair by the window. The air was damp and carried a faint musty odour, but it was a refuge, nonetheless. John realized how much he needed rest, not just for his body, but for his tormented mind. He closed his eyes for a moment, but the constant buzz of his racing thoughts made rest impossible. He knew he needed supplies. He was becoming hungry and certainly needed to clean himself up.

After ensuring Ethan was secure, John ventured out into the cold night air, pulling his coat tighter against the biting wind. The streets of Whitby were shrouded in an eerie calm, the distant, rhythmic crashing of the waves against the cliffs creating a haunting symphony. The moon cast a silvery glow over the cobblestone streets, turning the historic buildings into shadowy sentinels standing guard over the town.

As John walked, he passed rows of tightly packed houses, their brick facades dark and silent. A few streetlamps flickered, casting sporadic pools of light that only served to accentuate the surrounding darkness. The salty tang of the sea air filled his nostrils, mingling with the faint scent of fried fish from a nearby shuttered takeaway. The narrow streets twisted and turned, leading him closer to the seafront, where the cold wind whipped more fiercely.

He reached a small corner shop, whose neon sign buzzed and flickered, giving off an unnatural glow that battled the darkness. The shop was a relic from another era, its windows plastered with posters advertising local events and outdated specials. John pushed open the creaky door, the bell above jingling softly as he stepped inside.

The interior of the shop was a stark contrast to the night outside, brightly lit with fluorescent lights that buzzed incessantly. The shelves were sparsely stocked, with a few essentials lined up in neat rows. John grabbed a basket and methodically began collecting items. A toothbrush, toothpaste, soap, and a razor found their way into his basket, followed by non-perishable food items—canned beans, instant noodles, and a loaf of bread. He added a few bottles of water, the plastic rustling softly as they settled into the basket.

The boy at the counter was a bored-looking teenager, slumped over a mobile phone with a sullen expression. His greasy hair fell into his eyes, and a nametag reading

'Billy' was pinned to his faded polo shirt. The shirt itself looked like it had seen better days, the once vibrant colour now dulled and stained.

Billy barely glanced at John as he scanned the items, his movements mechanical and disinterested. The lighting above cast harsh shadows over his face, making his pallor look almost ghostly.

"Evening," John muttered, pulling out a crumpled wad of cash.

"Yeah, sure," Billy replied, his voice a monotone drone. He took the money without enthusiasm, his eyes never really focusing on John. The transaction complete, Billy handed over the change and a blue plastic bag.

John stuffed the supplies into the bag and made his way back out into the night. The bell jingled again as the door closed behind him, the sound oddly cheerful in the oppressive stillness of the town.

On his way back to The Seafarer's Rest, John decided to take a shortcut through a narrow, poorly lit alleyway. The walls of the surrounding buildings loomed high and close, the space between them claustrophobically tight. The ground was uneven, littered with debris that crunched under his feet.

Halfway through, the silence was shattered by a voice calling his name. It was soft, almost a whisper, but it froze him in his tracks. He spun around, heart pounding, but saw nothing but shadows shifting in the dim light. The alley seemed to close in around him, the darkness thickening as if trying to swallow him whole.

"John."

He spun around again, his heart still beating excessively.

A figure stepped out from the shadows in front of him,

blocking his path. "Hello, John," the man said in a weird, commanding tone.

John turned on his heels to retreat, but another man, identical to the first, blocked his way. Panic surged through him as he realized there were more—two identical figures to his left and right.

Suddenly, a voice whispered aggressively in his right ear, "Hello, John."

John's mind reeled. How was this possible? Five identical men now surrounded him, closing in.

In unison, they spoke. "We are The Five, John. We are The Hand, John."

"All good hands contain five fingers, John," the first man said.

"We can give with one hand, John," the second man continued.

"And we can take with the other, John," the third man added.

The fourth man, now inches from John's face, said, "If you want our help to give, John" — he then vanished, and a whisper sounded directly in John's ear — "then you must help us take, John."

"Five lives you must give us, John," they uttered as one horrifying choir, "and one life, we will give you in return, John."

The whispers had been growing louder, more insistent, ever since he'd crossed the threshold into this place. The Five had been patient, but now they demanded his full attention.

The voices were a chorus in his mind, each one distinct yet blending into an unsettling harmony that seemed to resonate with the very marrow of his bones.

"John … you've seen what we can do. You know what

we want. It's time to stop fighting. Time to accept what you are, what we need you to be …"

The voice that spoke was like shattered glass, sharp and cold, cutting through his resistance with ease. John felt the familiar chill creep up his spine, as though a hand had reached inside him, fingers curling around his heart. He swallowed hard, trying to steady his breath, but the dread was overwhelming.

"What … what do you want from me?" John's voice trembled, the words barely escaping his lips.

"Everything," the voice replied, soft but commanding, a dark promise of things to come. "Your pain, your rage, your loss … They have fed us, brought us closer to the world of the living. But it's not enough, John. We need more. We need your soul."

John squeezed his eyes shut, trying to block out the growing pressure in his head, but the voices only grew louder. They wove through his thoughts, turning memories of Sarah and Ethan into grotesque parodies, filling him with a twisted sense of purpose. He felt the last vestiges of his resistance crumbling, giving way to something much darker.

"Sarah ... Ethan ..." John's voice cracked as he uttered their names. The images of them, once so vivid, had been tainted by the malevolent presence of The Five. But even in this state, a part of him still clung to the love he felt for his family, the desperate need to do something, anything, to bring them back.

"You want them back?" one of the voices whispered, more seductive than the others, dripping with honeyed malice. "We can make that happen, John. You know we can. But you must do as we say, John. You must let us in. Fully."

John's heart pounded in his chest, his thoughts spinning wildly as he grappled with the impossibility of what they were offering. To see them again, to hold them, to feel whole—was it truly worth the cost?

"Yes," came the answer, almost as if it had been pulled from his own mind. "Accept us, and they will be yours again. Reject us, and you will lose them forever, condemned to wander this world alone, haunted by their absence."

He opened his eyes, staring into the darkness where he knew The Five were waiting, their forms just out of reach, barely perceptible, like a stain on the fabric of reality. The alleyway seemed to pulse around him, breathing in tandem with his ragged breaths.

"What ... what do I have to do?" John asked, the weight of his decision bearing down on him. His voice was barely more than a whisper, but the words felt final, sealing his fate.

"You know," they replied in unison, their voices mingling into a dreadful harmony. "Five lives is what we desire. You must give yourself to us, body and soul. And in return, we shall give you what you desire most, John."

John felt the tears well up in his eyes, the sorrow and fear gnawing at his resolve, but the thought of Sarah and Ethan—their faces, their smiles, the sound of their laughter—was enough to push him over the edge. He could not bear the emptiness any longer, the aching void that had consumed him since they were taken from him. If this was the price he had to pay to be with them again, then so be it.

"I accept," he said, his voice hollow, void of any hope or light.

As the last syllable faded into the ether, John felt

something inside him break, a tether to his old life snapping as the darkness consumed him whole. The world around him twisted, the walls bending and warping as reality itself seemed to buckle under the weight of the pact he had made.

He was no longer just John Morrison, the grieving father, the broken man. He was something else now, something far more dangerous. And as The Five receded into the shadows, their work complete, John knew there was no turning back.

He belonged to the darkness now, and the darkness belonged to him.

The alleyway suddenly fell silent and empty, leaving John alone and confused, his heart racing.

John stood there, trembling, his mind struggling to process what had just happened. The encounter left him feeling more desperate and unhinged. He knew that whatever forces he had invoked were real and powerful. The promise of help came with a terrifying cost, but in his grief-stricken state, he was willing to pay it.

Shaking off the unease, John quickened his pace, eager to put the alley and its disquieting presence behind him. He emerged back onto the cobblestone streets, the seafront's cold wind feeling almost welcoming in comparison to the stifling alley. John quickly made his way back to The Seafarer's Rest, clutching his bag of supplies. He unlocked the door to his room and entered, his hands shaking. He placed the bag on the dresser and sat on the edge of the bed, staring blankly at Ethan.

The encounter with The Hand weighed heavily on his mind. He had struck a deal with something beyond his understanding, something dark and malevolent. As the night wore on, John drifted into a restless sleep, haunted by the faces of The Five and the chilling whispers of their demands.

Chapter Eleven

Jack Palace sat in his office. The discovery of John Morrison's notebook had provided a crucial lead: repeated references to a mysterious online entity known as thevoiceofthehand. Jack's instincts told him this was no mere coincidence. Whoever this was had a significant connection to John's recent activities, and potentially, to the deaths surrounding him.

It was late, and the station was quiet—too quiet. Jack Palace leaned back in his chair, staring at the ceiling tiles, each one a patchwork of stains and cracks that told stories of their own. His desk was littered with case files, coffee cups, and the detritus of a man who spent more time working than living. But tonight none of it held his attention. Tonight all he could hear was the echo of a gunshot that had reverberated through his life like a thunderclap.

He closed his eyes, letting the sounds of the station fade away, and there it was—the crack of the shot, sharp and final, cutting through the chaos of that rainy afternoon. He could feel the gun in his hand, the recoil jolting up his arm, and see the man falling, a look of surprise and terror on his face. Jack hadn't had time to think, only to act, and that split-second decision had changed everything.

In the years since, he had tried to convince himself that it was necessary, that he had done the right thing. But in the dead of night, when sleep refused to come, the doubts crept in, whispering that maybe, just maybe, there had been another way. A way that didn't leave a little girl fatherless and him with a stain on his soul that no amount of justice could wash clean.

Jack opened his eyes and stared at the cluttered desk in front of him. The sound of the gunshot was gone, but its presence lingered, an invisible weight pressing down on him. He reached for John's notebook, something to drown out the memories, to keep the ghosts at bay. But as he flipped it open, he knew it was only a temporary fix. The past was patient. It would wait until he was alone again, in the quiet moments, to remind him of the cost of his choices.

And so, Jack did the only thing he could—he kept working, kept fighting, because stopping meant facing the echoes that haunted him. And that was something he wasn't ready to do. Not yet.

He spread John's notebook out before him, the worn leather cover giving off a faint musty odour. The pages were filled with scrawled handwriting, strange symbols, and fragmented thoughts. Each entry seemed to spiral deeper into madness.

The first few pages were relatively normal, lists of mundane tasks and brief reflections. But as Jack flipped through, the tone shifted. The handwriting grew more erratic, the entries more cryptic.

One page caught Jack's eye. It was filled with peculiar symbols—circles interlinked with triangles, lines crossing through spirals, all meticulously drawn in dark ink. Beside the symbols were words and phrases that seemed plucked from a nightmare: *soul binding, life reversal, eternal shadow.* The margins were crammed with small, frantic notes that seemed almost nonsensical: *Blood moon necessary, Voice commands obedience, Final sacrifice.*

Jack's eyes narrowed as he traced his fingers over a particularly dense section of text. Conversations were interspersed with these symbols, snippets of dialogue that read like a script from a horror film. The name thevoiceofthehand appeared repeatedly, always accompanied by instructions or commands.

One entry stood out, dated just a few days after Ethan's death:

Woke up to another message. 'thevoiceofthehand'. Can't shake the feeling that it's watching me. I tried to ignore it, but it knows ... it always knows. It says it can help me see Ethan alive again. I want to believe it. God, I miss him so much.

The handwriting was shaky, almost illegible, as if John's hand had been trembling as he wrote. Jack could feel the man's desperation bleeding through the ink. It was like watching someone sink in quicksand, each word pulling him deeper into the abyss.

Another entry, scrawled hurriedly, caught Jack's attention:

I did what it asked. It's not enough. It's never enough. It keeps asking for more. I know I shouldn't listen, but I have to. What if it's right? What if it's the only way?

Jack felt a cold sweat forming on his brow. He turned the page, each flip revealing more of John's unravelling sanity. There were no instructions about rituals or dark ceremonies, nothing so blatantly sinister, yet the implications were just as chilling. The messages from thevoiceofthehand were simple, insidious—an erosion of John's will, his sense of self.

The next entry was almost incoherent, the writing large and frantic:

The voice says I'm close. Closer than ever. Just need to let go, it says. Just need to let go of the world. Ethan's waiting, it says. Don't trust the doctors, don't trust anyone. They don't understand. They want to keep me here, in the dark. But I need to see Ethan. I need to know he's safe.

Jack's hands trembled as he closed the notebook for a moment, trying to compose himself. This was no calculated villain, no mastermind—this was a father losing his grip, falling prey to something he didn't understand. The true horror wasn't in what John had done, but in how he had been pushed to do it, one small step at a time.

Steeling himself, Jack reopened the notebook to the final pages. The entries were few, spaced out over several days. The handwriting had become almost childlike, scrawled with a blunt pencil, as if John had been too exhausted to hold a pen.

I saw something today. Just for a moment. I know it will work. The voice said it was a sign, that I'm getting closer. I have to keep going. Can't stop now. I'm so tired ... but I can't stop.

The entry near the bottom of the page was the hardest to read, the words smudged as if by a tear or a drop of water:

Ethan, I'm coming. I'll find you. We'll be together again. I just have to do what it says. It promised. It promised ...

Jack closed the notebook slowly, his breath catching in his throat. This wasn't just a case of a man driven mad by grief—this was a methodical breakdown, a manipulation by something or someone who had preyed on John's most vulnerable moments.

John's last note, shaky and smeared with what looked like tears, read: *Ethan, forgive me. I do this for us. I do this to save you.*

Jack placed down the notebook, his hands trembling. The magnitude of what John had been involved in was staggering. This wasn't just about a desperate father. This was about something far darker, something that had twisted John's mind and led him down a path of no return. The voice, the rituals, the symbols—it all pointed to a malevolent force that had sunk its claws deep into John's psyche.

He took a deep breath, steeling himself for what lay ahead. What would he find when they located John? A mad man or something more?

The tag 'thevoiceofthehand' appeared frequently, always in the context of guiding or instructing John.

Palace's investigation into the enigmatic figure began with a sense of grim determination and the kind of meticulous precision that had earned him his reputation. The quest to uncover the identity behind the cryptic online alias was more than just another task—it was a crucial piece of the puzzle in the desperate search for John and Ethan.

In the confines of his cluttered office at the Clough Road Police Station, Jack sat at his desk, a sea of case files and evidence bags strewn about. The office itself was a reflection of the chaos that surrounded his current case—a cluttered desk with half-empty coffee mugs, stacks of paperwork, and the occasional whirring of an overworked computer. The walls were adorned with pinned photographs, maps, and hastily scribbled notes connected by red strings, all contributing to the labyrinth of his mind's ongoing investigation.

The room smelled faintly of stale coffee and the metallic tang of stress, a combination that had become his olfactory signature over the years. The persistent hum of the police radio, mixed with the occasional clatter of keyboards from his colleagues, provided a background noise that was both comforting and maddening.

Jack reached out to the department's lead cyber investigator, a sharp-minded tech expert named Rachel.

"Rachel, I've got a new task for you," Jack said, his voice carrying the weight of urgency. "I need you to trace an online identity. The name is 'thevoiceofthehand'. They've been in contact with John Morrison, and I believe they hold critical information about our case."

Rachel McAllister was a formidable presence in the department, her sharp intellect and unyielding determination making her a cornerstone of the team. To those who knew her, she was a quiet storm—unassuming at first glance but with a mind that crackled like a live wire, always sparking with ideas and solutions.

Rachel stood at a modest 5'5", her stature almost deceptive when it came to her commanding intellect. She had an air of understated confidence about her, accentuated by her strikingly sharp features. Her hair was a cascade of raven-black waves, usually pulled back into a tight, no-nonsense bun that framed her angular face with a kind of rigid precision. Her eyes, a piercing green, were often hidden behind a pair of oversized glasses with thin black frames, which she adjusted with a deft flick of her fingers. They were eyes that could dissect a line of code or unravel a cryptic message with the same ease that one might open a book.

Rachel's clothing was functional yet stylish—a blend of practicality and subtle sophistication. She typically wore well-tailored blazers over sleek, fitted blouses, and her dark jeans or trousers spoke of a woman who was ready to move from her desk to the field with minimal fuss. Her boots, sturdy and polished, were scuffed from countless nights spent chasing digital ghosts. On her left wrist, she wore a silver bracelet—a simple piece that had belonged to her grandmother, a memento that tethered her to a past that was both cherished and formative.

Rachel's office was a sanctuary of controlled chaos. The room was much darker than Jack's, with the only illumination coming from the soft, pale glow of computer screens and the sporadic flicker of neon lights from an old, dust-covered clock. Walls lined with bookshelves were crammed with technical manuals, cryptography texts, and old case files, each meticulously organized yet showing signs of frequent use. A large mahogany desk dominated the centre of the room, its surface cluttered with an array of gadgets, cables, and sticky notes scribbled with cryptic reminders and hastily jotted ideas.

A pair of monitors sat on the desk, their screens filled with streams of code, digital maps, and an endless array of surveillance footage. In the corner of the room, a high-backed chair with worn leather provided Rachel with a perch from which she could survey her domain. A large window, covered with blinds that were always drawn halfway, allowed just enough light to illuminate the room while keeping prying eyes from peering in.

Rachel McAllister's journey to becoming the

department's lead cyber investigator was as unconventional as it was compelling. Born and raised in the small coastal town of Bridlington, she had always been drawn to technology. Her father, a retired naval officer, had instilled in her a fascination with codes and encryption from an early age, showing her the basics of Morse code and cryptographic puzzles as bedtime stories. Her mother, a librarian, had encouraged her to dive into books about early computer science and hacking, fostering an environment where curiosity was not just welcomed but encouraged.

Rachel's academic career had been marked by a series of impressive achievements. She had breezed through university, where she earned her degree in computer science with a joint honour in forensic analysis. Her time there was spent delving into the dark side of the digital world, a fascination that led her to intern with various cybersecurity firms and law enforcement agencies. Her skills had been honed in the crucible of a high-stakes internship, where she had cracked her first major case—a digital espionage scandal that had put her on the map.

When she had joined the police force, Rachel had quickly become known for her uncanny ability to unravel the most intricate of digital knots. Her reputation for excellence was built on long hours, an almost obsessive attention to detail, and a knack for staying one step ahead of those who would do harm. Her colleagues respected her not just for her technical prowess but for her unyielding commitment to justice.

Rachel's world was one where the digital and physical worlds intertwined, and her office was a reflection of that. Every case file and code sequence was a puzzle piece in a larger, ever-evolving picture. Her personal motto was simple but profound: "In the labyrinth of data, truth is the only light."

Rachel sat in the dim glow of her computer screen, the only source of light in an otherwise darkened room. The world outside had long since quietened, but inside, the air was thick with tension. She leaned forward, her face bathed in the cold blue light of the monitor, eyes narrowing as she typed with a speed that was deliberate and relentless. The internet, a vast and sprawling digital wilderness, was her hunting ground tonight, and she was determined to track down her prey: thevoiceofthehand.

This wasn't her first time delving into the shadows of the dark web, but it never got easier. The pathways were twisting and deceptive, designed to mislead and confuse, a labyrinth where only the most skilled navigators could find their way. Rachel's fingers moved with an expertise honed by countless hours of digital exploration, a subtle choreography that only the initiated could appreciate. She moved through layers of encryption, bypassing firewalls and proxies with the practised ease of someone who had long ago learned the language of code and deception.

Her first task was to trace the origins of the alias, 'thevoiceofthehand'. She knew better than to take anything at face value; this was the dark web, after all, where nothing was what it seemed. Each username, each post was a carefully constructed mask, a disguise meant to keep the curious at bay and the dangerous hidden in plain sight. But Rachel had a knack for peeling back those layers, for finding the truth buried beneath the lies.

She started by running a series of cross-references through specialized databases, tools designed to sift through the murky depths of the web and bring hidden data to the surface. Her screen flickered as she worked, displaying a chaotic mix of cryptic symbols, code strings, and fragmented posts from obscure forums. The digital landscape was a mess of noise, but within that noise, Rachel began to discern patterns.

Thevoiceofthehand had a presence, a footprint that, while faint, was unmistakable to a trained eye. The alias appeared in various forums dedicated to the occult and the esoteric, places where the conversations drifted from the mundane to the malevolent with unsettling ease. Discussions on necromancy, ancient rituals, and forbidden knowledge were common threads, and it became clear that this was no casual dabbler. The posts were meticulous, scholarly even, written with a precision that suggested not just knowledge but obsession.

Rachel leaned closer, her heartbeat quickening as she realized the depth of what she was uncovering. This was someone who didn't just study the occult—they lived it. She noticed recurring phrases in the posts, references to rituals she had only seen mentioned in the most obscure texts. And then there were the breadcrumbs, the small hints that thevoiceofthehand had deliberately—or perhaps arrogantly—left behind. It was as if they wanted to be found, but only by someone worthy.

One post in particular caught her eye, a lengthy treatise on a ritual to commune with the dead. The language was dense, filled with arcane references that would have confounded most, but Rachel read it with ease, her mind piecing together the implications. Whoever this was, they had crossed a line—a line that most wouldn't even dare approach.

But it was the IP address that changed everything. In the dark web, anonymity was sacred, and tracing an IP address was next to impossible. Yet with a combination of persistence, skill, and perhaps a touch of luck, Rachel managed to crack through the layers of encryption. What she found was a series of encrypted servers, a trail that led her deeper into the web's underbelly. It was a digital breadcrumb trail that wound its way to a small, almost forgotten town, a place with a history steeped in the occult.

Rachel's heart pounded as she realized where it was leading her: an obscure library, one that housed a collection of ancient texts and records, many of which had been lost to time. This was no ordinary library; it was a sanctuary for those who sought knowledge that the world had deemed too dangerous to preserve. It was not well known by the general public.

Her mind raced as she connected the dots. This was where thevoiceofthehand was likely holed up, or at the very least, where they had drawn much of their knowledge. She could almost picture them, huddled in a dark corner of that old, dusty library, surrounded by books bound in leather and secrets. The thought sent a shiver down her spine.

As Rachel's screen flashed with the final confirmation, she leaned back in her chair, letting out a breath she hadn't realized she was holding. She felt the stiffness in her neck and back, the physical toll of hours spent intense concentration. But there was no time for rest; she had to get this information to Jack.

She stood, stretching the muscles that had tightened during her marathon session, and crossed the room to where Jack was still poring over the latest case files. His brow furrowed as he looked up, but the tension in his face eased slightly when he saw her approach.

"Rach, you're a star! I don't know how you do it,"

Jack said, a mix of admiration and relief in his voice.

Rachel smiled, though it didn't quite reach her eyes. "It's not about how, Jack. It's about why. And right now, the why is more important than anything." She handed him the printout with the information she'd uncovered. "This is where you need to go. But be careful, Jack. I don't like what I've found, and I have a feeling we're only scratching the surface."

Jack's gaze darkened as he read over the data, his mind already jumping to the next steps. Urgency now gripped them both. As he gathered his notes and prepared to leave, the weight of what they were uncovering settled heavily on his shoulders.

Rachel watched him go, her mind still reeling from the digital journey she had just completed. She knew that the information she had unearthed was only the beginning, a key that could unlock something far more sinister than either of them had anticipated. And as the door closed behind Jack, Rachel couldn't shake the feeling that they were about to confront something ancient, something that had been waiting in the shadows for far too long.

Armed with this new information, Jack prepared for the next stage of the investigation. He knew that uncovering thevoiceofthehand's real identity would require more than just digital sleuthing; it would involve fieldwork and interviews. Jack's thoughts raced as he considered the implications of what he had uncovered. The stakes were high—John's desperate quest to bring back his son had led him to this shadowy figure, and Jack needed to get to the bottom of it quickly.

As he gathered his notes and prepared to leave the office, Jack felt a growing sense of urgency. The quiet hum of the office seemed to intensify, mirroring his own rising anxiety. He knew that every second counted, and the darkness that enveloped thevoiceofthehand was about to meet the relentless scrutiny of his investigative prowess.

Jack's plan was to visit the archives and dig deeper into the records and personal accounts associated with the occult community there. Each step in his investigation was calculated, each decision driven by the hope that he might find a crucial lead to help John, and potentially, save Ethan from the abyss into which they had been drawn.

But Jack needed to know more about John; he needed to know about the state he might be in. What he read in John's notebook had troubled Jack. He had someone else he needed to see first.

The pathologist's office was a cold, sterile place, the kind of room that seemed to swallow all warmth and life the moment you stepped inside. The air was thick with the faint scent of formaldehyde, a lingering reminder of the dead who had passed through here. Jack Palace had been in enough of these places to know that they weren't just rooms—they were thresholds, places where the living and the dead brushed up against each other in uneasy silence.

Dr Harvey Long, the pathologist, was a small, wiry man with thin, greying hair and a pair of glasses that perched precariously on the bridge of his nose. He looked up from his desk as Jack entered, his expression a mix of curiosity and concern.

"DI Palace," Long greeted, motioning for Jack to take a seat. "I understand you're here about John Morrison."

Jack nodded, lowering himself into the uncomfortable

chair opposite the coroner. The room seemed to grow colder as Lane opened a thick file, flipping through pages with practised precision.

"I've reviewed the reports," Long began, his voice clinical and detached. "Morrison's behaviour in the days leading up to his son's death was ... troubling, to say the least."

"Troubling how?" Jack asked, his voice rougher than he intended. He was tired, worn down by the weight of this case, and the pathologist's office felt like just another stop on a long dark road that seemed to have no end.

Long adjusted his glasses, leaning in slightly as if to emphasize his point. "There were several incidents reported by those close to him—strange actions, a growing obsession with occult symbols, isolation from friends and family. He was seen muttering to himself, drawing symbols on walls, and performing rituals that, frankly, made no sense. These aren't the actions of a rational mind, Detective Inspector."

Jack felt a chill creep up his spine, but he kept his voice steady. "You think he was losing it? Having a mental breakdown?"

The pathologist nodded slowly, his gaze fixed on the file in front of him. "Based on what I've seen, it's possible. Grief can do terrible things to a person's mind. In Morrison's case, it seems to have triggered something far more severe—a delusional disorder, possibly even psychosis. The loss of his son, the guilt, the desperation to bring him back ... it's all there, laid out in his actions."

Long paused, flipping to another page in the file before continuing. "What's particularly concerning is the level of obsession he developed with these occult practices. It's as if he was trying to find meaning in something, anything, that could justify his son's death. That kind of obsessive focus is a classic sign of someone who's losing touch with reality."

Jack absorbed the pathologist's words, feeling a heavy knot of unease settle in his gut. John's actions—the rituals, the symbols, the dark descent into a world that seemed to straddle the line between reality and nightmare—it all pointed to a mind unravelling, slipping further and further away from reason.

"But what if ..." Jack hesitated, the question sounding absurd even as it formed in his mind. "What if some of it was real? What if what he was seeing, what he was doing ... what if it wasn't just in his head?"

Long met Jack's gaze, his expression sombre. "Detective Inspector, I've seen people in the throes of psychosis who believed they were talking to angels, who saw demons in the corners of their rooms, who heard voices telling them to do unspeakable things. To them, it all felt real—more real than the world around them. But the truth is, their minds had created those realities as a way to cope with the trauma they couldn't process."

He closed the file with a decisive thud, leaning back in his chair. "I believe that's what happened to John Morrison. He was a man driven to the brink by grief and guilt, and his mind fractured under the pressure. What he saw, what he believed ... it was a manifestation of his own torment."

Jack left the pathologist's office with the file tucked under his arm, his thoughts a chaotic swirl of doubt and dread. He had come here looking for answers, but all he had found were more questions, more shadows to chase down dark alleys.

As he walked out into the pale afternoon light, Jack

couldn't shake the feeling that he was standing at the edge of something vast and terrifying, a precipice that dropped into a darkness too deep to fathom. Was John Morrison just a man broken by grief, or had he stumbled upon something far darker, something that had pushed him over the edge of sanity?

The line between reality and delusion had never felt so thin, so blurred. And as Jack continued down the street, the wind whipping around him like a cold whisper, he couldn't help but wonder which side of that line he was really on.

Chapter Twelve

John spent the next day in a state of torment, replaying the encounter with The Five over and over in his mind. The weight of the bargain he had struck was almost unbearable, like a lead weight strapped to his chest, compressing his every breath. He had agreed to kill five people as the cost of giving Ethan new life. The Five had spoken with a cold, unwavering certainty, and John knew there was no turning back. Even as the first light of morning began to creep over the rooftops of Whitby, the memory of those dead eyes and the sinister, almost serene voice haunted him. The picturesque town, usually a place of solace, now felt like a cage, its narrow streets twisting and turning into a labyrinth of despair.

He wandered through Whitby's cobbled streets, trying to make sense of what he had agreed to. His feet carried him aimlessly, past the quaint cottages and historic buildings, as though they were disconnected from his mind. The town, with its iconic abbey perched high on the cliff and the harbour that had once been a source of comfort, now seemed to mock him. Every face he passed seemed to be a potential victim, a candidate for the terrible task he had to complete. The notion sickened him, but it was also inescapable. The faces blurred together, nameless and insignificant, mere cogs in a machine that now demanded blood to keep turning.

John's emotions were a turbulent storm. He was consumed by grief and guilt over the death of his wife and the loss of Ethan. The promise of bringing Ethan back was a glimmer of hope in his otherwise dark existence, but the price was horrifying. Every thought was tinged with the knowledge that to save his son, he would have to destroy others. How could he reconcile that with any sense of morality? The question gnawed at him, but no answer came, only the ceaseless churning of his mind.

His journey took him along the winding path that led up to Whitby Abbey. The ruins, silhouetted against the grey sky, loomed over him like a sentinel of doom. Sarah had loved this place, often dragging him up here to take in the view, to breathe in the salty air, and to feel the history seep into her bones. He could almost hear her laughter echoing through the crumbling walls, a memory that now brought nothing but pain. The world felt drained of colour, the vibrant hues of his past replaced with the grey, suffocating fog of the present.

At one point, he found himself standing on the 199 steps, the steep stairway that led from the town to the abbey. He gripped the iron railing, his knuckles white, as he looked out over the town below. The harbour had a cluster of boats bobbing gently in the water, and the streets lined with shops and cafés were slowly coming to life. But there was no comfort in the familiar sights. They only served to remind him of everything he had lost. He turned away, unable to bear it any longer, and stumbled back down the steps, the ancient stone slick beneath his feet.

The rest of the day passed in a blur. He walked until his feet ached, until the sun dipped below the horizon and the town lights flickered on, casting long shadows that seemed to reach out for him. At a small corner shop near the harbour, he bought a pack of cigarettes, twenty Marlboro Lights, even though he hadn't smoked in years. The habit was something from his younger days, a relic of the time before responsibility had weighed him down, before life had hardened him into the man he had become. He lit one, the smoke curling around his face, and inhaled deeply, hoping it would numb the edges of his pain.

But the cigarette did nothing to dull the torment. Instead, it only served as a reminder of how powerless he was. The Hand had given him a task, and he would have to complete it. There was no other way. As the night deepened, he found himself back at the harbour, staring out at the dark, churning sea. The waves crashed against the stone pier with a relentless force, much like the thoughts that battered his mind. He sat on a bench, the cigarette burning down to the filter between his fingers, and tried to think of a way out, but there was none. His love for Ethan, the desperate need to see his son again, overpowered everything else.

That evening, as the last traces of daylight faded into the brooding, charcoal clouds above Whitby, John found himself drawn to the seafront. The town had a way of transforming at night, its quaint charm giving way to something darker, more mysterious. The cobbled streets, earlier bustling with tourists and locals, were now eerily silent, save for the occasional creak of a swinging sign or the distant murmur of voices from the pubs. The ancient stones beneath his feet were coated with a thin layer of mist, the air thick with the tang of salt and seaweed. The wind, sharp and relentless, cut through his thin jacket, but he welcomed the chill. It was something real, something tangible he could feel, unlike the torment gnawing away at his insides.

John's breath misted in front of him as he walked, each exhale a brief, ghostly apparition that dissolved into the night. The sound of the waves crashing against the jagged rocks below was a constant, rhythmic roar, punctuated by the occasional screech of a gull. The sea, a dark expanse of churning water, seemed to stretch on forever, merging with the sky at a horizon that was impossible to distinguish in the gloom. The tide was coming in, the waves growing in size and ferocity, as if the ocean itself was agitated and restless, much like the man walking along its edge.

The seafront was nearly deserted, the usual throngs of people reduced to a few shadowy figures huddled in doorways or trudging home, their faces hidden beneath hoods and scarves. The lights from the town, muted and sparse, cast long, wavering reflections across the wet pavement, creating the illusion of movement where there was none. The buildings that lined the promenade, old and weathered by years of salt air, seemed to loom over him, their windows dark and lifeless like the eyes of ancient, silent watchers.

As he walked, the smell of fish and hot oil drifted from a nearby chip shop, mingling with the briny scent of the sea. It was a familiar smell, one that usually brought comfort, but tonight it only made his stomach churn. He hadn't eaten all day, but the thought of food was repulsive, his appetite swallowed by the black pit of dread that had settled in his gut.

The moon, half-hidden by thick clouds, cast a pallid light over the landscape, giving everything a washed-out, otherworldly quality. The cliffs, rising up to his right, were shrouded in darkness, their contours barely visible against the sky. Somewhere in the distance, a foghorn blared, its mournful call echoing across the water, adding to the oppressive atmosphere.

John's mind was a chaotic swirl of thoughts, each one

more desperate than the last. He couldn't shake the feeling that he was being watched, that the shadows themselves were alive, creeping closer with every step. His thoughts drifted back to The Hand, to the terrible deal he had made. Was this what damnation felt like? A slow descent into madness, where every shadow held a threat, and every sound was a portent of doom?

It was then, as he rounded a bend in the promenade, that he saw it—a figure shuffling along the seafront, barely visible in the dim light. The figure moved with an unnatural gait, slow and deliberate, as if each step was a struggle. John's heart skipped a beat, a cold spike of fear shooting through him. The figure was hunched over, its face obscured by a wide-brimmed hat, and it wore a long, tattered coat that flapped in the wind. For a moment, John considered turning back, but something—curiosity, desperation, or perhaps something more sinister—compelled him to continue.

As he drew closer, the figure seemed to pause, as if sensing his approach. The wind picked up, howling between the buildings and whipping John's hair into his eyes. He pushed it back with a trembling hand, his gaze locked on the figure ahead. There was something familiar about the way it moved, something that tugged at the edges of his memory. But as hard as he tried, he couldn't place it.

"Who's there?" John's voice was hoarse, barely audible over the wind and waves. The figure didn't respond, didn't even turn around. It just stood there, at the very edge of the promenade, where the stone gave way to the open sea.

John hesitated, his heart pounding in his chest. Every instinct screamed at him to turn and run, to leave this place and never look back. But he couldn't. He was drawn to the figure, to the mystery of its presence here, on this desolate night.

Finally, as if sensing John's approach, the figure began to turn. The movement was slow, almost mechanical, and as the figure came into view, John felt his blood run cold. The face that met his gaze was not the face of a stranger. It was his own. Pale, gaunt, with hollow eyes that seemed to bore into his soul. The reflection of his own tormented, shattered self.

John stumbled back, his breath coming in short, panicked gasps. The figure raised a hand, and in that moment, John understood. The figure wasn't real. It was a manifestation of his guilt, his fear, his overwhelming sense of doom. It was The Hand's mark on him, a reminder of the deal he had struck, the terrible price he would have to pay.

He blinked, and the figure was gone, leaving nothing but the empty promenade and the sound of the crashing waves. John stood there for a long moment, his heart racing, the cold wind tearing at his clothes. He was alone again, but the fear lingered, clinging to him like the mist that swirled around his feet.

Slowly, he turned and began to walk back the way he had come, the weight of his decision pressing down on him with every step. Whitby's night had become his own personal purgatory, a place where the line between reality and nightmare had blurred beyond recognition. And somewhere out there, in the darkness, The Hand was waiting, watching, ready to collect its due.

As John walked, his intention was to head back to the relative sanctuary of his accommodation, but he knew he had been tasked with something sinister, and he knew it was too late to refuse. He had accepted his fate, and the fear of what would happen if he went back on his word was too much for John.

As John was battling his thoughts, his attention was drawn to another figure on the opposite side of the road. Any thoughts of handing himself in and losing Ethan forever vanished in an instant. He had a target now, and this one was perfect.

The figure in question was an unassuming homeless man, his clothes tattered and dirty, his hair matted. He moved slowly, his dragging steps heavy with exhaustion. John watched as the man turned and entered a nearby public toilet, the door creaking shut behind him. He wasn't sure if he was ready, but John knew what he had to do. He had agreed a terrible price, but if it meant seeing his child's sweet smile, his son's awkward, almost drunk-like steps, he would do it.

John's heart pounded in his chest as he approached the toilet. His mind screamed at him to stop, to turn back, but he pushed forward, driven by the promise of Ethan's return. He entered the dimly lit doorway to the toilets, the air thick with the smell of urine and bleach.

The public toilets were a nightmare of neglect, hidden away behind a decrepit amusement arcade on Whitby's seafront. The entrance, half obscured by graffiti and a heavy layer of grime, seemed to swallow the feeble light from a nearby streetlamp. Inside, the tungsten lights flickered erratically, casting a sickly yellow glow over the cracked tiles and corroded metal fixtures. The floor was a repulsive mix of wet sand, likely tracked in from the beach, and other, more dubious substances.

In one corner, the homeless man stood hunched over a grimy sink, the water running in a weak, sputtering stream as he tried to wash away the residue of the streets. His clothes were a patchwork of rags and old army surplus, layered against the coastal chill. A faded, oversized green jacket hung loosely over his thin frame, the fabric worn and torn in places. His hair was a matted mess of grey and brown, and his beard, unkempt and tangled, nearly obscured his weary, sunken eyes.

Once, this man had been someone—a factory worker, perhaps, or a fisherman who had fallen on hard times. Maybe he'd lost his job, his home, his family. The whispers of the past haunted him as he moved through his days, the world around him reduced to a series of survival tasks. The streets had been unkind, wearing down his spirit and leaving him a shell of his former self.

John walked further into the grimy room, the metal pipe he'd found by a lobster basket near the boats earlier that day cold and heavy in his coat pocket. The flickering lights seemed to sync with the rapid thud of his heart, each step he took echoing through the small, claustrophobic space. The air was thick with the acrid smell of urine and damp decay, a stench that clawed at his senses and made his stomach churn.

As John approached, the homeless man remained oblivious, focused on the small ritual of washing his face. The sound of the dripping tap was a rhythmic, mocking metronome that underlined John's every thought. His breathing grew rapid and shallow, his hands trembling as he gripped the pipe tighter.

"I'm sorry," John whispered, his voice barely more than a rasp, a confession meant for himself more than the man before him.

The homeless man turned slowly, confusion and fear dawning in his eyes. The dim light reflected in his gaze, a look of sudden, desperate understanding. But before he could react, John swung the pipe with all his strength. The metal struck with a sickening thud, the impact reverberating up John's arm and through his entire body.

The man crumpled to the floor, dark red blood streaming from a deep gash on his head, mingling with the filth on the tiles. John's mind was a storm of horror and urgency, each heartbeat pounding in his ears like a war drum. He swung again, the pipe connecting with another wet, crunching sound. And again. And again. Each blow sent tremors through his arms and dark thoughts through his mind.

The homeless man's body twitched once more, then lay still. Blood pooled around him, spreading out in a morbid halo. John's hands were slick with the warm, sticky liquid, the sight and smell of it overwhelming his senses. Tears streamed down his face, blurring his vision as he stared at the lifeless form before him.

John staggered back, dropping the pipe with a clatter that seemed to echo endlessly in the confined space. He was panting, each breath a ragged gasp that struggled to fill his lungs. Nausea surged within him, and he had to force himself not to retch. He had crossed a line, committed an unforgivable act, and the weight of it pressed down on him, threatening to crush his very soul.

Desperation kicked in, propelling him into motion. He moved to the sink, scrubbing his hands with a frantic urgency. The water ran pink, then red, swirling down the drain in a nauseating spiral. The smell of iron was thick in the air, making him gag as he tried to wash away the evidence of his crime. His hands felt raw, but no matter how hard he scrubbed, the blood seemed to cling to his skin, a dark reminder of the monster he had become.

With trembling hands, he wrapped the bloodied pipe in a wad of rough, tissue-thin paper from the nearest cubicle. He had to leave, had to get away before someone found him. As he stumbled out of the toilets, the cold night air hit him like a slap, a brutal reminder that there was no turning back.

John's breath fogged in the chill, a stark reminder of the warmth he'd left behind. He walked quickly, his footsteps echoing in the empty streets. Each step felt like a hammer blow, a cruel reminder of the deed he had just committed. His eyes darted around, scanning for any sign that someone had noticed, but the seafront was deserted, the streets empty and silent. The moon hung low in the sky, casting long, eerie shadows that seemed to dance in the corners of his vision.

He made his way back to The Seafarer's Rest, his pace quickening as his thoughts churned. The metal bar, wrapped hastily in tissue paper, felt heavy in his pocket, a burden he could no longer bear. He spotted a rundown bus stop ahead, its paint peeling and graffiti scrawled across its walls. The bin beside it overflowed with rubbish. With a quick, furtive glance around, John pulled the weapon from his pocket and shoved it deep into the garbage. The act felt final, like sealing away a piece of his own humanity.

His mind numb, his heart heavy, John continued his walk. The night was eerily quiet, the only sounds the distant crash of waves against the shore and the occasional rustle of leaves in the breeze. He passed closed shops and shuttered windows, the town asleep and oblivious to the horror that had just unfolded. He felt like a ghost, drifting through the streets, untethered from reality.

Back at The Seafarer's Rest, John slipped inside unnoticed. The old building creaked and groaned, as if acknowledging his return. He climbed the stairs slowly, each step a reminder of the weight he now carried. His room was as he had left it, a small sanctuary in a world gone mad. Ethan's lifeless body lay on the bed, a heart-wrenching sight that made John's throat tighten with emotion.

He collapsed onto the bed beside his son, tears streaming down his face. The sobs came uncontrollably, wracking his body as he grappled with the enormity of his actions. He had crossed a line, become something he never thought he could be. But through the haze of guilt and despair, he clung to the fragile hope that it would all be worth it, that somehow, in some way, his son would be returned to him.

The echoes of The Hand's voices reverberated in his mind, their sinister promises mingling with his own desperate thoughts. John lay on his bed, the springs creaking beneath his weight, the familiar sounds of the old building around him strangely distant, muffled by the pounding of his own heartbeat in his ears. His breath came in shallow, ragged gasps as he stared up at the ceiling, its peeling paint and spiderweb cracks forming a chaotic pattern that did nothing to calm his racing thoughts. The room felt oppressive, the walls closing in on him, as if the very space knew what he had done and was silently judging him.

The blood on his hands had been scrubbed clean, but no amount of washing could erase the memory of it—the warm, sticky sensation as it had seeped through his fingers, the way the homeless man's body had gone limp in his grasp, as if the life had been drained from it in an instant. John shuddered, pulling the threadbare blanket up to his chin, though it did nothing to stave off the chill that had settled deep in his bones. The room was cold, but it was not the kind of cold that could be remedied by mere blankets. This cold was internal, a creeping frost that had taken root in his soul, chilling him from the inside out.

His mind was a whirlwind of images, fragmented and disjointed, each one more horrifying than the last. He saw the man's face, etched with lines of hardship, his eyes wide with fear and disbelief in those final moments. The way his body had crumpled to the ground, a lifeless heap of rags, the brief struggle of his last breaths filling the air with a sound that John knew would haunt him forever. He had tried to forget it, to push the memory down deep where it couldn't hurt him, but it was no use. The man's face was burned into his mind, a permanent scar that would never fade.

John's thoughts were racing, tumbling over one another in a frantic, desperate attempt to rationalise what he had done. He had done it for Ethan, he told himself, repeating the words like a mantra. It was all for Ethan. The Hand had promised him, had assured him that this was the way, the only way to bring his son back. But even as he repeated those words, a sickening doubt gnawed at him. Was this really the only way? Was there not some other path he could have taken, some less horrifying way to reclaim what he had lost?

His stomach churned with nausea, and for a moment, he thought he might be sick. The bile rose in his throat, burning, but he swallowed it down, forcing himself to stay still. He couldn't afford to break down now. He had made his choice, and there was no going back. The Hand had been clear about that. There was no turning back.

As the minutes dragged on, the weight of exhaustion began to pull at him, his body craving the release of sleep even as his mind rebelled against it. He knew what awaited him in his dreams—dark, twisted nightmares born of guilt and fear, haunted by the spectre of the man he had killed. But he couldn't keep his eyes open any longer. The room began to blur, the edges of his vision darkening as sleep slowly, inexorably took hold.

The transition was seamless; one moment he was staring at the ceiling, the next he was plunged into the depths of his own mind, the dream world rushing up to meet him with all the force of a tidal wave. He was back in the alley, the night as dark and cold as it had been only hours before. The walls loomed high on either side, pressing in on him, the shadows thick and impenetrable. The air was heavy with the scent of decay, the stench of rubbish and unwashed bodies mingling with the metallic tang of blood.

And there, in the deepest part of the alley, where the light from the streetlamps couldn't reach, he saw him— the homeless man, standing upright as if nothing had happened, his eyes wide and empty, fixed on John with an intensity that made his blood run cold. The man's mouth moved, forming words that John couldn't hear, but he didn't need to. The accusation in those lifeless eyes was enough.

John tried to back away, but his feet wouldn't move. He was rooted to the spot, his legs heavy and unresponsive, as if they were made of lead. Panic surged through him, his heart hammering in his chest, but still, he couldn't move. The man took a step forward, then another, his movements slow and deliberate, his eyes never leaving John's. The shadows seemed to cling to him, like a cloak of darkness that followed him wherever he went, and with each step he took, the darkness grew, spreading outwards, swallowing the light, until the entire alley was plunged into pitch blackness.

John opened his mouth to scream, but no sound came out. He was suffocating, the air thick and heavy in his lungs, as the man drew closer and closer, until they were face to face. The man's breath was cold against John's skin, carrying with it the stench of death and decay, and those eyes—those lifeless, accusing eyes—bored into his soul, seeing everything, knowing everything.

"You did this," the man whispered, his voice low and rasping, a voice that didn't belong to the living. "You killed me."

John wanted to deny it, to scream that he had no choice, that he was forced into this, but the words stuck in his throat, choked by the overwhelming guilt that was consuming him. The man's hand reached out, fingers brushing against John's chest, and the touch was like ice, burning through his clothes, freezing him from the inside out.

Suddenly, the darkness was alive with whispers, voices that seemed to come from all around him, hissing and murmuring, growing louder and louder until they were a cacophony of sound, a deafening roar that filled his ears and drowned out his thoughts. They were voices of the dead, the forgotten, the damned, all crying out for vengeance, all demanding retribution for the life he had taken.

John squeezed his eyes shut, trying to block it out, but it was no use. The voices were inside his head, echoing off the walls of his mind, relentless and unyielding. The man's hand pressed harder against his chest, and John felt his heart stutter, his breath hitch in his throat. He couldn't breathe, couldn't think, couldn't escape the nightmare that had become his reality.

And then, just as suddenly as it had begun, it was over. The darkness receded, the voices faded, and John was left alone in his bed, drenched in sweat, his heart pounding erratically in his chest. He gasped for air, his hands clawing at the blanket as if it were a lifeline, something to anchor him to the real world, to pull him back from the brink of madness.

But even as he lay there, trembling and terrified, he knew that the nightmare wasn't over. It would never be over. Not until he had paid the price for the deal he had made, not until the darkness that had claimed him had taken everything. And as he finally drifted into a restless, haunted sleep, the image of the homeless man's lifeless eyes followed him, a ghost that would never let him go.

Chapter Thirteen

Jack Palace was in his office, the morning sunlight filtering through the blinds, casting stripes of light and shadow across his desk. He picked up the local newspaper, the paper's rough texture between his fingers a familiar sensation. His eyes scanned the headlines until one caught his attention: *Man Found Dead in Public Toilet in Whitby.*

He read the article slowly, his eyes lingering on each gruesome detail. It was a grisly story, one that crawled under your skin and set up camp there, a parasite of thought gnawing at your insides. The victim, a nameless drifter whose life had dissolved into the cracks of society, had been found in a beachside public toilet, his body mangled and face unrecognizable beneath a mask of blood and dirt. The homeless man had been brutally murdered, and the description of the scene was enough to turn anyone's stomach. For a moment, Palace felt a deep pang of sympathy for the victim, but he didn't link this incident with John. To him, it seemed like a random act of violence in a town that had seen its fair share of troubles. His mind was still fixated on the elusive John, who had vanished without a trace.

Jack felt a familiar tightness creeping up his chest, a sensation like cold fingers wrapping around his heart. He set the paper down, but his mind was already spiralling, a downward plunge into the dark recesses of his memory, a place he tried so hard to keep locked away.

The man's face—the one from that night—flashed in front of him, as clear as the day it happened, even though it had been years since. He could still smell the tang of gunpowder, feel the icy bite of the winter air, hear the hollow echo of his own voice shouting, "Drop the gun! Drop it now!"

The man hadn't listened, or maybe he hadn't heard. Either way, Jack had been in too deep, too far gone on adrenaline and fear to pause and consider the hesitation in the man's eyes. In the split second that followed, his instincts had kicked in—years of training distilled into a single, irrevocable action.

And then he saw her.

A little girl, no more than five years old, standing just a few feet away, her eyes wide and unblinking, as if the world had suddenly been ripped away from her and she was trying to figure out what was left. She looked at Jack, her gaze locking onto his, and in that instant, he felt something inside him shatter. It wasn't just her father's life he'd taken; it was her entire world. Good or bad, it didn't matter. Her life as she'd known it was gone in a single heartbeat.

He remembered the way she'd screamed—high and thin, the kind of scream that rips through you, tears you apart from the inside out, and Jack knew that sound would haunt him until the day he died.

Jack blinked, snapping back to the present, but the weight of that night clung to him like a shroud. He could still hear the girl's scream, still see the horror in her eyes. He could feel it every time he closed his own.

He glanced at the newspaper again but didn't pick it up. Instead, he stared at it, as if by sheer force of will, he could burn it to ash, erase the words, the images, the memories that clawed at the edges of his consciousness. But he knew it wouldn't work. It never did.

Palace's primary focus was on finding John. The police had been tracking John's movements through his phone, which had proven to be a valuable asset. The phone had pinged in various locations, creating a breadcrumb trail that the police had been following diligently. Palace knew that this was their best lead, and he felt it was only a matter of time before they closed in on John.

Setting the newspaper down, Palace felt a sense of anticipation tightening in his chest. He had been waiting for news of John's capture, knowing that the police were closing in on his location. The tension in the air was palpable, and Palace's mind raced with thoughts of finally bringing John in for questioning. He believed that once they had John, they could get to the bottom of the incident at the hospital and understand what had driven him to such desperate measures.

The police had traced the last known signal from John's phone to an industrial area on the outskirts of town. A large warehouse yard had been identified as the source of the signal. Police units, including armed response teams, were dispatched to the location. The warehouse yard was a sprawling area filled with lorries, shipping containers, and various industrial equipment, all bathed in the eerie glow of the setting sun.

Palace stood up from his desk, the weight of the case bearing down on him like a physical force. He shrugged into his worn leather jacket, the creak of the material a familiar comfort. Grabbing his keys and phone, he glanced one last time at the chaotic jumble of case files strewn across his desk, each one a piece of the puzzle he was determined to solve.

Palace exited his office and strode down the narrow hallway, the sound of his footsteps echoing off the tiled floor. The police station was a hive of activity, officers bustling about with purpose. He passed by the bulletin board cluttered with wanted posters and public notices, the familiar sights doing little to calm his racing thoughts. The fluorescent lights overhead flickered slightly, casting a harsh glow over the scene.

He nodded curtly to a few colleagues as he made his way to the exit, pushing through the heavy glass doors that led out into the car park. The cold, crisp air hit him, sharpening his senses. His dark blue Mustang was parked in its usual spot. He slid into the driver's seat, the engine roaring to life with a turn of the key. The radio crackled with updates from the ongoing operation, a constant reminder of the urgency of the situation.

Palace navigated through the familiar streets of Hull, the city a blur of grey and brick as he sped towards the industrial outskirts. He took Hedon Road, the main artery leading out of the city, his eyes scanning the road ahead while his mind raced with thoughts of John. The buildings became fewer and farther between, replaced by sprawling warehouses and industrial sites. The scent of saltwater from the nearby Humber Estuary mingled with the acrid smell of diesel and oil, a pungent reminder of the city's maritime heritage.

The route took him past the old docks, now mostly abandoned, their skeletal cranes standing as silent sentinels against the evening sky. He turned onto a narrower road, the streetlights casting long shadows on the pavement. The satnav on his phone guided him through a labyrinth of side streets and service roads, the city giving way to a landscape of industrial decay.

Finally, he arrived at the warehouse yard, its entrance flanked by rusting gates hanging askew on their hinges. The yard was a sprawling expanse of concrete, orange cones and roadwork diversion signs, littered with shipping containers and vehicles. The police had already established a perimeter, their vehicles parked strategically around the area. The flashing blue lights reflected off the metallic surfaces, casting an eerie glow over the scene.

Palace parked his car and stepped out, the gravel crunching under his boots. He approached the cluster of officers gathered near the entrance, their faces tense with anticipation. He exchanged a few brief words with the senior officer, his voice steady despite the adrenaline coursing through his veins.

"We've traced the signal to that lorry," the officer said, pointing to a large articulated vehicle with the faded logo of an old transport company. "We've got teams in position, ready to move in on your word."

Palace nodded, his gaze fixed on the lorry. He could feel the weight of the moment pressing down on him, the culmination of days of relentless pursuit. Taking a deep breath, he gave the signal to proceed. The officers moved in, their movements precise and coordinated.

As they closed in on the lorry, Palace followed closely, his senses on high alert. The tension was palpable, every sound amplified in the stillness of the yard. He watched as an officer climbed into the cab, his heart pounding in his chest. The search was methodical, each movement deliberate.

Minutes crawled by like wounded animals, each one dragging the weight of expectation behind it. Then, at last, the police officer emerged from behind the cab, his expression unreadable, his gloved hand gripping something small and dark. John's phone. It had wedged itself into the narrow crevice between the cab and the trailer, half-buried in grease and road dust, as if the truck itself had tried to swallow the evidence whole. The officers scoured every inch of the vehicle, their torches slicing through the dim interior, but there was no sign of John. He had vanished into the night, slipping through their fingers like smoke. And the phone, the only thing he'd left behind, was nothing more than a dead thing, holding no secrets, no answers—just cold, silent plastic. The disappointment was palpable as they realized their target had eluded them once again.

Palace felt a mix of frustration and concern gnawing at him. The discovery of the phone without John meant that he had likely discarded it to throw them off his trail. It was a clever move, indicating that John was still thinking clearly and was one step ahead of them. Palace knew that this setback meant they would have to rely on other means to track John down.

As he stood in the warehouse yard, the sounds of the search team echoing around him, Palace pondered John's state of mind. What was driving him? The incident at the hospital had been a desperate act, but now John was on the run, seemingly evading capture with calculated precision. Palace's instincts told him that there was more to this story, something darker and more complex than a simple escape.

The yard itself was a scene from a forgotten era, with rusting shipping containers stacked haphazardly and weeds growing through the cracks in the concrete. The air was thick with the smell of oil and decay. As Palace watched the officers continue their search, he resolved to redouble his efforts. He needed to understand what had pushed John to these extremes and find him before more lives were put at risk. The clock was ticking, and Palace knew that the next move could be critical in solving this perplexing case.

Chapter Fourteen

The sky above Whitby was a canvas of ominous clouds, their dark masses tinged with the fading hues of twilight. The salty air was thick with the scent of the sea, mingling with the faint aroma of fish from the nearby market stalls. Whitby Docks, usually bustling with activity during the day, had now taken on a more sinister atmosphere as night began to creep in. The place seemed almost deserted, save for a few late-working fishermen and the occasional seagull squawking overhead.

John walked along the cobblestone paths of the docks, his worn trench coat flapping in the cold wind, his eyes scanning the shadowy surroundings. The old wooden piers creaked under the weight of boats gently bobbing on the water. Rusted chains clinked softly against metal bollards, adding a haunting symphony to the night's sounds. The warehouses lining the docks were relics of a bygone era, their brick facades weathered and covered in ivy, windows darkened and broken like the hollow eyes of forgotten giants.

As John moved further into the maze of docks, he couldn't shake the feeling that he was being watched. He pulled his coat tighter around him, the chill of the evening seeping into his bones. His footsteps echoed on the damp cobblestones, each step amplifying his growing paranoia. He glanced over his shoulder, his eyes darting between the shadows cast by the dim streetlights.

"Who's there?" John's voice trembled as it cut through the eerie silence.

Only the gentle lapping of waves against the docked boats answered him. The hairs on the back of his neck stood up. He quickened his pace, the sense of being followed becoming almost unbearable. He passed by an old fishmonger's shack, its wooden planks rotting and paint peeling. The smell of decaying fish was overpowering, adding to his sense of unease.

Out of the corner of his eye, John saw a flicker of movement. He spun around, his heart pounding in his chest, but there was nothing there. Just the dim outlines of the boats and the dark, silent warehouses. The figure had disappeared into the shadows, leaving only the whisper of the wind to accompany John.

He took a deep breath, trying to calm his racing mind. He knew he couldn't afford to let paranoia get the best of him. He needed to stay focused, to complete his mission. But the docks, with their labyrinthine layout and oppressive atmosphere, made it difficult. Every creak, every rustle seemed magnified in the eerie stillness of the night.

John continued to walk, his senses on high alert. The occasional sound of a distant engine and the murmur of voices from a nearby pub drifted through the air, emphasizing the solitude of the docks. He approached a row of storage sheds, their doors slightly ajar, revealing glimpses of old fishing nets and rusty tools inside. The smell of damp wood and oil hung heavy in the air.

Suddenly, he heard a soft footfall behind him. He spun around again, his eyes wide with fear. This time, he saw the silhouette of a figure standing just beyond the reach of the nearest streetlight. The figure was cloaked in darkness, its features obscured. John's breath caught in his throat.

"Who are you? What do you want?" John's voice was more forceful, but no less terrified.

The figure remained silent, unmoving. Then, with a

swift, almost inhuman grace, it melted back into the shadows, disappearing from sight. John's mind raced. Who was this stalker? Why were they following him? The questions swirled in his head, adding to his mounting sense of dread.

Determined not to be intimidated, John steeled himself and pressed on. He knew he couldn't let fear derail his mission. The whispers in his mind, the promise of seeing Ethan alive again, drove him forward. He took a deep breath, trying to steady his nerves, and continued to navigate the docks, each step a testament to his resolve.

The docks stretched out before him, a maze of shadow and light, of history and decay. John knew he had to be careful, to stay vigilant. As he moved deeper into the darkness, the sense of being watched never left him, a constant reminder of the mysterious figure lurking just out of sight. But he pressed on, driven by the hope that somewhere, in the midst of this haunted place, lay the answers he desperately sought.

Yet as John ventured deeper into the labyrinthine docks, the shadows seemed to move with a life of their own. He caught glimpses of faces in the broken windows of the warehouses, eyes that seemed to bore into his soul. His mind began to play tricks on him, whispering doubts and fears that gnawed at his sanity.

John's thoughts spiralled into a whirlwind of paranoia. Was he truly being followed, or was his mind unravelling under the weight of his guilt and desperation? He thought of Ethan, his sweet boy, and clung to the hope that this nightmare would end with his son back in his arms. But the darkness of the docks seemed to seep into his very soul, twisting his perceptions and blurring the lines between reality and madness.

The figure reappeared, closer this time, its form more defined yet still cloaked in shadow. John's breath hitched as he took a step back, his heart hammering in his chest. The figure's eyes gleamed with an unnatural light, a cruel mockery of the hope that had driven John this far.

John shook his head, trying to dispel the apparition, but it remained, a constant reminder of his growing descent into madness. Was this figure real or a manifestation of his crumbling psyche? The docks seemed to close in around him, the familiar smells of salt and fish now mingled with the stench of fear and despair.

His footsteps echoed louder, the sound of his heartbeat a deafening drum in his ears. Each step forward was a battle against the encroaching darkness, both within and without. As he neared The Seafarer's Rest, the sight of the inn's warm lights was both a beacon and a taunt, promising solace while reminding him of the impossible choices he had made.

Finally, he stumbled into his room, collapsing onto the bed beside Ethan's lifeless body. Tears streamed down his face, each drop carrying the soul-crushing weight of his actions. He had crossed a line, become something he never thought he could be.

The room in the hotel was as cold as a morgue, the dampness from the sea air seeping through the cracked old window frames. John sat on the edge of the bed, staring blankly at the worn carpet beneath his feet. The silence in the room was thick and oppressive, the kind that wrapped around your throat and squeezed until you couldn't breathe.

He ran a trembling hand through his hair, the memories of the day swirling in his mind like a toxic brew. The alleyway, the homeless man, the sense that he was being watched—all of it felt unreal, like a dream he couldn't wake from. The weight of it pressed down on him, crushing his chest until he could barely stand it.

Then he heard it.

A faint noise from the bathroom, a soft rustling like the sound of a curtain moving in the breeze. John's heart skipped a beat, his breath catching in his throat. He turned his head slowly, staring at the closed bathroom door. The noise came again, a whisper of movement, and for a moment, John's mind raced with possibilities. Had someone followed him? Was he finally losing it?

He forced himself to stand, legs wobbling beneath him as he moved toward the door. The floorboards creaked ominously under his weight, each step sending a jolt of fear through his body. He reached out, his hand trembling as he grasped the cold metal knob, hesitating for a heartbeat before turning it.

The bathroom was dark, the only light coming from a faint sliver that seeped in from the window. The mirror above the sink was cracked, spiderwebs of glass glinting in the dimness. John's breath came in short, sharp gasps as he stepped inside, the air thick with the scent of mildew. His eyes darted around the small space, searching for the source of the noise, but there was nothing—just the silent, empty room.

He was about to turn and leave when he heard it again, closer this time, right behind him.

John whirled around, his heart hammering in his chest—and there he was. Ethan, standing in the doorway, bathed in the pale light of the room. The boy's hair was tousled, his face soft and round, just as John remembered. A small smile played on his lips, his eyes wide and innocent as they looked up at his father.

"Daddy," Ethan said, his voice as clear and sweet as it had been the last time John had heard it.

John's heart shattered into a thousand pieces. He fell to his knees, tears spilling from his eyes as he reached out to his son. This was impossible, it couldn't be real, but there he was—Ethan, alive and whole and standing right in front of him.

"Oh, God, Ethan," John sobbed, pulling the boy into his arms. He held him tight, feeling the warmth of his small body, the steady beat of his heart. "I'm so sorry. I'm so sorry I couldn't save you."

But as he clung to his son, something changed. The warmth in Ethan's body began to fade, replaced by a coldness that seeped into John's bones. He pulled back slightly, just enough to look at Ethan's face—and what he saw made his blood run cold.

Ethan's eyes had grown hollow, the once bright blue now dull and lifeless. His skin, once smooth and rosy, was turning grey, sagging against his bones like melted wax. His smile twisted into something grotesque, a sneer that sent a shiver of terror down John's spine.

"Why did you let me die, Daddy?" Ethan whispered, his voice no longer sweet but hollow and filled with malice.

John recoiled, stumbling backward as Ethan's small body began to disintegrate, the flesh crumbling into ash that sifted through his fingers. He reached out in a desperate attempt to hold on, but it was too late—Ethan's form collapsed into nothingness, slipping through his grasp like sand. The ash scattered across the cold tiles, and John was left kneeling on the bathroom floor, his hands grasping at empty air, his mind reeling from what he had just seen.

He collapsed, curling into himself as sobs wracked his body. His tears mingled with the dust on the floor, forming streaks of grey sludge that clung to his skin. The room around him seemed to shrink, the walls pressing in, suffocating him with the weight of his grief and guilt.

"Ethan ... no, no, no ..." John's voice cracked as he whispered the words over and over, a broken mantra that echoed off the cold, tiled walls.

But the boy was gone, just as he had been before—just as he always would be. John's chest heaved with the force of his despair, his mind teetering on the edge of a dark abyss. He had seen his son, touched him, but it had been a cruel illusion, a nightmare conjured by a mind that was breaking under the strain of his grief and guilt. The question that had haunted him for weeks now returned with a vengeance: was he losing his grip on reality?

John dragged himself to his feet, his legs shaking as he clutched the edge of the sink for support. He stared at his reflection in the cracked mirror, the face that looked back at him pale and gaunt, hollowed out by sleepless nights and the endless, gnawing pain of loss.

"What am I doing?" he whispered to his reflection, the words barely audible over the sound of his own laboured breathing. "This can't be real ... none of this can be real."

For a moment, he considered the possibility that he was going insane, that all of this—the rituals, the symbols, the voices in the dark—was nothing more than a desperate fantasy, a way for his mind to cope with the unbearable reality that his son was gone. The absurdity of it all hit him like a punch to the gut. He was a grieving father, lost in a nightmare of his own making.

But even as the doubt crept in, there was something else—a lingering sense that what he had seen, what he had felt, was real. It was as if the veil between worlds had thinned, allowing something dark and malevolent to slip through. John shook his head, trying to dismiss the doubts that gnawed at the edges of his mind, but they clung to him like shadows, refusing to let go. He could feel the madness pressing in, the line between reality and illusion blurring until he could no longer tell where one ended and the other began.

With a trembling hand, John reached out and touched the mirror, his fingers tracing the cracks that spiderwebbed across the glass. The reflection stared back at him, fractured and distorted, a twisted version of himself that seemed to mock his fear.

"I have to do this," he whispered, the words a desperate plea to whatever force was listening. "I have to bring him back ... I have to."

But as he stood there, staring into the broken mirror, the doubt lingered, a dark whisper at the back of his mind. And somewhere deep inside, John knew that the path he was on could only lead to one place—a place where the darkness was absolute, where the line between life and death, sanity and madness, had long since disappeared.

Chapter Fifteen

Jack Palace had seen his fair share of strange places in his line of work, but the Library of St Giles had an aura about it that was different. It was as though the very air surrounding the building was thicker, heavier, carrying the weight of countless secrets. The moment he stepped out of his car and onto the gravel path that led up to the library's entrance, he could feel it—the uneasy sensation of being watched, of unseen eyes following his every move.

The building was ancient, a relic from another time. Its weathered stone walls were covered in thick vines that clung like desperate hands, and the windows, small and clouded with age, were almost completely obscured by dust and grime. The large oak doors, blackened with years of exposure to the elements, loomed ahead, but as Jack approached, he found them shut tight, the iron knocker cold and unwelcoming.

He tried the handle—firm, unyielding, locked.

"Damn," Jack muttered under his breath, stepping back to survey the building once more. The library was closed. No lights on inside, no sign of life. Yet that feeling—like a pair of eyes boring into the back of his head—persisted.

Jack felt a cold shiver snake down his spine as he turned in a slow circle, scanning the empty grounds. The library stood at the edge of a dense, dark forest. The tall trees swayed gently in the breeze, their rustling leaves sounding like whispers. He couldn't see anyone, but he couldn't shake the sensation that he wasn't alone.

He cursed himself for not calling ahead, but Rachel's intel had been fresh, and he hadn't wanted to waste a moment. He had driven through the night to reach this place, and now here he was, standing in front of a building that seemed to defy him, as if daring him to try and pry open its secrets.

The wind picked up, causing the branches overhead to sway more violently. Jack felt the hairs on the back of his neck stand up. He took a step back from the door, then another, his instincts screaming at him to get away from this place, to leave whatever darkness lingered here well enough alone. But he had a job to do, and he wasn't the type to scare easily.

His phone buzzed in his pocket, and he pulled it out, glancing at the screen. It was Rachel.

"Jack, you at the library?"

"Yeah," Jack replied, his voice low. "But it's locked up. Feels like it hasn't been opened in years."

"The thought of that place gives me the creeps," Rachel admitted, her voice tinged with unease. "Be careful, okay? There's something … off about it."

"I know," Jack said, glancing around again. "I feel it too."

Rachel was silent for a moment before she spoke again. "Look, why don't you head into town, see if you can find someone who knows more about the place? Maybe it's just not open yet, or maybe there's another way in."

"Good idea," Jack agreed. "I'll let you know what I find."

He ended the call and pocketed his phone, casting one last look at the foreboding library before turning away. The gravel crunched under his feet as he walked back to his car, the sensation of being watched never quite leaving him. He glanced back over his shoulder a few times, half expecting to see someone—or something—peering out from behind one of those grimy windows. But the building remained still and silent.

Jack drove back down the narrow road that led to the village, his mind racing with possibilities. Whoever was behind thevoiceofthehand had ties to this place, of that he was certain. But what those ties were, and what they meant for John Morrison, was still a mystery.

The village itself was small, almost quaint, with a handful of shops and cottages lining the main street. At the centre was a small pub, The Red Fox, its sign creaking as it swayed in the wind. Jack parked his car and stepped out, taking a deep breath of the cool country air. The pub was as good a place as any to start asking questions, and besides, he could use a meal after the long drive.

The inside of the pub was warm and welcoming after the oppressive atmosphere of the library. The low ceiling beams were dark with age, and a fire crackled in the hearth, filling the room with a comforting warmth. A few locals sat at the bar, nursing pints of ale and chatting in low tones. They looked up as Jack entered, their eyes briefly sizing him up before returning to their conversations.

Jack made his way to the bar, where the barman, a stout man with a bushy moustache, greeted him with a nod. "What'll it be, mate?"

"Just a pint and whatever you've got for lunch," Jack replied, sliding onto a stool.

"Coming right up," the barman said, pulling a pint of amber ale from the tap. He set it down in front of Jack, then disappeared into the back to prepare the food.

Jack took a long sip of the ale, letting the warmth

spread through him. As he sat there, he couldn't shake the feeling that he was being watched, even here in the safety of the pub. He glanced around, but the locals seemed uninterested in him now, their attention focused on their own affairs.

After a few minutes, the barman returned with a steaming plate of shepherd's pie. "Here you go. Enjoy."

"Thanks," Jack said, picking up his fork. He took a bite, savouring the rich flavours. As he ate, he listened to the conversations around him, hoping to catch a snippet of useful information.

He didn't have to wait long. The man sitting two stools down from him, a grizzled old farmer with a weather-beaten face, leaned over and said, "You're not from around here, are you?"

Jack shook his head. "Just passing through. Was hoping to visit the library up the road, but it's all locked up."

The farmer grunted, his expression darkening. "Aye, that place is always locked up. Not many folks go there these days."

"Why's that?" Jack asked, his interest piqued.

The farmer took a sip of his beer, then set the glass down with a heavy sigh. "Strange things happen there, always have. That library's been there longer than anyone can remember, but it's never been a normal library, if you catch my drift."

Jack nodded, encouraging the man to continue.

"People say it's cursed," the farmer went on, lowering his voice. "Books in there that ain't meant to be read, knowledge that ain't meant to be known. The kind of stuff that gets into your head and won't let go. And the folks who do go there … well, they ain't quite right, if you know what I mean."

"Like who?" Jack pressed, his pulse quickening.

The farmer shrugged, his gaze drifting to the window as if expecting to see someone—or something—outside. "Can't say for sure. But I've seen men go in there who didn't look like they were from around here. Dressed all in black, like they were attending a funeral. And when they came out … they weren't the same. Eyes too wide, skin too pale, like they'd seen something they weren't supposed to."

Jack felt a chill run down his spine. "You ever see anyone who works there?"

The farmer shook his head. "Ain't no one who works there. Least, not that anyone's seen. It's just … there. Always has been. Like it's waiting for something."

Jack finished his meal in silence, mulling over what the farmer had told him. This place was steeped in darkness, and whatever was lurking inside that library, it had its hooks deep in John Morrison.

As he paid his tab and stood to leave, the farmer gave him one last piece of advice: "If you're smart, you'll stay away from that place. Nothing good ever came out of poking around in the dark."

Jack thanked the man and stepped out into the fading daylight, the pub door closing behind him with a creak. The wind had picked up again, carrying with it the scent of rain. He glanced back up the road, toward the distant shape of the library hidden among the trees.

Something was waiting for him there. Something that didn't want to be found.

But Jack Palace had never been one to turn away from the dark. And he wasn't about to start now.

Chapter Sixteen

Cassandra Lane sat in her plush, newly built flat, the glow from her laptop casting a pale light across her face. Her fingers hovered over the keyboard, her mind spinning with the tangled web of a story that had begun to consume her every waking moment. She could feel it in her bones, that tingling sensation that only came when she was on the brink of something big—something that could catapult her from a local reporter to a name that carried weight, one that stirred up equal measures of admiration and envy in newsrooms across the country.

The phone on her desk buzzed, shattering her focus. She snatched it up, eyes narrowing as she saw the caller ID. It was a number she recognized, one of those contacts buried deep in her phone under a name that wouldn't raise eyebrows but could provide gold when it mattered.

She answered with a practised coolness, and the voice on the other end crackled with the sort of excitement that only came from someone who knew they were about to deliver a juicy titbit.

"Cassie, you're not gonna believe this," the voice whispered conspiratorially.

She recognized the sound of the city in the background, the way it buzzed like an insect on summer nights—restless, alive, but always hiding something just beneath the surface.

"What have you got for me?" Cassandra asked, leaning back in her chair, trying to mask the eagerness she felt rising in her chest.

"It's about Morrison. They've been tracking his phone."

Her heart skipped a beat. "And?"

"They traced it to a warehouse yard on the outskirts of town. When they got there … nothing. Just the phone lying in the dirt like it had been tossed there."

Cassandra sat up straight, her pulse quickening. "No sign of him at all?"

"Not a damn thing. It's like he vanished into thin air."

She bit her lip, her mind already piecing together how to spin this into something her readers would eat up with a spoon. "You got any details on the warehouse? Ownership, history, anything?"

"Already on it. I'll send over what I can dig up, but I'm telling you, Cassie, this guy … he's smarter than we gave him credit for."

Cassandra smirked, already thinking ahead. "Let me know the second you get anything. And keep this quiet, alright? I don't want anyone else sniffing around this until I've had a crack at it."

"You got it. Just remember me when this thing blows up."

Cassandra hung up, her fingers immediately flying over the keyboard, the tap-tap-tap of the keys filling the room as she began to weave her narrative. She'd always been good at this, taking the raw material of reality and spinning it into something just a little more compelling, a little more dramatic. After all, people didn't want the truth—they wanted a story.

The cursor blinked at her, waiting, and then she began to type.

Title: The Vanishing Act: John Morrison's Descent into Darkness

John Morrison, once an unassuming family man, is proving to be far more cunning and dangerous than anyone anticipated. As authorities continue their manhunt, new details have emerged that paint a chilling picture of a man willing to go to any lengths to achieve his mysterious goals.

In a daring move that has left investigators baffled, Morrison's phone was recently tracked to an abandoned warehouse yard on the outskirts of the city. But when officers arrived, they found nothing but the device itself— discarded like a snake shedding its skin. There was no sign of Morrison, no trace of his next move.

It's clear that Morrison is more than just a grieving father. He is a man on the edge, orchestrating a twisted game that has law enforcement playing catch-up at every turn. And with each step he takes, the shadows around him seem to grow darker, hinting at a plan that goes far beyond anything we've seen before.

Sources close to the investigation suggest that Morrison may be involved in a network of underground activities, potentially linked to occult practices. While these claims are unconfirmed, they add another layer of complexity to an already terrifying saga.

What drives a man like John Morrison? Is it grief, desperation, or something far more sinister? As the hunt continues, one thing is clear: the man who was once just another face in the crowd has become a phantom, slipping through the fingers of those who seek to stop him.

But how long can he keep this up? And what will the cost be when he finally steps out of the shadows?

Cassandra paused, reading over what she had written. It was good—better than good. A creative fabrication straight from her own mind, she couldn't have known how close to the truth she really was. It was the kind of piece that would get people talking, speculating, feeding into the frenzy that had already started to build around the case. But more than that, it was the kind of piece that could solidify her place in the field, make her more than just another reporter.

She took a sip of her cold coffee, grimacing at the bitterness. As much as she hated to admit it, there was something about John Morrison that fascinated her. He wasn't just another criminal on the run. He was a man who had been pushed to the brink, someone who had seen the edge and chosen to leap off it. There was a darkness in him, a depth that she couldn't help but be drawn to, like a moth to a flame.

She thought about the last time she'd written a story with this kind of intensity, the way it had gripped her, kept her awake at night, pacing her flat, her mind spinning with possibilities. It had been years, too many, since she'd felt that fire. And now here it was again, burning bright and hot, threatening to consume her if she wasn't careful.

Cassandra leaned back in her chair, her thoughts drifting. She wondered what it would be like to meet John Morrison, to sit across from him and see the man behind the headlines. What would she find? A monster? A victim of his own circumstances? Or something else entirely, something that defied the neat categories her articles always fell into?

She shook her head, forcing herself back to the task at hand. She needed to stay focused, keep the story moving forward. There was still so much she didn't know, so many pieces of the puzzle that were missing. But that was part of the thrill, wasn't it? The chase, the hunt, the never-ending search for the truth—or at least, a version of it that would keep her readers hooked.

As she returned to her article, refining sentences, adding more dramatic flair, Cassandra couldn't shake the feeling that this story was going to take her places she hadn't anticipated. It was more than just a news piece; it was a gateway into something darker, something that both excited and terrified her.

And as much as she tried to deny it, there was a part of her that wanted to follow John Morrison down that dark path, to see where it led, to understand the madness that had taken hold of him.

Because in the end, wasn't that what she was always looking for? The truth behind the story, the reality that lurked in the shadows, just out of reach?

Cassandra smiled to herself, the thrill of the chase tingling in her veins. This was what she lived for—the darkness, the mystery, the tantalizing promise of a story that would keep her up at night.

And with John Morrison, she had a feeling she was about to find it.

Chapter Seventeen

It was early morning in Whitby, the air crisp and cool with a light mist rolling in from the sea. John, feeling the weight of his actions and living with the growing stench of Ethan's decaying body, decided to take a walk to clear his mind. His thoughts raced as he made his way through the quiet streets, the echoes of his footsteps the only sound accompanying him.

He paused by a bench near the harbour, the grey water lapping gently against the stones. The newspaper in his hand rustled as he unfolded it, his eyes scanning the front page until they landed on a familiar name. *Cassandra Lane.* His jaw tightened, the name itself enough to set his teeth on edge. She had been writing about him for weeks now, feeding the public whatever lies she thought would sell the most papers, whatever scraps of half-truths she could twist into something salacious.

John's eyes narrowed as he read the latest article, his breath coming faster with each word. She had written about the warehouse, about the phone he had deliberately discarded as a decoy. But it wasn't just the facts that angered him—it was the way she had spun them, the way she had turned him into a character in some twisted story, a phantom slipping through the cracks. He could almost hear her smug tone in the words, feel the satisfaction she must have felt typing them out.

John Morrison, once an unassuming family man, is proving to be far more cunning and dangerous than anyone anticipated.

She didn't know the half of it. But it was the next part that made his blood boil, the part where she insinuated he was involved in some sort of occult practice.

Sources close to the investigation suggest that Morrison may be involved in a network of underground activities, potentially linked to occult practices.

He could almost hear the click of her keyboard, see the smirk on her face as she made up whatever bullshit she needed to keep her readers hooked.

Occult practices? Underground activities? He wasn't some deranged lunatic. Everything he did had a purpose, a reason. But to her, he was just a headline, a chance to get her name in lights, to climb the ladder out of whatever backwater newsroom she was stuck in.

John's hands shook as he crumpled the paper, the ink smudging against his fingers. She had no idea what she was talking about. She had no idea who he really was, what had driven him to this point. She didn't care about the truth—only the story. But he could set her straight. He could show her the real John Morrison, make her understand what was at stake, why he had to do what he was doing.

Or maybe … maybe she needed to be taken care of, just like the others. Maybe she was another loose end that needed tying up before things got too out of hand. The thought settled in his mind, dark and heavy, like a storm cloud gathering on the horizon. He wasn't a killer by nature, but she was pushing him, forcing him into a corner with her lies and her smears. And if it came down to it, he would do what needed to be done.

He clenched his fists, staring down at the crumpled newspaper. His breath was coming in short, angry bursts now, his heart pounding in his chest. "Bitch," he muttered under his breath, his voice low and venomous. He threw the paper onto the ground, letting it lie there like the trash it was.

He glanced up, his eyes narrowing as they fixed on the path ahead. The 199 steps to the abbey loomed in the distance, the ancient stone steps winding their way up the hillside like a stairway to another world. John took a deep breath, steeling himself. The article was just noise, a distraction. He had more important things to focus on, more pressing matters to deal with. But still, the thought of Cassandra Lane lingered, a thorn in his side that he couldn't quite ignore.

As he began to climb the steps, the cold air biting at his cheeks, John made a silent vow. He would deal with her, one way or another. And when he did, she would regret ever putting his name in print.

The abbey loomed above him, dark and foreboding against the pale morning sky. He kept climbing, his steps steady, determined. There was work to be done, a plan to see through. And nothing—certainly not some nosy journalist—was going to stand in his way.

Each step seemed to echo in his mind, amplifying his turmoil. Reaching the top, he paused to catch his breath and take in the sweeping view of the harbour below. The morning light cast a golden hue over the water, the boats bobbing gently. John's mind swirled with questions: Had he truly lost his mind? Was this the only way to bring Ethan back?

The abbey loomed ahead, an ancient, imposing structure that seemed to harbour countless secrets. As he stood there, lost in contemplation, an elderly priest approached him. The cemetery adjacent to the abbey was shrouded in a thin layer of mist, gravestones peeking through like the broken teeth of a long-dead giant.

Father Michael was a man whose past was as weathered and shadowed as the ancient stone walls of

Whitby Abbey. Born Michael O'Sullivan in the small, windswept village of Dunmore, Ireland, his early years were steeped in a mix of rustic simplicity and simmering turmoil. His father, a fisherman who often took to the bottle, was a harsh and unpredictable man. His mother, a devout Catholic, found solace in her faith and in Michael, her quiet, introspective son.

From a young age, Michael had sought refuge in the small village church, captivated by the stories of saints and martyrs. The church, with its flickering candles and scent of incense, became his sanctuary from the stormy atmosphere at home. It was here, amidst the solemnity of the stone altar and the soft murmurs of prayer, that he first felt the stirrings of a divine calling.

By the time he was seventeen, Michael had decided to dedicate his life to the service of God. He left Dunmore, with its crumbling cottages and relentless sea winds, and entered the seminary. The seminary years were arduous, filled with long hours of study and contemplation. Yet Michael found solace in the rigorous routine, the chants of the liturgy, and the quiet moments of reflection.

Ordained at twenty-five, he was sent to a small parish in Belfast during the height of the Troubles. It was here that Father Michael's faith was tested in the crucible of violence and hatred. He became a beacon of hope in a city torn apart by conflict, offering comfort to both Protestant and Catholic alike. The stories of those he ministered to and their tales of loss, despair, and fleeting hope etched deep lines of sorrow and wisdom into his face.

After years in Belfast, seeking a quieter life, Father Michael was transferred to St Mary's Church, a stone's throw from the ruins of Whitby Abbey. The move was supposed to be a respite, a chance to find peace in the serene, historical surroundings of the abbey overlooking the tumultuous North Sea. Whitby, with its narrow, winding streets and brooding cliffs, was a welcome contrast to the urban turmoil of Belfast.

At St Mary's Church, Father Michael's days were filled with the mundane and the mystical. He tended to his parishioners, performed the daily offices, and found solace in his faith's ancient rituals. The community respected him, drawn to his quiet strength and the depth of his compassion. His small cottage, nestled among the graves of long-forgotten souls, was a haven of tranquillity and contemplation. Inside, it was a reflection of his life: humble, cluttered with books on theology and relics of his faith. The scent of incense often mingled with the aroma of tea, a small comfort in his solitary life.

But even in Whitby, shadows of his past lingered. Memories of Belfast and the faces of those he couldn't save haunted his dreams. There were times he questioned his faith, times when the silence of the abbey seemed to echo with unanswered prayers. Yet he persevered, believing that in the darkness, there was always a flicker of light, a whisper of hope.

Father Michael had always been drawn to those in pain, perhaps because he understood it so intimately. His eyes, kind but piercing, had seen the depths of human suffering, and his heart carried the weight of countless confessions. It was this deep well of empathy that made him approach John on that fateful morning, sensing the turmoil behind the young man's haunted gaze.

Father Michael, noticing the distress etched on John's face, offered a gentle smile. "Good morning, my son. You seem troubled. Is there something weighing heavily on your mind?"

John looked at the priest, his eyes haunted and tired. He hesitated before speaking, his voice barely above a whisper. "I ... I don't know what to do. Everything is falling apart."

Father Michael nodded understandingly, his eyes filled with compassion. He was a tall, gaunt figure with wisps of silver hair escaping the confines of his black clerical collar. His face, lined with the years of comforting parishioners and battling his own demons, bore the kind of genuine empathy that made people want to pour out their souls to him.

"Why don't we go inside? It's starting to rain, and we can talk over a cup of tea," he suggested, gesturing toward a narrow path that led to a small, modest cottage nestled beyond the graves.

John nodded, grateful for the offer. As they walked, Father Michael spoke in soothing tones. "My name is Father Michael. I've been here at the abbey for many years. Sometimes, sharing your burdens with someone else can help lighten the load."

The priest's cottage was an old, weather-beaten structure with ivy creeping up its stone walls. Inside, it was cozy and cluttered, filled with books and relics of faith. The smell of old wood and incense lingered in the air, mingling with the aroma of the tea that Father Michael was preparing. The kitchen was a small, quaint space with a wooden table and mismatched chairs, reflecting the priest's humble life.

"What's your name, my son?" Father Michael asked, setting the teapot on the stove.

"John," he replied, his voice shaky. "My name is John."

Father Michael smiled warmly. "It's nice to meet you, John. Now, tell me, what has brought you so much pain?"

John hesitated, struggling to find the words. "I've lost everything. My wife ... my son. I don't know how to keep going."

The priest's expression grew even more sympathetic. "Loss can be an unbearable burden. It's natural to feel lost and alone. But remember, there is always hope, even in the darkest of times."

John looked down at his hands, the whispers in his mind growing louder. "Sometimes, I hear voices. They tell me to do things ... terrible things."

Father Michael set the teapot down and turned to face John, his eyes filled with concern. "Voices can be frightening, but they are not always real. Sometimes, our grief and pain can make us hear things that aren't there. You must find strength within yourself to resist them."

John nodded, trying to absorb the priest's comforting words. But the whispers persisted, growing more insistent. "Think of Ethan," they urged. "You can see him again. Just kill the priest!"

Father Michael continued to speak, his voice calm and reassuring. "You are not alone, John. There are people who care about you, who want to help you through this difficult time. Have faith, and don't let the darkness consume you."

The priest turned back to the counter. The voices in John's mind screamed at him, urging him to act. Father Michael hummed a hymn softly as he prepared the tea, completely unaware of the inner battle raging within John. His heart pounded in his chest as he stood up, moving silently behind Father Michael.

As the priest reached for the teapot, John made his

move. With a quick, desperate motion, he wrapped his arm around the priest's neck, squeezing tightly. Father Michael struggled, his hands clawing at John's arm, but the younger man's grip was unrelenting.

"I'm sorry," John whispered, tears streaming down his face. "I'm so sorry."

Father Michael's struggles weakened, and finally, his body went limp. John released his grip, letting the priest's lifeless body fall to the floor. Panting, he looked down at what he had done, the reality of his actions hitting him like a tidal wave.

The room around him seemed to close in, the shadows deepening and the air growing cold. The whispers subsided, leaving only a deafening silence. Panicked, John knew he had to get back to Ethan. He fled the cottage, running down the path toward the town.

As he emerged onto a quiet street, he nearly collided with a woman walking her dog. Her eyes widened in shock as she took in his dishevelled appearance and frantic demeanour. "Are you alright?" she asked, her voice tinged with concern.

John didn't answer, pushing past her and continuing to run. The woman, puzzled and alarmed, decided to investigate. She made her way to the priest's cottage, calling out as she approached. When she received no response, she cautiously entered and found the lifeless body of Father Michael.

The woman, her face pale and hands trembling, immediately pulled out her phone and called the police.

"Hello? I need to report a murder. I ... I found a priest, and he's dead. Please hurry!"

Chapter Eighteen

Jack Palace pulled up outside the small, quaint residence of Eve, John's mother. The house was a single-storey cottage with a garden bursting with colourful flowers. Jack sat alone in his car, the rain drumming a relentless rhythm on the roof. The windshield wipers swished back and forth, clearing the glass in smooth, mechanical strokes, but his mind was far from the storm outside. It was miles away, in a crumbling block of flats on the wrong side of town, where a little girl had stared at him with eyes that would haunt him forever.

Those eyes—they were the first thing he saw whenever he closed his own, like a brand burned into his memory. Wide, unblinking, frozen in that terrible moment when he had pulled the trigger. He could still see the way she clung to her mother, her tiny hands gripping at the fabric of her shirt, desperate for protection from a world that had shown her nothing but cruelty. Jack had been the one to take her father away, to end his life with a bullet. Self-defence, they called it. Justified. But Jack knew better. There was no justification for the fear he had seen in that child's eyes.

The car's interior was cold, the heater doing little to chase away the chill that settled in his bones whenever he thought of that day. It was one of many ghosts that followed him, a constant reminder that the line between hero and villain was as thin as a razor's edge. He clenched the steering wheel, the leather creaking under the pressure. No matter how many cases he solved, no matter how many lives he saved, that little girl's eyes would always be there, a silent judge and jury.

Jack shook his head, trying to dispel the memories. He

had a job to do, and there was no room for ghosts. But as he started the engine and pulled away from the curb, he knew that the past wasn't something you could just drive away from. It was always there, lurking in the shadows, waiting for the quiet moments to strike.

The radio in his car blared out a news report about a murder in Whitby, but before the details could be divulged, Palace turned off the engine and stepped out.

Eve's home stood at the end of a winding, tree-lined lane on the outskirts of Hull in the village of Swanland, a relic from a bygone era of Victorian charm and quiet isolation. The lane, flanked by ancient oaks and sycamores, seemed to swallow the sound of passing cars, creating a cocoon of tranquillity that felt almost otherworldly. The large, detached cottage had ivy creeping up its brick façade, weathered from years of enduring the elements.

Outside, the property was enclosed by a wrought-iron fence, its black paint chipped and faded from years of exposure. The gate creaked mournfully as it swung open, revealing a cobblestone path leading to the front door. The garden was overgrown, with wildflowers and unkempt shrubs creating a chaotic yet picturesque display of colours. A stone birdbath, cracked and stained by time, stood sentinel amidst the greenery, a place where birds occasionally alighted before taking flight.

The house itself was a grand but slightly dilapidated structure. It had tall, narrow windows with leaded glass that filtered the sunlight into fractured patterns across the interior. The roof was steeply pitched, adorned with curling, blackened tiles that hinted at the age of the building. A large bay window protruded from the front, its wooden frame showing signs of peeling paint and neglect.

Inside, the house was a labyrinth of old-world charm and faded elegance. The entryway, with its creaky floorboards and patterned wallpaper, led into a grand hallway lined with dusty, antique photographs and the occasional faded portrait of long-forgotten ancestors. The walls, adorned with floral wallpaper that had seen better days, held the remnants of an era when the house had been the pride of the neighbourhood.

The living room was a cozy but cluttered space. It featured a large stone fireplace with a mantle cluttered with knick-knacks: porcelain figurines, tarnished silver photo frames, and a clock with hands frozen in time. The furniture was a mix of old and worn—a faded velvet settee, armchairs with sagging cushions, and an oak cabinet crammed with dusty books and old china. Heavy curtains framed the windows, their once-vibrant colours now dulled by years of sunlight.

In the corner of the room, a grandfather clock ticked rhythmically, its sound a constant reminder of the house's long history. The smell of aged wood and the faint aroma of lavender, a remnant of Eve's love for old-fashioned potpourri, hung in the air. The floors were covered with intricate though threadbare rugs that had been woven in patterns now mostly hidden beneath layers of dust.

The kitchen, accessible through a swing door, was small but functional, with worn linoleum tiles and a large battered table at its centre. The cabinets were old-fashioned, with brass handles that had lost their lustre, and the countertops were lined with jars of preserves and dried herbs. There was a small stove, its enamel chipped, and an ancient refrigerator hummed softly in the background, providing a sense of faded practicality. The room smelled of stale bread and the lingering scent of past meals, a hint of the life that had once thrived here.

The house, despite its grandeur, bore the marks of time and neglect. It was a place steeped in memories, where the past clung to the walls and the silence spoke of lives lived and lost. For John, it was a tangible reminder of a simpler time, a sanctuary that had once been filled with warmth and love but now stood as a haunted reminder of what was lost.

Eve herself was a petite woman in her late sixties, with kind eyes and a gentle, nurturing demeanour. She was a woman of delicate grace, with a slender frame and an air of faded elegance that suggested a past filled with genteel activities and social soirées. Her hair, once a vibrant blonde, had mellowed into a soft silver that she wore in a slightly dishevelled bun. Her eyes, a deep blue, were the colour of stormy seas and held a wisdom and melancholy that spoke of a life deeply lived. Her skin, now creased with age, bore the marks of time—gentle lines at the corners of her eyes and a softness that spoke of years spent in contemplation and quietude.

Eve dressed in a manner reminiscent of her youth, favouring floral prints and pastels, which were often adorned with delicate lace or embroidery. She habitually wore sensible, well-worn shoes and vintage brooches that were more heirlooms than accessories. Her style was a reflection of her personality—unpretentious, yet deeply personal.

She greeted Jack with a warm, if weary, smile and invited him inside.

"Please, come in, Detective Inspector," she said, her voice soft but steady. "Would you like some tea?"

"Thank you, Mrs Morrison. Tea would be lovely,"

Jack replied, taking a seat on the velvet sofa.

Eve bustled off to the kitchen, and Jack took the opportunity to survey the room. His eyes fell on a photograph on the mantelpiece—John, his wife Sarah, and their son Ethan, smiling on a sunny beach.

Eve returned with a tray, setting it down on the coffee table. "Here we go," she said, pouring the tea. "So, how can I help you?"

Jack took a cup and sat back, his expression serious. "I'm here to ask about your son, John. We've been trying to locate him, and we believe he might be in a lot of trouble."

Eve's face fell, her eyes glistening with concern. "Oh, John. He's been through so much since Sarah died. It's like he's lost a part of himself."

"Can you tell me more about that?" Jack asked gently.

Eve sighed, her hands trembling slightly as she held her teacup. "Sarah's death was devastating for him. She passed away six months before Ethan, both from the same illness. John was inconsolable. He kept asking why people couldn't be brought back to life. Why did Sarah have to die? Why not someone else in her place?"

Jack listened intently, noting the anguish in Eve's voice. "Did he ever mention anything specific about bringing people back to life?"

Eve nodded slowly. "He became obsessed with the idea. He'd talk about it constantly, as if he could somehow find a way to reverse what had happened. It broke my heart to see him like that."

As Eve got up to fetch more sugar, Jack's eyes wandered back to the photo on the mantelpiece. When she returned, he pointed to it. "Where was this taken?"

Eve smiled sadly. "Whitby. It was Sarah's favourite

place. She loved the Dracula novel and all the history there. They went often, especially after Ethan was born. It was their special place."

Jack froze, his mind racing. Two deaths in Whitby in the past three days—this couldn't be a coincidence.

"Thank you, Mrs Morrison. You've been very helpful," Jack said, standing abruptly. "I need to go."

Eve looked puzzled but nodded. "Please find my son, Detective Inspector. Help him if you can."

Jack nodded, determination set in his features as he hurried out the door, the connection between John's troubled past and the recent murders in Whitby becoming all too clear.

Chapter Nineteen

Cassandra Lane had always been good at finding the cracks in the facade. Whether it was a politician's polished veneer or a grieving family's desperate need to believe their loved one was still out there, she had a knack for seeing the truth that others couldn't—or wouldn't—face. It was a talent that had made her one of the most feared investigative journalists in the business, and it was the same talent that had drawn her into the tangled, dark web of John Morrison's story.

As she sat in her cramped, cluttered office, the light from her computer screen cast sharp shadows across the walls, exaggerating the piles of notes and files that seemed to grow daily. She was exhausted, her body humming with the kind of jittery energy that came from too many cups of bad coffee and too few hours of sleep. But exhaustion wasn't enough to stop her. Not when she was this close.

Cassandra had been following John's story for weeks now, ever since the tragic incident at the hospital. But it wasn't just the horror of what had happened that kept her up at night; it was the feeling that there was something more, something lurking beneath the surface that no one else had seen. The idea that John, desperate and broken as he was, had reached out to something far darker than she had originally imagined.

She had to know more, and that meant she needed help—discreet, illegal help. She thought of Rosie, a hacker she'd worked with before. Rosie wasn't cheap, and she wasn't exactly trustworthy, but she had a skillset Cassandra needed. After a few brief exchanges over encrypted messaging, they arranged to meet in a dingy bar on the outskirts of the city. The place was half empty, the air thick with the smell of stale beer. It was the kind of place where no one asked questions.

Rosie was already there when Cassandra arrived, seated in a shadowy corner booth. She looked up as Cassandra approached, her expression a mixture of amusement and mild suspicion.

"Didn't think I'd hear from you again," Rosie said, her voice low and raspy, the product of too many late nights and too many cigarettes.

Cassandra slid into the booth opposite her, placing an envelope on the table between them. "I need information," she said simply.

Rosie arched an eyebrow, tapping the envelope with one slender finger. "You always do. What's it about this time?"

Cassandra leaned in, her voice slipping into a conspiratorial murmur. "I need you to dig up everything you can on John Morrison's recent online activity. I don't care if it's buried six passwords deep or hidden in the dark corners of the web—find it. Anyone he has spoken to. I need to know who they are, where they're based, and what they want. Anything you can get your hands on."

She watched Rosie's eyes widen, a flicker of curiosity sparking behind the tired lines of long hours and caffeine jitters. Cassandra leaned back, trying to ignore the chill creeping up her spine. It felt too much like breathing life into a shadow, pulling something dangerous into the light. But she needed answers—needed the truth clawed free from whatever hole it was hiding in. And if anyone could do it, it was Rosie.

Rosie's usual look of boredom was replaced by something sharper. "You know I don't do freebies, Lane."

Cassandra pushed the envelope across the table, her heart beating a little faster as she did. She'd dipped into her savings for this, money she'd been putting aside for a rainy day. But this was bigger than a rainy day. This was a hurricane. "There's five grand in there. Consider it a down payment."

Rosie's eyes gleamed as she took the envelope, slipping it into her bag without a second glance. "You're serious about this, aren't you?"

Cassandra nodded, her throat tight with tension. "Just find out what you can."

Rosie gave her a quick, almost mocking salute before sliding out of the booth and disappearing into the shadows. Cassandra watched her go, feeling a mixture of anticipation and dread settling in her gut. She had a bad feeling about this, but there was no turning back now.

It didn't take long for Rosie to get back to her. Cassandra was in her office, staring at her computer screen, when the message came through—two lines of text with an attachment.

Library of St Giles. Ask about 'thevoiceofthehand'. You'll find what you're looking for there. Be careful.

The address was in a small, nearly forgotten town miles away, a place with a reputation for its historical connections to the occult. It was the kind of town that people avoided, the kind that didn't show up on maps unless you knew exactly where to look. Cassandra felt a cold shiver run down her spine as she read the message. She knew she should feel triumphant, but instead, all she felt was a growing sense of unease. Still, she couldn't let it go. She had to see it through.

The drive to the Library of St Giles was long and silent, the road winding through dense, ancient forests that seemed to close in around her as she drove. The town itself was little more than a cluster of old buildings huddled together as if for protection. The library was at the edge of town, its rear backing into the treeline of the forest, an imposing stone structure that loomed over the surrounding houses like a sentinel from another time.

Cassandra parked her car and stepped out into the cool, damp air. The sky above was overcast, the clouds hanging low and heavy, as if they were watching her. She walked up the steps to the library, each footfall echoing in the stillness. The door creaked as she pushed it open, the sound reverberating through the empty building.

The Library of St Giles stood like a monolith at the edge of the forgotten village, a building seemingly untouched by time yet marked by the weight of centuries. Its stone walls were dark and weathered, mottled with patches of moss and lichen that crept up under the vines like skeletal fingers grasping for the past. Gargoyles perched on the corners of the roof, their grotesque faces frozen in eternal snarls, as if they were guarding something precious—or something cursed.

The entrance was a pair of heavy oak doors, so old that the wood had splintered and warped, making them creak ominously as Cassandra pushed them open. They groaned as if in protest, revealing the cavernous interior that swallowed her in shadow. The scent of damp stone and old parchment filled the air, a smell so thick and heavy it felt almost tangible, like walking through a fog of ancient secrets.

Inside, the library was a maze of towering shelves, each one crammed with books that looked as though they had been forgotten by the world. The shelves were made of dark polished wood that gleamed faintly in the dim light, their surfaces etched with strange, indecipherable symbols that might have been decorative—or might have been something more. The books themselves were an eclectic mix, their spines cracked and worn, their titles faded or missing entirely. Some were bound in rich, dark leather, while others were wrapped in brittle cloth that threatened to disintegrate at the slightest touch.

The ceiling loomed high above, lost in shadows, supported by massive stone columns that seemed to grow out of the floor like the trunks of ancient trees. Stained glass windows, dulled by layers of dust, filtered what little daylight there was into a murky, coloured haze that cast strange patterns on the floor. The light was so faint it seemed almost reluctant to enter, as if it too feared what lay hidden within these walls.

The library was eerily quiet, the kind of silence that pressed in on you from all sides, amplifying the sound of your own heartbeat. The only noise came from the occasional rustle of pages as a draught slipped through the cracks in the stone or the soft creak of a floorboard as Cassandra moved deeper into the labyrinth. The place had an unsettling energy, as though the very walls were alive, pulsing with a silent, malevolent hum that vibrated in the back of her skull.

In the centre of the library, a grand reading table stood beneath a massive chandelier that hung precariously from the ceiling. The chandelier was covered in cobwebs, its candles long since melted into hardened drips of wax that clung to the iron frame like stalactites. The table was cluttered with forgotten tomes, some of which had been left open, their pages yellowed and brittle. Whoever had last used this table had been in a hurry, judging by the haphazard arrangement of books and the scattered notes written in a spidery hand.

There were more secluded corners, hidden alcoves where the light barely reached and where the shadows seemed to deepen unnaturally. In these recesses, the books grew older, their covers more ornate, their titles more obscure. It was in one such corner that Cassandra found herself, drawn to a particular shelf that seemed to exude a quiet menace. The books here were different— thicker, bound in dark leather that was cool to the touch. Their spines were marked with symbols that made her skin crawl, sigils and runes that felt wrong, as if they shouldn't exist in this world.

As Cassandra pulled one of the books from the shelf, she noticed the dust motes swirling in the air, illuminated by a sliver of light that had managed to slip through the stained glass. They floated lazily, as if time had slowed to a crawl in this place, as if the very air resisted the intrusion of the outside world. The book in her hands was heavy, its pages crackling like dry leaves as she turned them. The text was in a language she didn't recognize, the letters twisted and sharp, almost painful to look at.

The deeper she ventured into the library, the more oppressive the atmosphere became, as if the building itself were watching her, waiting for something. She couldn't shake the feeling that she was being followed, though every time she glanced over her shoulder, she saw nothing but the rows of silent, indifferent books. But the sensation persisted, gnawing at the edges of her mind, making her nerves tingle with a mix of fear and anticipation.

This was no ordinary library. It was a place where knowledge came at a price, where the walls held onto secrets that could drive a person mad. And yet despite the growing dread that settled like lead in her stomach, Cassandra couldn't stop. She had come too far, and the answers she sought were buried somewhere in this tomb of forgotten words and forbidden lore.

Eventually, she found the section of the library where the shelves were filled with books on the occult, forbidden knowledge that had been hidden away from the world. She felt a cold sweat break out on her forehead as she pulled a book from the shelf, its pages yellowed with age.

As she flipped through the pages, a piece of paper fluttered out and landed on the floor at her feet. Cassandra bent down to pick it up, her hands trembling slightly. It was a handwritten note, the ink smudged and faded, but still legible. It read:

Thevoiceofthehand will lead you to what you seek but beware the price.

Cassandra stared at the note, her mind racing. Who had written this? And more importantly, what price were they talking about?

She felt a sudden rush of fear, a primal instinct telling her to leave, to get out of that library and never look back. But she couldn't. She was too close now, too deep into this dark, twisted web to walk away. She stuffed the note into her pocket and continued to search the shelves, her mind filled with the echoes of ancient secrets and the distant, foreboding voice of the hand that had drawn her here.

All the time she was in there, Cassandra Lane was being watched, obsessively.

The Library of St Giles was run by a man named Alistair Kane, a figure as enigmatic and unsettling as the library itself. Alistair was tall and gaunt, with skin so pale it seemed almost translucent, stretched tightly over his sharp, angular features. His hair was silver, though not with age—Alistair had always looked like he had one foot in the grave, even as a young man. Now, in his sixties, he had the air of someone who had seen too much, someone who knew more than was good for him.

His eyes were a piercing shade of blue, so intense that they seemed to bore into your soul when he looked at you. They were the eyes of a man who had spent too much time in the company of ancient, forbidden knowledge, eyes that held secrets darker than the ink on the pages he guarded so fiercely. When he spoke, his voice was low and raspy, as if it hadn't been used in years, and it carried with it the weight of countless unsaid things.

Alistair Kane had been the caretaker of the library for as long as anyone could remember. Some said he had inherited the position from his father, and his father before him, but there were no records to prove it. In fact, there were no records of Alistair Kane at all—no birth certificate, no family history, nothing. It was as if he had sprung from the shadows themselves, a spectre bound to the library and its dark purpose.

He was seldom seen outside the library, and when he was, it was only in the dead of night, moving silently through the narrow, deserted streets of the village like a ghost. He had no known family, no friends, no connections to the outside world. It was whispered among the townsfolk that he never left the library for long, that he slept there, ate there, and most unsettling of all, that he sometimes spoke to the books as if they could hear him.

Alistair was a man of few words, and those who did

cross his path often felt a chill in his presence, as if the air around him was somehow colder. He moved with a deliberate slowness, his long, bony fingers always clutching a book or a piece of parchment. His clothes were as old-fashioned as the library itself—an immaculate black suit that looked like it had been tailored in another century and a starched white collar that peeked out from under a high-buttoned vest.

But it was his knowledge that truly set him apart. Alistair Kane knew every inch of the library, every book, every secret it contained. He could recite entire passages from the most obscure and arcane texts, texts that had been forgotten by time or purposely hidden away. He was the gatekeeper of knowledge that no one else wanted to possess, the keeper of secrets that could unravel a mind.

Cassandra Lane had heard the name Alistair Kane before, but never in connection with the library. He was a shadowy figure whispered about in the kind of circles journalists either chased or avoided, depending on their appetite for trouble. She'd come across his name while digging into a story about missing persons—people who'd gone looking for answers and never come back. Kane had been mentioned offhand, a footnote in a larger mystery, a man who could unearth knowledge no one else could. Some called him an archivist, others a broker of secrets, but everyone agreed on one thing—whatever he found for you came at a price.

It wasn't until she stepped into the library that the pieces clicked together, the name she'd scribbled in an old notebook suddenly carrying a new and heavier weight. Alistair Kane wasn't just some information dealer operating in the shadows. He was *this*. The library. And now she was standing right in the middle of it.

As Cassandra finally came face to face with him, she felt a shiver run down her spine. Alistair was standing behind a massive oak desk, his fingers steepled in front of him, those unnervingly blue eyes fixed on her as if he had been expecting her all along. He did not greet her with words, but with a slight nod, his expression unreadable.

"I'm looking for something," Cassandra said, trying to keep her voice steady under his gaze.

Alistair tilted his head slightly, his thin lips curling into a faint, almost imperceptible smile. "Everyone who comes here is," he replied, his voice as dry as the pages of the books surrounding them. "The question is, are you prepared to find it?"

There was no trace of warmth in his words, only a quiet, almost predatory curiosity. It was as if he knew what she was after, knew how dangerous it was, and was testing her resolve. Cassandra felt her pulse quicken, but she squared her shoulders and met his gaze head-on.

"I am," she said, though the words felt heavier than she had intended, laden with the gravity of the situation.

Alistair studied her for a moment longer before he slowly rose from his chair, his movements deliberate, almost ritualistic. He gestured for her to follow as he turned and led her deeper into the labyrinth of shelves. As they walked, the shadows seemed to grow thicker, the silence more oppressive, until it felt like they were the only two people left in the world.

"I have what you seek," Alistair said finally, his voice barely more than a whisper, "but be warned, knowledge comes with a cost. And what you learn here ... you cannot unlearn."

Cassandra nodded, her mouth dry but her determination unwavering. She had come too far to turn back now. Whatever lay ahead, whatever secrets the library held, she was ready to face them. It would appear she had been granted access to the normally closed building for a reason.

Cassandra Lane stood before Mr Kane, her breath coming in short, quick bursts. The man before her was old, impossibly old, his skin stretched tight over the contours of his skull like parchment. His eyes were dark and bottomless, and as he spoke, it felt as though they were drawing her into an abyss where all sense of time and reality began to slip away.

"The Five," he whispered, his voice like the dry rustling of dead leaves in a forgotten graveyard. "They are the ones who can make the impossible possible, Cassandra. They are the keepers of secrets older than this world itself, and they have the power to grant any desire ... for a price."

Cassandra swallowed hard, her throat tight. The air in the room felt thick, suffocating, as though it was infused with the weight of countless unspoken sins. She had come here seeking answers about John Morrison, but what she had found was something far darker, something that threatened to consume her just as it had consumed him.

"What do they want with him?" she asked, her voice trembling despite her best efforts to remain calm. "What did John do to get mixed up with them?"

The old man chuckled, a sound that sent shivers down Cassandra's spine. "John Morrison, like many before him, was desperate. Desperation is the gateway, the key that opens the door to The Five. They find those who are teetering on the edge, those who have lost hope, and they offer them a way out. John was promised the impossible—a way to bring his son back from the dead. But in return, he had to offer something of equal value."

"What could be of equal value to a child's life?" Cassandra's words came out sharper than she intended, a mix of fear and anger twisting in her gut.

The old man's smile widened, a ghastly sight that made her stomach churn. "The Five have their own ways of measuring worth, my dear. Sometimes it's not just what is given, but what can be taken away. John offered up more than just his soul; he offered a piece of himself, the very essence of who he was. And now The Five have their hooks in him. They won't let go until they've drained him dry, until he's nothing more than a shell, a puppet to their will."

Cassandra took a step back, the weight of the man's words pressing down on her. She thought of John, of the broken man he had become, and of the monstrous lengths he had gone to in his misguided attempt to save his son. "And you want me to do what?" she asked, her voice barely above a whisper.

The old man leaned forward, his eyes gleaming with a hunger that made her skin crawl. "I want you to tell the world, Cassandra. Tell them about The Five. Tell them that they can have anything they desire—love, power, revenge. The Five will grant it all, for the right price. You will be their voice, their messenger."

Cassandra recoiled at the thought. "Why would I do that? Why would I help them?"

The old man's expression turned cold, his eyes narrowing to slits. "Because, Cassandra, The Five do not ask—they demand. And if you refuse, they will take what they want from you, whether you offer it willingly or not. But if you comply, they may grant you a favour of your own. Anything you desire, for a price."

Cassandra's mind raced. She thought of her own struggles, the darkness that had haunted her for years. The thought of having it all erased, of being free from her pain, was almost too tempting to resist. But she knew the cost would be too high.

She straightened, summoning all the courage she had left. "I won't do it," she said firmly. "I won't be their pawn."

The old man's smile faded, his eyes turning cold and hard. "You think you have a choice?" he hissed. "You don't know the power they hold, the power I hold. You will do as they command, Cassandra, or you will suffer."

Cassandra turned on her heel, her heart pounding in her chest as she hurried towards the door. She could feel the old man's gaze burning into her back, and she knew that this was far from over.

As she stepped out into the night, the cold air hit her, but it did little to calm the storm of fear and anger raging inside her. The Five were real, and they were coming for her, just as they had come for John Morrison.

Cassandra's footsteps echoed in the silent night, each one a hollow, muffled thud that seemed to carry the weight of the terror lodged in her chest. The air was cold and sharp, but it did little to dispel the dark, oily fear that clung to her like a second skin. Her heart was pounding so loudly she thought it might burst, each beat reverberating in her ears, drowning out the rational thoughts that tried to claw their way to the surface.

She walked quickly, almost running, the image of the old man's gaunt face burned into her mind like a brand. His voice—dry and rasping, like sandpaper on bone—kept replaying in her head, whispering promises of power, of untold desires fulfilled by The Five. She shuddered, pulling her coat tighter around her, as if that could keep out the chill that had seeped into her very soul.

The Five. The name alone was enough to twist her stomach into knots, to make her mind reel with the possibilities of what they were, of what they could do. These weren't just legends or ghost stories told around campfires. They were real. Tangible. And they had their claws in John Morrison, twisting him into something dark and unrecognizable.

And now they had set their sights on her.

The thought was enough to send a fresh wave of fear crashing through her, but beneath that fear, something else was stirring, something she didn't want to acknowledge. It was a whisper, soft and insidious, curling around her mind like smoke. *What if* ...

She stopped walking, her breath hitching as she stood under the dim glow of a streetlight. The world around her was silent, the night deep and endless, but inside her mind, a storm was raging. *What if you could use them?* The thought was so vile, so terrifying, that she almost gagged on it, but it was there, lurking in the corners of her mind, refusing to be ignored.

She could feel the darkness of it, the wrongness of even entertaining the idea. The Five were monsters—*monsters*, she reminded herself—and yet ... She bit her lip, her eyes wide as she stared at the cracked pavement beneath her feet, the realization creeping in like a sickness.

What if ... she thought again, almost unwillingly. What if she *did* write the story? What if she told the world about The Five, about the impossible promises they could fulfil? What if she became the voice that carried their dark message to the masses?

She could be more than just a journalist. She could be a legend. The most sought-after, the most powerful. The world would know her name, her byline, her face. She would be untouchable, her words gospel, her stories the most talked about, the most feared.

The fear that had gripped her heart began to loosen its hold, replaced by something darker, something that whispered of power and ambition. She imagined it—her name in headlines, her stories leading every news channel, every major publication scrambling to get a piece of her. *Cassandra Lane*, the woman who uncovered The Five, who brought them to the light.

She could almost taste it, the fame, the power. The money. She could have it all.

But then, just as quickly as the thought came, another followed, slamming into her like a freight train. *But at what cost?*

Her hands began to shake, and she quickly stuffed them into her coat pockets, her breath coming out in ragged gasps. She couldn't do it. She couldn't let herself be drawn into their web, no matter how tempting it was. No matter how much she wanted what they were offering.

Because once she crossed that line, there would be no going back. The Five would own her, just as they owned John. They would twist her desires, manipulate her ambitions until she was nothing more than a puppet dancing on their strings.

The realization hit her like a punch to the gut, and she stumbled back, her eyes wide with fear. She couldn't let them in. She couldn't let them take her, too. But the seed had been planted, the dark temptation lingering at the edges of her mind, whispering of possibilities too tantalizing to ignore.

She shook her head violently, trying to clear her thoughts, trying to banish the darkness that threatened to consume her. She couldn't let herself think like that. She had to be strong. She had to fight.

But as she continued down the empty street, the whispers followed her, a constant reminder of the price that could be paid, of the power that could be hers. And deep down, buried beneath the layers of fear and resolve, a small, insidious voice kept whispering, *what if?*

And with every step, she felt herself slipping further into that darkness, into the dangerous allure of The Five, knowing that the fight was far from over. And knowing, too, that the hardest battle was not with them, but with herself.

Chapter Twenty

John stood in the cramped bathroom, his hands gripping the edges of the sink so tightly that his knuckles had turned bone white. The cold porcelain surface grounded him, a fleeting anchor against the storm raging in his mind. He had barely slept—another night of tossing and turning, his thoughts circling like vultures over the carcass of his sanity. The dark bags under his eyes seemed to sink deeper with each passing day, pulling his face into a haggard, hollow expression that even he barely recognized anymore.

He turned the tap on, letting the water run until it was as cold as the grave, before splashing his face repeatedly, hoping to wash away the fatigue, the fear, the relentless thoughts that gnawed at his brain like hungry rats. Droplets clung to his skin, trailing down his face and dripping from his chin as he stared at the swirling water in the sink, listening to the steady hypnotic drip of the taps.

With a deep breath, John forced himself to look up at the mirror, expecting to see the familiar wreck of a man he had become. But what he saw instead made his blood run cold.

His reflection stared back at him, but it wasn't him— not really. The face in the mirror was his, but it wore an expression that twisted his features into something grotesque, something wrong. A grin stretched across his face, wide and unnatural, the corners of his mouth pulling back too far, as if someone had hooked invisible strings into his cheeks and yanked. His eyes gleamed with a dark, malevolent joy, the kind of look you'd expect from a predator who had just cornered its prey.

John's heart hammered in his chest, each beat thudding against his ribcage like a drum signalling his doom. He blinked, hoping the sinister grin would vanish, that it was just a trick of the light, a product of his exhausted mind. But when he opened his eyes again, the grin remained, more pronounced now, almost mocking.

"Who ... who are you?" he whispered, his voice cracking, barely audible over the sound of his own racing pulse.

The reflection's head tilted slightly, the smile widening even further, an impossible stretch of lips and teeth that sent a wave of nausea rolling through John's gut.

"He's waiting for you, John," the reflection whispered, its voice a rasping hiss that crawled into his ears like a thousand spiders. "Just let me in."

John's breath caught in his throat, and for a moment, he couldn't move, paralyzed by the sheer horror of what he was seeing. The thing in the mirror—the thing wearing his face—wasn't just smiling now. It was leaning closer, as if trying to push through the glass, to breach the fragile barrier between them. Its eyes, so familiar yet so alien, bore into his, filled with a malevolent hunger that made John's skin crawl.

"No!" John shouted, his voice a desperate, guttural cry as he lashed out. His fist connected with the mirror with a sickening crunch, the glass shattering under the force of the blow. Pain exploded in his hand, sharp and hot, as shards of glass rained down around him, clinking and skittering across the floor like broken promises.

He stumbled back, clutching his bleeding hand, his breath coming in ragged gasps. The mirror was in ruins, jagged pieces clinging to the frame, reflecting fractured images of the bathroom. The sinister grin was gone, replaced by the fragmented, bewildered face of a man on the brink of collapse. His real face.

John's knees buckled, and he sank to the floor amidst the scattered glass, his chest heaving with each laboured breath. He stared at the blood trickling from his knuckles, the red rivulets mixing with the cold water that dripped from the tap. The pain in his hand was real, tangible, but what about everything else? What about the voice? The grin? The words that had slithered out of the reflection's mouth like a serpent's tongue?

"Am I ... am I going insane?" he muttered, his voice barely more than a whisper, lost in the small sterile room. The question hung in the air, unanswered, echoing in the hollow spaces of his mind.

He couldn't shake the feeling that something was wrong, something deep inside him that was fraying at the edges, pulling apart the threads of his reality. The lines between what was real and what wasn't had begun to blur, smudging together like wet ink on a page. Had the reflection spoken to him, or was it just another hallucination? Was he truly hearing voices, or was his mind playing cruel tricks on him, a punishment for his desperation, his obsession, his guilt?

John pressed his bleeding hand to his chest, trying to calm the wild beating of his heart, but the fear, the doubt, the creeping sense that he was slipping further into madness, wouldn't leave him. It clung to him like a shadow, whispering dark thoughts into his ear, thoughts he didn't want to entertain but couldn't silence.

He was alone in that bathroom, surrounded by broken glass and the remnants of a shattered mirror, but he couldn't shake the feeling that he wasn't alone at all.

Something was watching him, waiting for him to break completely, to give in, to let it in.

John didn't know how much longer he could hold on.

Loud banging at the door jolted John from the lonely battle with his own mind in that bathroom, the room that seemed to grow smaller with each passing second. The harsh sound ricocheted off the grimy walls, mingling with the relentless whispers that had taken up residence in his mind. Disoriented and groggy, he stumbled to the door, opening it just a crack. On the other side stood an irate woman, her presence filling the narrow hallway with a suffocating sense of dread.

The landlady stood there, a stout, immovable figure in the dimly lit hallway. Her face, perpetually twisted into a scowl, seemed carved from stone. Deep lines etched her forehead, the marks of years spent scowling at the world. Her eyes, small and piercing, glowed with a fiery intensity that could burn through steel. They were the kind of eyes that saw everything, missed nothing, and offered no forgiveness.

Her greying hair was pulled back into a tight, unforgiving bun that sat atop her head like a crown of iron. It was a style that hadn't changed in decades, a relic of her younger days when discipline and control were her guiding principles. Wisps of hair escaped the bun, framing her face like strands of barbed wire. She wore a floral housecoat, faded with time, the once vibrant colours now muted and dull. It was belted at the waist, emphasizing her stout figure. Over it, she had a worn mustard-coloured cardigan, its pockets sagging with the weight of keys, a notebook, and various odds and ends. On her feet were a pair of sensible black orthopaedic shoes, polished to a shine.

Her hands, calloused and strong, were planted firmly on her wide hips. Her fingers, adorned with cheap rings that pinched the skin, tapped impatiently against her sides. The veins on the backs of her hands stood out, a roadmap of a life lived with relentless determination. Around her neck, she wore a locket, tarnished with age, its contents a secret she guarded fiercely.

Her name was Agnes Cavanaugh, a woman who had spent the last thirty years managing the Seafarer's Rest, a decrepit hotel that had seen better days long before she took over. Born in a small village outside of Whitby, Agnes had known hardship from a young age. Her father had been a fisherman, lost at sea when she was just a girl, leaving her mother to raise her and her three siblings alone. The family scraped by, living hand to mouth, and Agnes learned early on the value of hard work and thrift.

As a young woman, she had dreams of escaping the drudgery of her life. She moved to the town of Whitby, hoping for a fresh start. She took a job as a maid at the Seafarer's Rest, working her way up to manager over the years. Her dreams of escape faded, replaced by a steely resolve to make something of herself in the only way she knew how. She never married, her stern demeanour and unyielding nature driving away any suitors. The hotel became her life, its creaking floors and peeling wallpaper a testament to her dedication and her isolation.

Agnes had seen it all: the drunks, the down-and-outs, the lost souls who drifted in and out of the Seafarer's Rest. She prided herself on keeping order, maintaining a semblance of respectability in a place that seemed to defy it. Her rules were strict, her punishments swift, and she ruled the hotel with an iron fist. The locals respected her, though few truly liked her. She was a fixture, an unchanging part of the town's landscape, as much a part of Whitby as the abbey ruins on the hill.

As she stood there, glaring at John through the narrow crack of the door, she was the embodiment of authority and suspicion. Her eyes flicked past him into the shadowy room, her nose twitching at the unpleasant odour wafting out. She had dealt with tenants like John before, and she knew trouble when she saw it.

"What is going on in there?" she demanded, her voice sharp and accusing. The words echoed down the hallway, a challenge and a warning. Agnes Cavanaugh was not a woman easily deceived, and she was not about to let this latest tenant disrupt the uneasy peace of her domain.

"I said, what on earth is going on in there?" she demanded, her voice slicing through the oppressive atmosphere like a knife. "I've been getting complaints about a terrible smell coming from your room! What are you doing in there?"

John's heart began to hammer in his chest, a frantic drumbeat that matched the tempo of the whispers swirling in his head. He tried to compose himself, forcing a weak smile that felt more like a grimace. "I'm sorry, love. I've just been a bit ... under the weather. I'll clean up right away."

The landlady's eyes narrowed, her suspicion deepening. She pushed against the door, her stout frame straining as she tried to force her way in. "I need to inspect the room. Now. We can't have this kind of thing going on here!"

John's grip tightened on the door, holding it shut with a strength born of desperation. Panic surged through him as the whispers in his head grew louder, more insistent, a cacophony of sinister voices.

"She's going to alert someone," they hissed, each word a dagger in his mind. "She's going to stop you from helping Ethan. You're going to get caught!"

John's breath came in ragged gasps. He knew he couldn't let her in, couldn't let her see what lay beyond the door. His mind raced, searching for an escape, a way to silence the voices and keep his secret safe. But the landlady was relentless, her determination as solid as the door he clung to.

"Move aside or I'll call the police!" she threatened, her voice rising to a shrill pitch.

John's vision blurred with fear, and in that moment, something inside him snapped. The whispers melded into a single, deafening roar, drowning out all reason. He had to act. He had to protect his secret. He had to keep helping Ethan, no matter the cost.

And as he stood there, caught between the relentless landlady and the dark demands of his own mind, John knew that whatever happened next would change everything.

"Think of Ethan," they urged. "You can't let her ruin everything. Do something, John!"

He swallowed hard, his mind a chaotic whirlpool of desperation and dread. He knew he had to act quickly, but his thoughts were fragmented, and his hands trembled as he tried to maintain control.

"Please," he said, his voice strained and desperate. "Just give me a few minutes. I promise I'll take care of it."

But the landlady was relentless, her face inches from his as she pushed harder against the door. John could see the resolve in her eyes, the determination to uncover whatever secret lay behind his door.

The whispers reached a fever pitch, blending into a singular, deafening command. "Do it now, John!"

With a surge of adrenaline, John pushed back, slamming the door shut and locking it swiftly. The landlady banged on the door with renewed fury, her shouts muffled but still audible.

"You can't do this! Open up! Open this door right now!"

John leaned against the door, his chest heaving with rapid breaths. He felt the weight of his predicament pressing down on him, the gravity of his choices bearing heavily on his soul. The room around him seemed to close in, the shadows lengthening as the whispers continued their insidious assault.

"Get rid of her, John. For Ethan. For your son."

His eyes snapped open, resolve hardening in his gaze. He knew what he had to do, even if it meant crossing lines he never thought he'd approach. His love for Ethan, the desperate need to bring his son back, overshadowed every other consideration.

Chapter Twenty-One

As the landlady's hand pushed over the threshold, her keys still jingling in the lock as she tried to wedge the door open, John reacted swiftly. He slammed the door on her hand with all his might. The sickening crunch of bones breaking echoed in the narrow hallway, followed by a piercing scream of agony from the landlady. Her fingers, now mangled and twisted, were pinned in the doorframe.

Without hesitation, John yanked the door open and grabbed her.

The cheap synthetic fabric of her housecoat rustled with every movement, and her face was round and flushed, perpetually framed by a pair of thick, cheap glasses that magnified her small piggy eyes.

"John? What are you—" she began to yell, her voice as grating as her unwanted presence.

But he didn't let her finish. Something inside him snapped, a tension that had been coiling tighter and tighter since the moment he had struck that godforsaken deal. He moved in a blur, closing the distance between them before she could even register the danger.

His hands shot out, fingers digging into the soft, flabby flesh of her ears. The skin was greasy with sweat, and her earrings—tacky gold hoops—dug into his palms as he yanked her forward with a force that sent a jolt of pain shooting through her skull. She screamed, a high-pitched, guttural sound that echoed off the walls of the tiny room.

John silenced her the only way he knew how. He reared back and brought his forehead crashing down into her face with all the force he could muster. There was a sickening crunch, the sound of cartilage giving way as her nose shattered beneath the impact. Blood sprayed out in a crimson arc, splattering across his face, warm and sticky.

She made a garbled sound, something between a scream and a moan, her hands flailing weakly against his chest, but John wasn't done. He drove his head forward again and again, each impact reverberating through his skull, each crack of bone against bone more satisfying than the last.

The landlady's face crumpled like wet paper, her features losing their shape with every blow. Her glasses shattered, shards of glass embedding themselves in her cheeks and brow, her nose flattening into a grotesque pulp. Blood poured from her broken face in rivers, pooling in the creases of her neck, soaking into the collar of her housecoat. The smell of copper and sweat filled the room, mingling with the stench of decay that had permeated her life for so long.

John could feel the resistance in her body waning, the fight draining out of her with each blow, but he couldn't stop. He was a man possessed, driven by something far beyond his control, something that whispered to him in the darkest corners of his mind, telling him that this was necessary, that this was what had to be done.

The sounds of the assault were grotesque, wet, and meaty, like someone repeatedly slamming a mallet into raw, butchered meat. Her skull finally gave with a sickening, hollow crack, her head lolling back, her eyes—those piggy, magnified eyes—rolling up into her head, showing nothing but whites stained with blood.

And then, just as suddenly as it had started, it was over. John let go, his hands trembling, slick with blood and bits of flesh. The landlady slumped to the floor in the corner of John's room, her body twitching spasmodically, the final vestiges of life fleeing her broken form. Her face was a ruin, a hideous, unrecognizable mask of blood, bone, and gore. Her mouth hung open, jaw slack, a few yellowed teeth visible through the mess, her breath a gurgling rattle as blood filled her throat.

The room was silent save for John's laboured breathing and the slow, steady drip of blood hitting the threadbare carpet. His heart pounded in his chest, the adrenaline slowly ebbing away, leaving behind a cold, hollow numbness. He stumbled back, his legs suddenly weak, the enormity of what he had done crashing down on him like a tidal wave.

He wiped a hand across his face, smearing the blood even further, his mind racing but unable to latch onto any coherent thought. All he could see was the broken, lifeless form of the woman before him, the blood pooling around her, seeping into the fabric of the chair, the room. The horror of it threatened to overwhelm him, but he pushed it down, burying it deep where it couldn't reach him.

This was for Ethan, he reminded himself, trying to steady his shaking hands. This was necessary. But even as he repeated the words, he knew they rang hollow, drowned out by the image of the woman's shattered face, a grotesque mask that would haunt him for the rest of his days.

He stared at the lifeless body at his feet, a mix of horror and resignation washing over him. He knew there was no turning back now. The landlady was dead, her blood on his hands. He had crossed the line again, driven by the desperate need to bring Ethan back, and there was no undoing it.

Taking a deep, shuddering breath, John forced himself to move. He needed to get out, to escape before anyone discovered what he had done. With every step, the magnitude of his actions bore down on him, but he pushed it aside. He couldn't afford to break down now.

John's mind raced as he hastily packed up his belongings once more. His hands trembled, slick with a mix of sweat and residual blood from his latest act of desperation. He grabbed a damp towel from the bathroom and quickly tried to wash as much blood off himself as he could. The cold water did little to remove the stains of his guilt.

He threw his few remaining clothes into a duffel bag, along with his laptop and the ritual book that had led him down this dark path. Every moment felt like an eternity as he moved frantically around the room. His heart pounded in his chest, the whispers in his mind growing louder with each passing second.

John approached the drawer where Ethan's tiny body lay. To him, Ethan still looked the same as he always had—innocent, angelic, his little boy. He couldn't see the reality of the situation. In truth, Ethan's body was decomposing. The skin was bloated and discoloured, the eyes sunken deep into their sockets, a macabre shadow of the vibrant child he had once been.

"Come on, buddy. We're getting out of here," John whispered, his voice choked with emotion. He gently lifted Ethan out of the drawer, cradling him tenderly against his chest. His mind blocked out the horrible reality, replacing it with the image of his healthy son. The smell, though pungent and overwhelming, was ignored by John's desperate mind.

With Ethan in his arms, John ran for the door. He snatched the landlady's car keys from the counter, her accusations and threats still echoing in his ears. The guilt of what he had done to her weighed on him, but the urgent need to escape overpowered any remorse.

The hallway outside the room was eerily quiet, the only sound John's hurried footsteps. He reached the landlady's car, a beaten-up blue Audi A4, parked just outside the B&B. The car was old but reliable, a vehicle that had seen many years of service. John quickly opened the back door, laying Ethan gently on the back seat and securing him with the seatbelt, as if he were still alive and needed the protection.

John hurried to the driver's side, his hands trembling as he fumbled for the keys. The duffel bag hit the passenger seat with a heavy thud, a grim reminder of what lay within. He slid behind the wheel, his breath coming in ragged gasps, and jammed the key into the ignition. The engine sputtered to life with a reluctant growl, the car shuddering as if it too sensed the darkness that clung to him like a second skin.

He cast one last look at the B&B, its quaint charm now overshadowed by the horror and guilt that tainted it. The sight of it sent a shiver down his spine, and he wrenched the car into gear, tires crunching over the gravel like bones underfoot. As he pulled away, the rearview mirror showed the house growing smaller, its silhouette disappearing into the early morning fog.

John's hands gripped the steering wheel with white-knuckled intensity, his eyes darting between the road and the mirror. He navigated the narrow streets of Whitby, the town still cloaked in pre-dawn shadows. The cobblestone roads seemed to stretch endlessly, winding past silent shops and shuttered windows. The streetlights cast eerie pools of yellow light, illuminating the path before him in a series of disconnected fragments.

He turned onto Church Street, the cobblestones giving way to slick asphalt. The car's headlights cut through the mist, revealing the ghostly outlines of ancient buildings, their stone facades pocked and weathered by centuries of salt air and storms. He sped past the old church, its steeple a black finger pointing accusingly at the sky, and made a sharp left onto Skinner Street.

The whispers of The Five echoed in his ears, an insidious chorus that demanded more sacrifice. His heart pounded, a frantic rhythm that matched the engine's growl. He passed by the deserted marketplace, the stalls empty and forlorn, the scent of the sea mingling with the faint odour of rotting fish. His mind raced with conflicting emotions, a tempest of fear, guilt, and desperate hope.

The voice of reason, small and feeble, tried to break through the fog of his delusion. "This is wrong," it whispered, a thin thread of sanity in the chaos. "You've lost touch with reality."

John shook his head violently, as if trying to dislodge the voice from his mind. He couldn't afford to listen, not now. He had to focus on the road ahead, on the dark clouds gathering on the horizon, mirroring the storm brewing in his soul.

He hit the outskirts of town, the houses giving way to open fields and the winding roads of the North Yorkshire countryside. The car's tires hummed against the road beneath, the rhythm almost hypnotic. John's eyes darted to the mirror again, half-expecting to see the shadows of pursuers closing in. The whispers grew louder, more insistent, urging him on.

He pushed the accelerator harder, the car lurching forward as he tore down the road. The landscape blurred past, a mix of green fields and dark woods, the sky above turning a sickly grey. The voice of reason was nearly drowned out now, a distant echo in the cacophony of his thoughts.

John's mind flickered with images of Ethan, his son's face a beacon of light in the darkness. He clung to that image, to the hope that this nightmare would end with Ethan back in his arms, alive and well. But even as he drove on, a part of him knew the truth. He had crossed a line, stepped into a world of madness and blood, and there was no turning back.

The road stretched out before him, an endless ribbon of uncertainty. He drove on, into the gathering storm, the whispers of The Five his only companions on the journey into the unknown.

Chapter Twenty-Two

Jack Palace gripped the steering wheel of his car as he sped along the coastal road from Hull to Whitby. The world around him was still steeped in the eerie calm of dawn, the horizon just beginning to blush with the first hints of sunlight. The North Sea stretched out to his right, a vast and unfeeling expanse that mirrored the turmoil within his own mind, which was racing, piecing together the clues that had led him here. The murders in Whitby, the connection to John's favourite place, and the sense of desperation in Eve's voice all pointed to one thing: John was in Whitby. The road ahead wound through the rugged landscape, flanked by rolling moors that seemed to stretch on forever, their loneliness broken only by the occasional cluster of sheep or the hunched silhouette of a farmhouse.

The drive felt like a journey through a haunted landscape, the scenery a blur of muted greens and greys, punctuated by the occasional twisted tree or weather-beaten signpost. Whitby loomed somewhere ahead, the ancient town shrouded in history and secrets, a place where the line between reality and nightmare seemed perilously thin. Jack had been here before, many times, but never with the weight of a manhunt pressing down on him like this.

His hunch had brought him here, that instinctive pull that seasoned detectives learned to trust after years of following breadcrumbs and gut feelings. John Morrison's descent into madness had led him to Whitby, a place that held significance for John in ways Jack couldn't fully grasp. There was something about this town that had drawn John, something that whispered to him in the dark, fuelling his descent into violence. Jack didn't need to understand it to know that he had to stop him.

The constant vibration of the car engine was a steady companion, a metronome to his thoughts, until the sudden ringing of his phone shattered the quiet.

He glanced at the screen, saw it was from the station, and quickly answered, "Palace here."

"Jack, it's Peters. We've got some updates on your case."

"Go ahead," Jack said, his grip tightening on the steering wheel.

Peters was a seasoned officer, a man with thirty years on the force and the scars to prove it. He had seen it all, from gang wars to serial killers, and his voice carried the weight of that experience. He had mentored Jack when he was a rookie, teaching him the ropes of detective work, the importance of patience, and the value of gut instincts. Now, as Jack sped towards the looming nightmare, he needed all that experience and more.

"We received a call about an hour ago. A local landlady was found dead in her establishment. It looks like she was savagely attacked. A witness mentioned she confronted a tenant about a smell coming from his room shortly before she was killed."

Jack's heart sank. "Do we have a description of the tenant?"

"Yes, it matches John Morrison. But that's not all. There was another incident earlier this week. A priest was murdered, and a witness saw a man fitting John's description running away from the scene."

Jack's mind raced, the pieces of the puzzle coming together like jagged shards of glass. "Two murders in one week," he muttered. "John's losing control."

"It seems that way," Peters replied. "The local police are swarming the area, but we thought you should know. You're already on your way there, right?"

"Yeah, I'm about thirty minutes out," Jack said, his voice tight with urgency. "I'll head straight to the landlady's place and then the church. Send me the addresses."

"Will do. Be careful, Jack. This guy is dangerous and unpredictable."

"I know. Thanks for the heads-up." Jack ended the call and exhaled slowly, his thoughts a tumultuous mix of concern, determination, and dread. John, once a loving father and husband, was now a fugitive, driven to madness by grief and a twisted sense of hope.

The call from Peters still echoed in his ears, the veteran officer's voice tinged with the kind of weariness that came from seeing too much. A landlady, dead in her own establishment, brutally murdered after confronting a tenant about a smell. The priest, a man of God, left to bleed out on the cold stone of his own church. Two lives snuffed out in a matter of days, and John was the common thread. The realization settled over Jack like a suffocating blanket—John wasn't just on the run anymore. He was spiralling, losing control in the most horrific way possible.

As he drove, the rhythmic hum of the engine became a dull background noise to the cacophony of thoughts racing through his mind. The narrow roads twisted and turned, each bend revealing another stretch of desolate countryside. The sun was a pale disc in the sky now, its light struggling to pierce the thick clouds that clung to the coast. Jack's mind replayed the details of the case over and over, trying to find some pattern, some clue that he might have missed.

He had left Hull in the dead of night, the city's familiar streets fading into the rearview mirror as he headed east. The darkness had felt like a shroud, wrapping around him as he drove through sleeping villages and past fields blanketed in mist. The isolation had been almost comforting, the solitude giving him space to think, to prepare himself for what lay ahead. But now, as he neared Whitby, that comfort was gone, replaced by a growing sense of dread.

He thought of Eve, her voice trembling with fear when she had called him earlier, the desperation thick in her words. "You have to find him, Jack," she had pleaded. "You have to stop him before it's too late." She had sounded so different from the confident, vibrant woman he remembered, her voice hollowed out by worry and guilt. She was afraid of what John might do next, of how far he would go in his madness. And Jack was afraid too—not just for the potential victims, but for John himself, for what little remained of the man he had once been.

The road began to narrow as it wound its way into Whitby, the town's ancient buildings rising up from the mist like spectres from another time. The abbey loomed on the hill above, its Gothic ruins stark against the morning sky, a reminder of the town's long, dark history. Jack couldn't shake the feeling that he was driving straight into a trap, that this town held something more sinister than just the crimes of a broken man.

As he pulled onto Church Street, the old B&B came into view, its once-cheerful facade now marked by the shadow of death. Jack parked his car a short distance away, his hand lingering on the key for a moment before he turned off the engine. The silence that followed was deafening, broken only by the distant cries of seagulls and the rhythmic crashing of waves against the harbour walls. He sat there for a moment, staring at the building, trying to steel himself for what he might find inside.

His thoughts drifted to his own family—his kids, their laughter, the warmth of their home. He thought about how easily that could be taken away, how a single act of violence could shatter everything he held dear. The thought of it twisted like a knife in his gut.

Jack's duty was clear, but the lines between right and wrong were blurring with every passing mile. John wasn't just a suspect; he was a man unravelling, a man driven by grief and a desperate need to fix something that couldn't be fixed. But that desperation was dangerous, deadly, and Jack knew he had to be the one to put an end to it, no matter the cost.

Chapter Twenty-Three

As John sped down the winding country road heading south, tears streamed down his face like rivers of despair. His grip on the steering wheel was painfully tight, his thoughts a chaotic whirlwind of regret and horror. The gruesome scenes he had left behind clawed at his mind, leaving him questioning his sanity. What was happening to him? What was he becoming?

The road ahead stretched out like a twisted serpent, deserted and foreboding. The early morning light cast eerie shadows through the dense canopy of trees, their branches reaching out like skeletal fingers. The air was thick with the scent of damp earth, mingled with the faint, metallic tang of his own fear. Birds sang their mournful tunes, a stark contrast to the cacophony of guilt and madness echoing in John's head.

His vision blurred with tears, making the road a shimmering, uncertain ribbon. Each passing mile seemed to drag him deeper into an abyss of his own making. The memories of his wife and son, once comforting, now haunted him with relentless intensity. Their faces, twisted in expressions of shock and pain, flickered like a macabre slideshow before his eyes.

Suddenly, a small lay-by appeared up ahead, a brief respite from the endless torment of the road. John veered towards it, the gravel crunching under the tires like the grinding teeth of some unseen beast. The car shuddered to a stop, and he killed the engine, plunging the world into a thick, oppressive silence.

John rested his head on the steering wheel, his shoulders heaving with sobs that wracked his body. The weight of his actions pressed down on him like a physical force, squeezing the air from his lungs. He felt as if he were drowning, each breath a desperate, gasping struggle against the tide of his own guilt.

His mind flashed back to the landlady's lifeless eyes, the priest's final, futile struggle. The whispers of The Five were a constant, insidious presence, urging him on, promising that just two more sacrifices would bring Ethan back. But with every horrific act, the promise seemed more and more like a cruel, unreachable mirage.

The lay-by was a small, forgotten patch of land, overgrown with weeds and littered with the detritus of neglect. An old, rusted sign leaned precariously, its faded letters barely legible: Rest Stop. The irony was not lost on John. There would be no rest for him, no respite from the nightmare he had unleashed.

He lifted his head, staring through the windshield at the mist rising from the damp ground, swirling in ghostly tendrils. The world outside was a blur, a landscape of shadows and phantoms. His heart pounded in his chest, a relentless drumbeat of fear and desperation.

John's thoughts turned inward, to the man he had once been and the monster he feared he was becoming. He remembered the joy of holding his newborn son, the warmth of his wife's embrace. Those memories seemed like fragments of a distant, unreachable past, taunting him with their simplicity and peace.

"God, what have I done?" he whispered, his voice a broken, trembling thing. The tears came harder now, a torrent of sorrow and self-loathing. He had crossed a line, committed acts that could never be undone, and the realization was a crushing weight on his soul.

Outside, the birds continued their indifferent serenade, the morning light slowly dissolving the shadows. But for

John, there would be no dawn, no new beginning. The road ahead was shrouded in darkness, and the only certainty was the inexorable pull of his own despair.

"Should I turn myself in?" John whispered to himself, the words barely audible. "Am I insane?"

He was lost in his turmoil when a sudden knock on the window jolted him back to the grim reality. He jerked his head up, eyes wide with fear and confusion. Standing outside, illuminated by the dim grey morning light, were The Five. Identical men, their expressions cold and impassive, stared back at him with eyes that seemed to pierce his soul. Each figure was tall and gaunt, their skin a deathly pale, their features eerily symmetrical. They wore dark suits that seemed to absorb the light, making them appear as if they were carved from the very shadows themselves.

John's heart pounded in his chest as he fumbled to unlock the door, his hands trembling. His mind raced, a chaotic jumble of fear and desperation. Before he could react, a voice from behind him sent a chill down his spine, freezing him in place.

"Stick to the plan, John."

He whipped his head around, his eyes wide with shock. One of The Five sat calmly in the back seat, his presence a manifestation of John's darkest fears. His voice was smooth, almost hypnotic, yet it carried an undertone of sinister intent that made John's blood run cold.

John gasped, whipping his head forward again only to find another of The Five in the passenger seat. This one leaned closer, speaking in a calm, almost soothing voice that belied the horror of his words.

"Two more, John, for your son," the man said, his eyes

boring into John's with an intensity that made him feel as if his very soul was being laid bare. The man's gaze was unrelenting, a bottomless void that promised both salvation and damnation.

John's tears stopped, replaced by a cold, steely determination that gripped his heart like a vice. The despair and fear that had consumed him were now replaced by a single, unyielding thought: Ethan. Ethan was all that mattered. He nodded mechanically, the decision made, his movements robotic and devoid of emotion. He started the car again, the engine's growl echoing the turmoil within him.

As he pulled back onto the road, the figures of The Five disappeared, fading into the ether as if they had never been there at all. Yet their presence lingered, a haunting spectre that shadowed his every thought. The whispers of their voices echoed in his mind, urging him forward, promising that just two more lives would bring Ethan back to him.

John's grip on the steering wheel tightened, his knuckles white with the force of his resolve. His mind was a battleground, the whispers of The Five clashing with the small, insistent voice of reason that still tried to break through. But the promise of seeing his son again was too powerful, too overwhelming to ignore.

The road stretched out before him, a dark and twisting path that seemed to lead straight into the abyss. The landscape blurred past, a nightmarish blend of reality and hallucination. Every shadow seemed to move, every flicker of light a harbinger of The Five's return. The weight of his actions pressed down on him, suffocating him, yet he drove on, propelled by a twisted sense of hope and duty.

As the miles rolled by, John's thoughts grew darker, more fragmented. He could feel his sanity slipping away, piece by piece, consumed by the relentless demands of The Five. His heart ached with the weight of his decision, yet he couldn't stop. He wouldn't stop. For Ethan, he would do anything.

The journey continued, a descent into madness and despair. The road, once a symbol of escape and freedom, had become a conduit for his nightmares, a path leading inexorably to the next sacrifice. And all the while, the whispers of The Five echoed in his mind, a constant reminder of the price he had to pay, the blood he had to spill.

In that moment, as he drove through the waking nightmare of his own making, John Morrison was no longer the man he had once been. He was a vessel for The Five's dark will, a father driven to the brink by love and loss. And as the sun broke through the clouds, casting long shadows across the desolate landscape, he knew there was no turning back. The horror had only just begun.

Unbeknownst to John, a lorry driver had parked his truck a little further down the road, having stopped for a rest. The driver, a burly man in his late fifties, had a face weathered by years on the road. His name was Frank Henderson, a man with a history as long and winding as the highways he travelled. Frank had a bushy salt-and-pepper beard that seemed to obscure half his face and a pair of thick glasses perched on his nose, giving him an owlish look. He wore a faded trucker cap emblazoned with the logo of a long-gone trucking company, a flannel shirt with the sleeves rolled up to his elbows, and a pair of well-worn jeans. His boots, scuffed and stained, had seen more miles than most people's cars.

Frank had started his journey early that morning from Newcastle, hauling a load of building supplies destined for a site near Scarborough. He had been on the road for nearly six hours, the monotony of the drive broken only by a brief stop for coffee and a sandwich. Feeling the fatigue set in, he had pulled over into a lay-by to rest his eyes for a bit before continuing on his way. The lay-by was a quiet spot, bordered by dense woods on one side and a low stone wall on the other, offering a view of the rolling hills beyond.

As Frank settled back in his seat, he noticed a blue saloon car pull over a short distance ahead. He watched curiously as the driver, a dishevelled-looking man, got out and seemed to be talking to himself, gesticulating wildly. Frank squinted, trying to make sense of what he was seeing. When the man opened the car door, Frank's blood ran cold. He could see the still form of a child in the back seat, unmoving.

Frank's heart pounded in his chest. He knew he had to act. He grabbed his phone with a calloused hand and dialled 999, his thick fingers trembling slightly as he hit the buttons. The phone rang twice before a calm, professional voice answered.

"Emergency services, what is your emergency?"

"There's a man acting really strange, talking to himself, and there's a baby in the back of his car. I'm worried for the child's safety. He's driving a blue saloon, number plate ... let me see ..." Frank peered through his windshield, squinting to read the plate. "The number plate is LC54 KRD. We're on a lay-by off the A171, about ten miles south of Whitby."

The dispatcher's voice remained steady. "Can you

describe the man for me?"

"Yeah," Frank said, his voice gruff. "He's mid-thirties, I'd say, with dark hair and a pretty wild look about him. Looks like he hasn't slept in days. He's wearing a dark jacket and jeans."

"Thank you, sir. Can you stay on the line while I dispatch officers to your location?"

"Sure thing," Frank replied, his eyes never leaving the blue car. His mind raced back to his own kids, now grown and living their lives far from the cab of a truck. The thought of any child in danger was enough to stir a protective instinct deep within him.

Minutes passed like hours as Frank waited, watching the man in the parked Audi. He saw the man's desperate, frantic movements, and his gut told him this situation was bad, really bad. The dispatcher kept him calm, asking occasional questions, but mostly just providing a steady voice on the other end of the line.

Frank watched as the man in the blue Audi seemed to come to a decision. His movements became more frantic, and suddenly, he started the car again. The engine roared to life, and the car peeled out of the lay-by with a spray of gravel, heading back onto the main road and quickly disappearing into the distance. Frank's heart pounded in his chest, a mix of fear and helplessness washing over him.

"He's gone," Frank said into the phone, his voice shaking slightly. "The car just took off heading south on the A171."

"Stay where you are, sir," the dispatcher instructed calmly. "Officers are en route to your location. They will need your statement."

Frank sighed, his broad shoulders slumping as he

ended the call. He climbed out of his lorry and leaned against the hood, the morning air cold and sharp against his skin. The countryside around him was eerily quiet, the peacefulness at odds with the turmoil in his mind. He kept seeing the child's lifeless body in the back seat, the haunted look in the man's eyes.

The wait for the police felt interminable. Frank replayed the scene over and over in his mind, questioning if there was something more he could have done. He scanned the horizon, hoping against hope that the man would come to his senses and return, but knowing deep down that was a fantasy.

Finally, the sound of approaching sirens broke the silence. Two police cars pulled into the lay-by, their lights flashing, but there was no urgency now, only grim determination. The officers approached Frank, their faces set in serious lines.

"Mr Henderson?" one of them asked, a young officer with sharp eyes and a reassuring presence. Frank nodded.

"Yeah, that's me. I was the one who called."

The officers took his statement, asking for every detail he could remember. Frank told them about the blue saloon, the man's erratic behaviour, and the still form of the child in the back seat. He described the man's appearance, his wild eyes, and the way he seemed to be talking to himself. The officers took notes, their expressions growing more grave with each piece of information.

As Frank spoke, he noticed an older officer, standing a bit apart from the others, watching him closely. The officer had a weathered face, etched with lines of experience and sorrow. When Frank finished his account, this officer stepped forward.

"Thank you, Mr Henderson," he said, his voice rough but kind. "You've done the right thing. We'll find him. We'll make sure that child is safe."

Frank nodded, but a gnawing doubt remained in his gut. He watched as the police cars drove off, their lights fading into the distance. He climbed back into his lorry, the cab now feeling like a confessional booth. He sat there for a moment, the engine idling, his mind a whirl of worry and guilt.

As he pulled back onto the road, heading south towards his delivery point, Frank couldn't shake the feeling that he had just had a glimpse into the abyss. The road ahead seemed darker, the miles stretching out into an uncertain future. He clutched the wheel tightly, his thoughts heavy with the weight of what he had seen and the hope that he had made a difference, however small, in the vast, uncaring world.

Chapter Twenty-Four

The Seafarer's Rest was a crumbling relic of a bygone era, a three-story building that hunkered down on the edge of Whitby's harbour like a weary sailor who had seen too many storms. The paint on its facade was peeling away, leaving behind mottled patches of weathered wood that seemed to absorb the gloom of the overcast sky. The windows were grimy, half-covered by torn lace curtains, and the sign above the door—once a vibrant blue—was now a faded, chipped reminder of the building's better days. The scent of brine and rot clung to the air, mixing with the faint, oily stench of fish from the nearby docks.

Jack pulled his car into the narrow alley beside the inn, the tires crunching over the loose gravel as he parked. The tension in his chest tightened like a noose as he cut the engine. His stomach churned with unease as he stepped out of the vehicle, his boots sinking slightly into the damp ground.

He approached the entrance, noting the way the door creaked on its rusted hinges as he pushed it open. The interior was dimly lit, and the walls were lined with old nautical memorabilia—faded photographs of ships, a rusting anchor mounted above the bar, and a lifebuoy hanging from a nail—but the place had a feeling of neglect, as if the very walls were closing in on themselves, suffocating under the weight of disuse.

Jack flashed his warrant card at the officer on duty. The area at the bottom of the stairs was cordoned off with police tape, officers bustling around, collecting evidence.

"Detective Inspector Palace," he said, his voice gravelly with exhaustion. "I'm here about the Morrison case."

The officer, a young woman with a serious expression, nodded and lifted the tape for him. "Go right up, sir."

Jack nodded, his jaw clenched as he made his way to the stairs. The wood beneath his feet creaked with every step, the sound echoing down the narrow corridor like the crack of distant gunfire. The air grew colder as he ascended, the chill seeping into his bones, mixing with the dread that knotted his gut.

Room 302 was at the end of the hallway, the door ajar, hanging by a single hinge. A faint, metallic smell wafted from within, the unmistakable scent of blood. Jack paused, taking a steadying breath before pushing the door open wider. It groaned in protest, revealing the small, dimly lit room beyond.

The first thing he saw was the landlady.

She lay sprawled on the floor, her body twisted at an unnatural angle, her head turned toward the ceiling. But it was her face—dear God, her face—that sent a jolt of horror through Jack's system. It was a ruin of shattered bone and torn flesh. Her nose had been obliterated, reduced to a gory pulp that left a jagged hole where it had once been. Blood had congealed in thick black rivulets across her cheeks, mixing with shards of glass that had embedded themselves in her skin. One of her eyes was swollen shut, a dark, purplish mass of bruised flesh, while the other stared blankly at the ceiling, its glassy surface reflecting the room's dim light.

The once-white floral housecoat she wore was stained with dark, coagulated blood, the pattern of flowers barely visible beneath the gore. Her arms were splayed out beside her, fingers curled into claws as if she had tried to fend off the attack, but her strength had failed her. The floor around her head was slick with blood, spreading out in a macabre halo.

Jack's throat tightened as he stepped closer, his pulse hammering in his ears. He had seen death before—he was no stranger to violence—but this … this was something else. This was madness. The brutality of it, the sheer savagery, turned his stomach. He could feel the bile rising in his throat, the taste of acid on his tongue as he fought the urge to retch.

His eyes drifted to the small bed in the corner, unmade and covered with a thin, threadbare blanket. A few scattered belongings were piled on the bedside table—an empty bottle of whiskey, a crumpled pack of cigarettes, a notebook with pages hanging loose from its spine. The room was otherwise bare, devoid of any personal touches, as if its occupant had lived there in body only, leaving his soul behind long ago.

Jack turned his gaze back to the landlady, his thoughts churning with questions. What the hell had driven John to this? What kind of madness could compel a man to destroy another human being with such ferocity? He could almost hear the wet thud of a blunt object meeting bone, the sickening crunch that had echoed through the room as John's rage consumed him. The thought of the murdered priest flashed through his mind, and he wondered if this had been inevitable, if John had been spiralling toward this point from the moment he'd struck that godforsaken deal.

He knelt beside the woman, his hands shaking as he reached out to check for a pulse, even though he knew there wouldn't be one. Her skin was cold, the blood sticky against his fingers. He pulled back, wiping his hand on the edge of his coat, feeling the weight of the horror settle deep in his chest.

This wasn't just about recovering a body anymore. This was about stopping a man who had lost everything, a man who had nothing left to lose. A man who was willing to kill again.

Jack stood, his resolve hardening. There was no time to waste. He had to find John before anyone else ended up like the woman on the floor. Before the madness consumed him completely.

"DI Palace," a voice called from behind him. Jack turned to see Constable Daniels, a seasoned cop Palace knew from when they worked together in Hull, with greying hair and a sombre expression. "Good to see you. It's a real mess in here."

"Tell me about it," Jack muttered, stepping deeper into the room. "Any observations I should be aware of?"

"Blunt force trauma," Daniels said, his voice a low rumble. "Probably that cast iron skillet over there, but I need to look into it further." He pointed to a heavy pan discarded in the corner, its surface slick with gore.

Jack nodded, his jaw tight. "Any witnesses?"

"None who saw the act itself," Daniels replied. "But a couple of guests reported hearing a commotion. By the time anyone got upstairs, Morrison was gone."

Jack stood, his gaze lingering on the dead woman's face. "And the kid? Ethan?"

Daniels shook his head. "No sign of him. We think Morrison took him when he fled."

"Damn it," Jack muttered under his breath.

Jack began methodically searching through the drawers, tossing aside socks, shirts, and toiletries as he worked. Each empty compartment added to his mounting frustration. He needed a clue, some indication of where

John might have gone next. As he rifled through the bedside table, his fingers brushed against something hard and smooth. He pulled out a small leather-bound journal similar to one he had found previously, its pages crammed with more of John's erratic handwriting. It was a diary of sorts, but the entries were far from coherent.

The notebook was an artefact of a mind teetering on the brink of madness. Jack flipped through its pages, his eyes narrowing at the fevered scrawlings. The writing was erratic, punctuated by paranoid ramblings and sketches of symbols that seemed to pulse with a life of their own. Each page was a glimpse into John's unravelling psyche, dominated by references to a group called 'The Five'. They appeared to be both separate entities and a single, malevolent force, whispering dark instructions to John.

Jack's breath quickened as he read about a ritual and something cryptically referred to as *the offering over water*. The words were jagged, almost tearing through the paper in their intensity. The final entry made Jack's blood run cold:

The Five have spoken. The offering must be made over water. Only then can Ethan return to me.

The significance of 'over water' struck Jack like a bolt of lightning. Whitby was a coastal town, with the North Sea lapping at its shores. The harbour, the piers, the cliffside abbey—all places where John might attempt to complete his dark ritual. The clock was ticking, and Jack knew that every second brought John closer to his goal.

Snapping the notebook shut, Jack felt a surge of urgency. He bolted down the stairs, the weight of his responsibility pressing down on him. Outside, he found Daniels directing the scene.

"Daniels," Jack barked, his voice cutting through the chatter. "I need a team to start searching the coastal areas immediately. Focus on the harbour, the piers, any place with a view of the sea. John's planning something—an offering. We can't let him complete it."

Daniels nodded, his expression grim as he relayed the instructions over his radio. Jack felt a brief surge of relief, knowing that help was mobilizing, but he couldn't afford to waste any more time. He sprinted to his car, the notebook still clutched in his hand.

As he sped toward the harbour, the landscape blurred past him in a kaleidoscope of greens and greys. The coastal road wound through dense patches of forest, their dark canopy casting eerie shadows on the pavement. Jack's mind was a whirlpool of thoughts, the cryptic mentions of The Five and their twisted demands gnawing at him. He gripped the steering wheel, the words from the notebook echoing in his mind. What kind of ritual required an offering over water? And what exactly was John planning to sacrifice?

The road straightened as he approached the outskirts of Whitby, the smell of salt and seaweed growing stronger with each passing mile. Jack's eyes flicked to the clock on the dashboard—every minute counted. He imagined John's frantic, desperate actions, driven by a delusional hope that performing this ritual would somehow bring Ethan back. The madness of it chilled Jack to the core.

Finally, the area Jack was headed to came into view, its quaint buildings and narrow streets a stark contrast to the dark storm brewing in Jack's mind. He navigated through the winding lanes, making his way toward the harbour. Fishing boats bobbed gently in the water, their masts swaying in the morning breeze. The air was thick with the cries of seagulls and the distant hum of maritime activity, but Jack felt an oppressive weight hanging over everything.

He parked the car and stepped out, scanning the area with a sharp, practised eye. The harbour stretched out before him, a labyrinth of piers and docks. He could see officers already starting their search, moving with determined efficiency.

Jack approached one of the officers, a tall man with a serious demeanour. "Detective Inspector Palace," he said, introducing himself. "I need you to focus on any secluded spots, places where someone might go to carry out a ritual. We don't have much time."

The officer nodded, understanding the gravity of the situation. Jack continued down the pier, his mind racing. He couldn't shake the feeling that he was on the edge of something monumental, something horrifying. The clues pointed to a desperate man, willing to go to any lengths for a twisted sense of salvation.

As he walked, the words from the notebook echoed louder in his mind, a haunting refrain that drove him forward. The sea lapped quietly against the wooden pilings, the waves whispering secrets he was desperate to uncover. Jack's resolve hardened. He would stop John, not just to save Ethan, but to prevent the darkness from claiming another victim. The path ahead was fraught with danger, but Jack Palace was determined to see it through to the bitter end.

Chapter Twenty-Five

Cassandra Lane sat in her office, the air thick with the scent of old paper and stale coffee. The room was a chaotic mess of ambition and drive, a reflection of her own relentless pursuit of the next big story. Notes and photographs were scattered across the desk, and half-empty coffee cups lined the shelves, a snapshot of countless late nights spent chasing leads. The low hum of her computer screen was the only sound, filling the silence as she sifted through her latest findings.

Her sharp green eyes were glued to the monitor, scrolling through the notes from her recent interview with the nurse who had cared for Ethan Morrison. The conversation had been frustratingly vague, full of hints that danced around the truth but never quite landed. Yet Cassandra knew she was close—so close to the story that could catapult her to the top. John Morrison's case was a goldmine, and she wasn't about to let it slip through her fingers.

Her phone buzzed on the desk, pulling her attention away from the screen. She reached for it without hesitation, her heart skipping a beat as she saw the message notification. The number was unfamiliar, but that didn't matter. In her world, anonymous tips were the lifeblood of a groundbreaking story.

She opened the message, her eyes narrowing as she read:

John Morrison's next move will be linked to the river. Be there before the police. – An Insider.

A thrill shot through her. This was it—a fresh lead, a chance to get ahead of the competition and deliver the story everyone wanted. Cassandra's mind raced with possibilities. The riverbank? It was the perfect setting for another grim twist in the Morrison saga. She could already see the headline: *Morrison's Deadly Path— Exclusive Details from the Scene.*

The idea of being first on the scene, capturing the raw tension before anyone else, made her pulse quicken. She didn't stop to question the source of the message. The promise of a scoop was too tantalizing to resist.

Cassandra leaned back in her chair, a smile playing at the corners of her mouth as she began to plan. But before she could get too far, she was interrupted by the sound of footsteps approaching. It was Jeremy, one of her colleagues—a younger journalist still cutting his teeth on crime stories.

"Cass, you look like you've just hit the jackpot," Jeremy said, leaning against the doorframe. His casual tone couldn't mask his curiosity. Cassandra was known for her ruthless drive, and any sign of excitement from her usually meant something big was about to break.

She turned to him, her green eyes glinting with barely contained excitement. "I might have just got a lead that could blow this Morrison case wide open," she said, holding up her phone. "An anonymous tip. They're saying Morrison's next move is going to be by the river. If I can get there before the cops, it's going to be huge."

Jeremy raised an eyebrow. "The river, huh? That sounds ... ominous. You sure it's legit?"

Cassandra shrugged, her smile not wavering. "You never know with these things, but it feels real. And if it is, it's the kind of story that could put me on the map. I'm not about to let someone else get there first."

Jeremy nodded, a flicker of admiration in his eyes. "Well, you've got a nose for these things. Just be careful, okay? Morrison's not exactly the kind of guy you want to surprise."

"Don't worry," Cassandra said, waving off his concern. "I'm not about to rush in without thinking. I'll do some digging, maybe see if I can find anything else that backs up the tip. But if this pans out ..." She trailed off, letting the potential glory hang in the air.

Jeremy smiled, giving her a thumbs-up before heading back to his desk. Cassandra watched him go, her thoughts already spinning with possibilities. She needed to prepare, to get everything in place for when she made her move. There was no way she was letting this opportunity slip by.

Meanwhile, miles away, John Morrison sat in the front seat of the landlady's stolen car, a burner phone lying on the seat beside him. He stared at the screen, his mind cold and calculating. He had sent the message knowing exactly how Cassandra Lane would react. She was predictable, driven by ambition, blinded by the need to be first, to be the one who broke the story.

John smiled, a dark, twisted grin that didn't reach his eyes. He could see it all unfolding in his mind: Cassandra, rushing to the riverbank, thinking she was about to scoop the biggest story of her career, only to find herself tangled in a web she couldn't escape. He had no intention of meeting her tonight—no, that was too soon. But he was patient. He would let her think she was on to something, let her excitement build, until the time was right.

For now, the game was just beginning. And Cassandra Lane had just become another piece on his board, a pawn to be moved and manipulated as he saw fit. He didn't need to worry about her digging too deep—she would see what he wanted her to see, nothing more. When the time came, she would be exactly where he needed her to be.

Back in her newsroom, Cassandra was oblivious to the dark plans forming in John's mind. She was already preparing, gathering her gear, her heart pounding with anticipation. The thrill of the chase was intoxicating, and she was ready to dive in headfirst.

But for now, she would bide her time, doing the legwork, setting the stage. And when the moment came, she would be ready to capture the story of a lifetime—or so she thought.

Chapter Twenty-Six

John pulled off the main road and into the gravel car park of a small roadside café. The sign above the entrance read 'Millie's Diner', the faded letters barely legible against the peeling paint. The building itself was a relic from another era, with a rusted tin roof and windows that hadn't been cleaned in years. An old neon sign buzzed intermittently, casting an eerie green glow over the entrance.

Inside, the diner was a time capsule from the 1950s. Red vinyl booths lined the walls, their seats cracked and patched with duct tape. The tables were covered in yellowing Formica, each one adorned with a glass sugar dispenser and a chipped salt and pepper shaker. The linoleum floor was scuffed and worn, the pattern long since faded. The air was thick with the smell of stale coffee and frying bacon, mingled with a hint of mildew.

John shuffled to a booth near the back, his mind a chaotic whirl of thoughts. The whispers of The Five had grown quieter, but they were still there, lurking in the corners of his consciousness. He sank into the booth and buried his face in his hands, trying to shut out the noise.

A soft voice interrupted his reverie. "What can I get you, love?"

John looked up to see a waitress standing beside his table. She was in her late forties, with curly ginger hair pinned up in a messy bun. Her face was lined with age, but her green eyes sparkled with a kindness that seemed out of place in such a rundown diner. She wore a powder-blue uniform dress, cinched at the waist with a white apron that was smudged with flour and grease. A nametag on her chest read 'Ellen'.

"Just coffee," John muttered, not meeting her eyes.

Ellen nodded and walked away, her shoes squeaking on the linoleum floor. She returned a moment later with a steaming mug of coffee, setting it down in front of him with a gentle smile. "You look like you could use something stronger," she said, her voice tinged with concern.

John forced a weak smile. "Coffee's fine. Thanks."

Ellen lingered, her eyes studying him with a mixture of curiosity and sympathy. "You passing through, or are you headed somewhere specific?"

John hesitated, his mind racing for an answer that wouldn't raise suspicion. "Just passing through," he said finally. "Needed a break from the road."

She nodded, her expression softening. "I know how that is. Been working here for twenty years, seen all kinds of folks come and go. Some are running from something, others are searching for something. And some, well, they're just lost."

Her words hit John like a punch to the gut. He looked down at his coffee, the black liquid swirling in the mug like a dark vortex. "I guess I'm a little of all three," he admitted, his voice barely above a whisper.

Ellen's eyes filled with empathy. "We all get lost sometimes, love. The trick is finding your way back."

John looked up at her, his eyes haunted. "What if there is no way back?"

Ellen sighed, her gaze distant. "I lost my husband ten years ago. Cancer. For a long time, I didn't think I'd ever find my way back. But life has a way of surprising you. You just have to keep moving forward, one step at a time."

John nodded, her words resonating with a part of him

that he thought had long since died. "Thanks," he said quietly.

Ellen patted his hand. "Anytime, pet. You take care of yourself, okay?"

As she walked away, John stared into his coffee, the steam rising in ghostly tendrils. For a brief moment, the whispers of The Five were silent, and he felt a flicker of something he hadn't felt in a long time: hope.

He finished his coffee, left a few bills on the table, and stood up to leave. As he walked out of Millie's Diner and back into the harsh light of day, he felt a sense of determination settle over him. He didn't know what lay ahead, but he knew he had to keep moving forward, one step at a time. The path was uncertain, but for the first time in a long while, he felt like he might be able to find his way back.

John climbed into his car, the engine rumbling to life with a low growl. He glanced at the diner one last time, the empty car park stark against the fading afternoon light. Millie's Diner stood alone, an island of desolation on this forgotten stretch of road. As he adjusted his rearview mirror, his heart nearly stopped.

There they were. The Five. Their faces were pale and expressionless, eyes as dark as voids. They seemed to flicker in and out of existence, like shadows caught between worlds. John's breath caught in his throat, his hands trembling on the steering wheel.

"John," they whispered in unison, their voices merging into a single, eerie chorus. "She's alone. It's perfect. Think of Ethan. Think of your son."

John squeezed his eyes shut, trying to drown out their voices. But their words seeped into his mind, insidious and unrelenting.

"She's seen you, John," they continued. "You can't leave loose ends. This is the way. It's the only way. For Ethan."

He opened his eyes and stared at his reflection in the mirror, the ghosts of The Five hovering just behind him. His face was a mask of torment, the weight of their demands pressing down on him like an iron shroud.

He knew what they wanted. And deep down, a part of him understood. He couldn't let anyone interfere. He couldn't risk losing Ethan forever. With a resigned sigh, he cut the engine and stepped out of the car, the gravel crunching under his feet with each slow, deliberate step.

The diner door chimed softly as he re-entered. The warm scent of coffee and bacon hung in the air, a stark contrast to the cold resolve in his heart. Ellen looked up from behind the counter, her kind eyes lighting up with surprise.

"Back so soon?" she asked with a smile. "Did you forget something?"

John didn't answer. He walked slowly, methodically, towards her. The whispers of The Five grew louder, their words echoing in his mind like a sinister mantra.

"Do it, John. She's alone. It's perfect."

Ellen's smile faded as she saw the look in his eyes, a look of haunted resignation. She stepped back, her hands trembling. "Is everything okay?"

He stopped in front of her, his gaze fixed on the floor. "I'm sorry," he whispered, his voice breaking. "I have to do this. For Ethan."

Tears welled up in Ellen's eyes, but she didn't move. "Please, you don't have to do this. We can find another way."

But John was beyond reason. The whispers of The

Five were all he could hear, their demands driving him forward with a relentless force. He reached out, his hand shaking, and Ellen's face crumpled with fear and sorrow.

Outside, the world carried on, oblivious to the tragedy unfolding within Millie's Diner. The wind rustled the leaves, the sun dipped lower in the sky, and somewhere far away, a child's laughter echoed faintly on the breeze.

But in that small, forgotten diner, time stood still as John took the first step towards his dark and inevitable fate. The whispers of The Five had won, and in that moment, John knew there was no turning back. He was lost, a pawn in a game he barely understood, driven by a desperate hope that somehow, in the end, it would all be worth it. For Ethan.

John's heart pounded in his chest as he stepped closer to Ellen. The diner, once a sanctuary of warmth and comfort, now felt like a suffocating cage. The whispers of The Five were becoming a relentless drumbeat driving him to the edge of his sanity.

Ellen's eyes widened with fear, her back pressed against the counter as if she could somehow melt into it and disappear. "Please, you don't have to do this," she pleaded, her voice trembling.

But John couldn't hear her over the insistent commands in his mind.

In one swift, desperate motion, John lunged forward, the mug Ellen carried slipping from her grasp and clattering to the floor with a sharp crash. His hands found her throat, his fingers digging into the soft flesh with a force that surprised even him. The warmth of her skin, the feel of her pulse fluttering beneath his grip, made him hesitate for just a heartbeat.

But the whispers wouldn't allow him to stop.

"For Ethan," they chanted, relentless.

Ellen's eyes went wide with terror, her mouth opening in a silent scream. Her hands flew up, clawing at his wrists, her nails raking across his skin in a desperate attempt to break free. The pain was sharp but distant, as if it were happening to someone else. John's grip only tightened, his nails biting into her flesh. Tears blurred his vision, but he could still see the panic in her eyes, the disbelief, as the life drained from them, moment by agonizing moment.

Her struggles grew weaker, her movements more frantic and disjointed, sending a tray crashing to the floor, silverware clattering in every direction. The sound seemed to echo endlessly in the small space, mingling with the hiss of the coffee machine and the faint strains of music from the jukebox.

Ellen's lips moved soundlessly, forming words that never came. Her eyes pleaded with him, begging for mercy, but there was none left in him. The last vestiges of his humanity slipped away as her body gave one final, shuddering gasp. Her legs buckled beneath her, and she crumpled to the floor like a broken doll, her head striking the edge of the counter with a sickening thud.

John staggered back, his hands trembling uncontrollably. He stared down at Ellen's still form, the reality of what he'd done crashing over him like a tidal wave. Blood trickled from the corner of her mouth, pooling on the linoleum beneath her head, mixing with the shards of broken glass from the mug. Her eyes, once so full of life, were now empty, staring up at him with an expression frozen in horror.

He had crossed a line from which there was no return. The whispers fell silent, leaving a void filled only with the sound of his ragged breathing and the faint, distant wail of a siren approaching. The room seemed to close in around him, the walls pressing in, suffocating him with the weight of his actions.

John's knees buckled, and he collapsed into a booth, his head in his hands. The warmth of her skin still lingered on his fingers, a ghostly reminder of the life he had just snuffed out. He could feel the bile rising in his throat, the taste of acid burning his tongue. He had done it. He had killed again for Ethan.

But at what cost?

He stumbled out of the diner, the bell above the door chiming innocently as he exited. The world outside seemed unchanged, indifferent to the horror he'd left behind. The sun had dipped below the horizon, casting long shadows that seemed to reach out and clutch at him.

John climbed into his car, his body moving on autopilot. His mind was a storm of conflicting emotions—guilt, fear, and a grim resolve. He started the engine, the rumble a grotesque counterpoint to the silence that now enveloped him. He needed to get away, to a place near home, maybe to Beverley. The name of the town loomed large in his mind, a destination that somehow felt both ominous and inevitable.

The tires crunched over the gravel as he pulled onto the road, heading south. The route was a winding ribbon of asphalt cutting through the darkened countryside. Trees lined the road, their gnarled branches casting eerie shadows in the headlights. John's grip on the steering wheel was vice like, his gaze fixed on the road ahead but his mind replaying the scene in the diner over and over.

He drove past deserted fields and silent farmhouses, the landscape a blur of darkness and fleeting patches of moonlight. Each mile marker brought him closer to Beverley, but the destination felt like a lifetime away. The weight of his actions bore down on him, but the whispers had promised that it was the only way, the only path to see Ethan again.

As he approached the outskirts of Beverley, the town lights flickered on the horizon, a beacon in the night. John's heart was a leaden weight in his chest, his mind a tumultuous sea of regret and determination. He had no idea what awaited him in Beverley, but he knew he couldn't stop now. Not when he was so close. Not when Ethan's voice seemed just a whisper away.

The road stretched out before him, a dark and lonely path, much like the one he'd chosen. And as John drove towards whatever fate awaited him, the shadows seemed to close in, a silent testament to the darkness that had taken root in his soul.

John pulled into a quiet road on the outskirts of the town and put his seat back. He was exhausted. He checked on Ethan in the rearview mirror, then closed his eyes.

Chapter Twenty-Seven

The morning fog hung thick over Whitby, clinging to the town like a shroud. Jack Palace could barely see a few feet in front of him as he navigated the narrow cobblestone streets, the sea breeze biting at his face. The town was a maze of twisting alleys and ancient buildings, their weathered facades staring blankly at him through the mist. Whitby had always been a place that seemed to exist halfway between the past and the present, a town where history was as tangible as the stones beneath his feet.

Jack pulled his coat tighter around him as he approached the first location on his list: the harbour. The water was dark, almost black, lapping against the old wooden docks with a rhythmic, sinister slosh. He could hear the faint creaking of boats tethered to the pier, their masts swaying gently in the wind. Jack paused for a moment, staring out at the expanse of the North Sea, its surface churning with an almost malevolent energy. It was as if the ocean itself held secrets, whispering them to the town in the dead of night.

He turned to the group of local officers standing nearby, their faces etched with a mixture of determination and unease. These men were used to dealing with the oddities of Whitby—the strange weather, the occasional unexplained disappearance—but the fear that John Morrison was stalking their town had shaken them to their core.

"Alright, listen up," Jack said, his voice cutting through the mist like a knife. "We need to cover every inch of this harbour. I want you to split into teams and search the water's edge, the boats, and any nearby buildings. If you see John Morrison, don't approach him directly. Call it in and wait for backup. He's dangerous, and we can't afford any mistakes."

The officers nodded, their breath visible in the cold air. They moved out in pairs, their flashlights cutting through the fog as they began their search. Jack watched them for a moment before turning on his heel and heading towards the riverbank, the next location on his list.

The Esk River wound its way through Whitby like a dark ribbon, its surface smooth and still, reflecting the overcast sky. The banks were lined with reeds and old stone walls, remnants of a time when the river had been the lifeblood of the town. Now it seemed almost forgotten, a quiet place where shadows gathered in the corners and the silence was broken only by the occasional cry of a seagull.

Jack crouched by the edge of the river, his eyes scanning the water for any sign of disturbance. It was hard to shake the feeling that something was watching him, something old and malevolent lurking just beneath the surface. He shook his head, trying to focus. This was no time for superstition—he needed to find John before anyone else got hurt.

He barked orders to another group of officers, instructing them to search along the riverbank and check for any signs of recent activity. "Look for footprints, anything out of place," he said, his voice tense. "If he's been here, there'll be some kind of trace. But remember—stay sharp. He's not in his right mind, and he could be anywhere."

The officers nodded grimly and set off down the path that ran parallel to the river, their boots crunching on the gravel. Jack stayed behind, his eyes narrowing as he scanned the surrounding area. He felt like he was missing something, some crucial detail that was just out of reach. The frustration gnawed at him, a constant, dull ache that wouldn't let go.

After hours of fruitless searching, with no sign of John, Jack found himself standing near the mouth of the river where it spilled out into the sea. The sky was growing darker, the day slipping away, and the sense of urgency was mounting. He couldn't afford to let John slip through his fingers again.

It was then that a voice broke through his thoughts—a low, gruff voice with a Yorkshire accent thick as molasses. "You lookin' for somethin' particular, officer?"

Jack turned to see an old fisherman standing by a small boat, his weathered face creased with curiosity. The man was hunched, his hands rough and scarred from years at sea, but his eyes were sharp, glinting with a knowledge that only came from a lifetime in this town.

"Yeah," Jack replied, walking over to the man. "I'm looking for someone—a man named John Morrison. Have you seen anyone suspicious around here?"

The fisherman shook his head slowly, the brim of his cap casting a shadow over his eyes. "Can't say I have. But if it's strange goings-on you're interested in, you might want to have a word with Lydia Bone. She's the one who knows all the old stories and legends around here. If there's somethin' off, she'll know about it."

Jack felt a flicker of hope. "Where can I find her?"

"She lives up near the old church," the fisherman said, pointing towards the rising hill where the ruins of St. Mary's loomed. "But she'll likely be at the library now, cataloguing her bits and pieces. If anyone can tell you about the shadows in this town, it's her."

"Thanks," Jack said, already pulling out his phone. He dialled the number of one of the officers. "Get someone over to the library. Find Lydia Bone and bring her to the station. Tell her it's urgent."

The officer on the other end confirmed the order, and Jack hung up, his thoughts racing. Lydia Bone—he hoped she could shed some light on whatever was driving John, whatever had turned a once-loving father into a monster.

As Jack made his way back to the police station, he couldn't shake the feeling that time was running out. The mist seemed to thicken, the town closing in around him as he walked, the narrow streets winding like a labyrinth. Whitby felt alive, like a beast slowly waking from a deep slumber, and Jack was being drawn into its heart.

The police station was a squat, unremarkable building at the edge of town, its brick walls worn and weathered by years of salt air and wind. It was a place that had seen its share of trouble, but nothing like this. The front entrance was flanked by old iron railings, rusted and bent, and the windows were narrow, as if the building itself were trying to keep the darkness at bay.

Jack pushed open the heavy wooden door and stepped inside. The interior was just as dreary as the exterior— dim lighting, scuffed floors, and the faint smell of mildew that seemed to cling to everything. The place was a far cry from the bustling station in Hull, but it would have to do.

He made his way to the incident room, where maps of Whitby were spread out on tables, red pins marking the locations they had already searched. Officers were hunched over paperwork, the tension in the room palpable as they tried to piece together the puzzle of John Morrison's movements.

Jack sat down at one of the tables, his eyes scanning the maps. He had a sinking feeling that they were missing something—something crucial. And until Lydia Bone arrived, all he could do was wait and hope that the shadows hiding in Whitby would finally give up their secrets.

Some time later, he sat in the cramped interview room, the smell of stale coffee and damp paper permeating the air. The room was dimly lit, the overhead fluorescent light flickering with an annoying buzz that matched the relentless pounding in his head. He'd been up for nearly twenty-four hours straight, chasing a ghost through the winding streets and cliffs of Whitby, a town that seemed to breathe secrets from its ancient stone walls.

Across from him sat Lydia Bone, the local historian he'd contacted in desperation. She was a petite woman with sharp features and an even sharper intellect, her dark eyes gleaming with a mixture of curiosity and concern. She leaned forward, her fingers tracing the edges of an old leather-bound book she had brought with her—a tome that looked as ancient as the abbey ruins looming over the town.

"Jack," Lydia began, her voice soft but laced with urgency, "you asked me about 'The Five'. The origins of that myth are deeply rooted in the dark history of this region. We're talking about tales that go back centuries, whispered among fishermen and passed down through generations. The Five were said to be a group of men who made a pact with forces they barely understood. It was a twisted version of the Faustian bargain. They sought power, influence, and immortality—not in the traditional sense, but in a way that defied the natural order."

She paused, her gaze drifting to the book as if it held all the answers. "The legend says they were granted these things, but at a terrible cost. Their souls were bound to the waters of Whitby, cursed to roam the earth in search of others to join them, to feed the dark force that had granted them their desires. It's said that anyone who learns of their story and believes in their power can become susceptible to their influence. It's as much about belief as it is about the curse itself."

Jack nodded, absorbing the information, but a part of him struggled to reconcile this old-world superstition with the modern-day horrors John Morrison was unleashing. "So, you're saying John might have read this somewhere, maybe stumbled across the story, and in his grief and madness, started believing it?"

Lydia sighed, her fingers tapping the book lightly. "It's possible. People in a state of psychological distress can latch onto these kinds of ideas, especially if they're looking for some sort of meaning or explanation for their suffering. If John believed he was somehow connected to The Five, or even that he could resurrect them, it could explain his actions. But Jack ..." She hesitated, her eyes searching his face. "There's something more to this. These stories—they've persisted for a reason. I'm not saying I believe in them, but you can't dismiss the power of belief itself. For John, this could be very real."

Jack leaned back in his chair, the leather creaking under his weight. His eyes drifted to the window and saw the sun beginning to rise, casting long shadows over the town. "I hear you, Lydia. But there's something about this that doesn't sit right with me. It's too convenient, too ... neat." He ran a hand through his hair, his mind churning with unease. "John was always a rational guy, a man of science. Even after the tragedy with Ethan, I can't see him just losing himself to some old legend. There might be something else—something we're not seeing yet."

Lydia tilted her head, considering his words. "Maybe you're right. But whatever it is, Jack, you need to be careful. If John truly believes in this, if he's convinced that he's part of something larger, he could be capable of anything."

Jack stood, the conversation leaving him more unsettled than before. "I appreciate the history lesson, Lydia. It gives me something to work with, at least. But I've got to keep looking. John's out there, and every minute we waste could mean another life lost."

Lydia nodded, her expression grave. "Good luck, Jack. And if you need anything else, you know where to find me."

Jack left the station, the cold morning air biting at his skin as he joined the small army of officers combing through Whitby. They had scoured the coastline, the riverbanks, even the shadowy alleys that crisscrossed the town. Jack found himself standing by the harbour, the waters below churning restlessly against the ancient stone walls. The search was methodical, precise—every inch of the town was being covered. But something gnawed at Jack, a voice in the back of his mind whispering that they were missing the point.

As the day wore on and the search dragged into the afternoon, the tension among the officers grew. There were no signs of John, no traces of his passing, just the endless stretch of water that seemed to mock their efforts. Jack's phone buzzed with updates—nothing conclusive, nothing that brought them any closer to finding him.

He finally called it off, the frustration weighing heavy

on his shoulders. There was no point in continuing a fruitless search. The town was holding its breath, waiting for the next strike, and Jack knew they couldn't keep chasing shadows.

As he walked back to his car, the grey clouds overhead thickening, Jack made a decision. It was time to head back to Hull, regroup, and figure out the next move. He'd got nowhere in Whitby, just a history lesson that left him with more questions than answers and a gut feeling that John was playing a much more dangerous game than they realized.

Jack slid into the driver's seat, his fingers gripping the steering wheel. The image of John's face, once full of warmth, now twisted by madness, haunted him. And Lydia's words echoed in his mind. If John truly believed he was part of something greater—something dark and ancient—then they were dealing with more than just a man gone mad.

As he started the car and pulled away from the town, heading back towards Hull, Jack couldn't shake the feeling that they were running out of time. Whatever John was planning, it was far from over. And the next time they crossed paths, Jack feared it would be in the shadow of something far more sinister than a simple case of grief and delusion.

Chapter Twenty-Eight

John entered the Screwfix store located in the industrial estate of Beverley, the fluorescent lights casting a harsh glow on the rows of neatly organized shelves. The air smelled of metal and sawdust, a scent that reminded him of simpler times, before everything had spiralled into this nightmare. His mind was a fog of despair, the whispers of The Five a constant hum in the background, now interspersed with thoughts of ending it all. He felt like he was drowning, caught between the haunting memories of Ethan and the monstrous acts he'd committed.

The store was quiet, save for the occasional clinking of tools and the low murmur of the radio playing a classic rock station. John wandered the aisles, his movements slow and deliberate, as if in a trance. He picked up a heavy-duty screwdriver, its cold, metal handle feeling solid in his trembling hand. He added padlocks to his basket, their weight a small but tangible burden. Finally, he selected a long length of chain, the clinking links echoing ominously in the quiet store. Each item was a step closer to the end, a part of the plan that had taken shape in his tormented mind.

At the counter, the cashier gave him a polite nod, completely unaware of the turmoil behind John's hollow eyes. John forced a weak smile as he paid, the transaction feeling surreal, like he was watching someone else perform these mundane tasks. The plastic carrier bag felt unnaturally heavy as he left the store, the automatic doors sliding shut behind him with a soft whoosh.

John Morrison stepped out of the Screwfix store, the plastic bag in his hand rustling softly in the cool breeze. He glanced up at the sky, overcast with a thick blanket of clouds that threatened rain. The day was grey, washed out, and cold—perfect, he thought, for what he had in mind.

Inside the bag, the weight of the screwdriver, chain, and padlocks felt heavier than it should have. Each item was a step closer to something he had never wanted to become, a man teetering on the edge of humanity, driven by forces he could barely control. But John had convinced himself long ago that this was no longer about choice. Choice had been stripped away from him, peeled back layer by layer until all that remained was a raw nerve, throbbing with pain and rage.

Outside, the industrial estate was a maze of large, grey buildings, their utilitarian design a stark contrast to the chaos in John's mind. Rows of delivery trucks and cars were parked haphazardly, the faint sound of machinery droning in the background. The sky was overcast, casting a dull, oppressive light over the scene. It felt like the world was mirroring his internal despair.

As he walked across the car park, his footsteps echoing off the asphalt, John pulled out his phone and finished typing the message to Cassandra Lane. He had chosen his words carefully, cloaking them in the veneer of anonymity. He pretended to be an insider, someone who knew John Morrison's every move.

John Morrison will be at the Humber Bridge by nightfall. Be there if you want the scoop of a lifetime.

He paused for a moment before pressing send, his thumb hovering over the screen. There was a part of him, deep down, that still clung to a sliver of humanity. A part of him that recoiled at the thought of what he was planning. But that part had grown quieter over the past weeks, drowned out by the deafening roar of his grief and anger.

He sent the message and slipped the phone back into his pocket, feeling a pang of regret that quickly twisted into something darker. Cassandra Lane had been relentless in her pursuit of him, twisting the truth to suit her narrative, painting him as a monster in the eyes of the world. Maybe she was right. Maybe he had become the very thing she wrote about in her articles.

But it hadn't always been like this. John could still remember a time when he was just a man—a husband, a father. When his days were filled with warmth and laughter, when the only battles he fought were against the mundane trials of everyday life. But that life was gone, torn away by something that felt like fate, though it was far more insidious. And now Cassandra Lane had chosen to write his story for him, to turn his tragedy into a spectacle, feeding it to her readers as just another headline.

John's hands tightened around the bag. He could feel the roughness of the chain through the thin plastic, the cold metal of the padlocks, and he imagined them around Cassandra's wrists, her ankles. He imagined the terror in her eyes as she realized the truth, that she had become part of the very story she had been so eager to exploit.

A wave of sadness washed over him, mingling with the rage that had taken root in his heart. He hadn't wanted to hurt anyone—not really. But life had cornered him, pushed him to this point where the only way forward was through the bodies of those who had wronged him, at least by his fractured thinking, and if not wronged him, those that stood in the way of what he desired, what he needed: Ethan. He had tried to be strong, to hold on to the remnants of the man he used to be, but each death had chipped away at that resolve, leaving something hollow and desperate in its place.

Cassandra had lied about him, twisted his story into something grotesque, and for what? For a few more clicks on her articles? For a fleeting moment of fame? John's jaw clenched as he imagined her smirking behind her keyboard, safe in the knowledge that she was untouchable. But she wasn't untouchable. No one was.

If he had to kill her, then so be it. If his hands were already stained with blood, what difference would one more life make? The thought sickened him, but it also filled him with a grim determination. Cassandra had made herself part of his story, and now she would face the consequences.

As he walked, the people around him blurring into a meaningless background, John felt a strange sense of calm settle over him. He had a plan, and he would see it through to the end. There was no turning back now.

The Humber Bridge loomed in his mind like a dark promise, and by nightfall, he would be there, waiting. Waiting for Cassandra to arrive, drawn by her own curiosity and ambition, never suspecting that she was walking into a trap.

And when it was all over, when her lies had finally caught up with her, maybe then John would find some measure of peace. Or maybe he would finally lose himself completely, the man he used to be nothing more than a distant memory, swallowed whole by the darkness.

But that was a problem for later. For now, there was only the plan, the weight of the bag in his hand, and the cold certainty that Cassandra Lane wouldn't be writing any more lies about him. Not after tonight.

With a final glance at the cloudy sky, John continued

walking, his footsteps steady and sure as he headed towards his inevitable confrontation with the woman who had dared to make his pain her story.

As John approached his car, he noticed a burly tradesman standing nearby, glaring at him. The man was dressed in overalls, his muscular frame suggesting a life of physical labour. His face was red with anger, and his fists were clenched at his sides. John's heart skipped a beat, a pang of anxiety shooting through him. He quickened his pace, his mind racing with how to explain Ethan's condition if it came to that.

The tradesman seemed to sense John's unease and took a step forward, his glare intensifying. "Oi, you! What's your problem?" he shouted, his voice echoing off the concrete walls of the buildings around them.

John clutched the plastic bag tighter, his knuckles turning white. "Nothing, I … I'm just leaving," he stammered, his voice barely above a whisper.

The tradesman, a hulking figure of a man, stood at about six feet four with broad shoulders and a chest that seemed to barrel outward, sculpted from years of hard labour. His hands were calloused, the kind that had seen countless hours gripping tools and lifting heavy loads. His face was rugged, marked by deep lines and a permanent scowl that hinted at a life of hardships. His brown eyes burned with a fierce intensity, and a thick beard streaked with hints of grey framed his weathered face. His overalls, once a vibrant blue, were now splattered with paint and grease stains, a testament to the countless jobs he'd tackled. His name was Trevor Higgins, and he had a reputation in Beverley as a man who didn't back down from a fight. He was a father of three, with a temper as fiery as his love for his kids.

Trevor had started his day early, delivering supplies across the industrial estate. He had just pulled over for a quick break, sipping on a lukewarm coffee from his thermos, when he noticed the car and the frantic man. Something about the way John had been talking to himself had piqued Trevor's curiosity, and when he spotted the baby in the backseat, alarm bells went off in his head.

Trevor marched towards John, pointing angrily at the car. "Hey! What the hell is wrong with you? There's a baby in there, and he doesn't look well at all!"

John's heart pounded, but he tried to keep his voice steady. "I'm helping him. He's ... he's sick. I'm taking care of him." He tightened his grip on the screwdriver inside the bag, hoping the situation would de-escalate.

"Helping him?" Trevor's voice rose, incredulous and furious. "You call locking a baby in a car helping him? You're out of your mind!" He advanced on John, his eyes wild with rage. "I'm calling the police right now, and if you try anything, I'll make sure you regret it!"

Before John could respond, Trevor grabbed him by the throat and shoved him against the side of the car. The impact knocked the wind out of him, and for a moment, John's vision blurred. The tradesman's grip was tight, his face inches from John's, teeth bared in a snarl.

In a flash of desperation, John dropped the bag but kept hold of the screwdriver. His movements were quick and driven by a primal instinct to survive. With a swift motion, he drove the screwdriver into Trevor's side. The first strike elicited a grunt of pain, and the tradesman's grip loosened. John struck again and again, the screwdriver plunging into flesh with sickening precision. Trevor's eyes widened in shock and agony with each thrust, his strength ebbing away.

The tradesman staggered back, blood seeping through his overalls. He clutched his side, trying to stem the flow, but his efforts were futile. He fell to his knees, gasping for breath, his eyes fixed on John with a mixture of disbelief and pain.

John's mind was a maelstrom of horror and guilt, yet a dark, cold resolve gripped him. He had crossed another line from which there was no return. The whispers of The Five were a deafening chorus in his mind, their approval almost palpable. He took a step back, his breath coming in ragged gasps, the screwdriver slick with blood still clutched in his hand.

Without another glance at the dying man, John scrambled to his car. He threw the bloodied screwdriver onto the passenger seat, started the engine, and peeled out of the car park. The industrial estate blurred past him, a monotonous landscape of grey buildings and lifeless machinery. He drove with a single-minded focus, the road a dark ribbon unfurling towards the horizon.

The route out of Beverley was a winding path, the overcast sky casting long shadows that seemed to claw at the car as it sped past. Trees lined the road, their branches like skeletal fingers reaching out to snare him. John's thoughts were a chaotic whirlpool of fear, guilt, and the ever-present whispers promising that this was all for Ethan. His hands gripped the steering wheel with a vice-like intensity as he tried to outrun the demons nipping at his heels.

He drove for what felt like hours, the monotonous thrum of the engine and the rhythmic beat of the tires against the asphalt his only companions. Finally, John's path to familiar safety came into view, a patchwork of old stone buildings and narrow streets. John's heart raced as he navigated the labyrinthine roads, searching for a place to hide, to think, to make his final move. The cold reality of his actions pressed down on him like a weight, but the whispers wouldn't let him rest. They urged him onward, promising that there was no turning back now.

Chapter Twenty-Nine

Cassandra Lane sat at her cluttered desk in the dim light of her cramped flat, her eyes scanning the latest draft of her article with a mix of satisfaction and exhaustion. She wore a fitted dark green blouse that brought out the sharpness in her emerald eyes, and a pair of black jeans that clung to her lean figure. A half-empty cup of coffee sat beside her, the steam long gone, leaving only the cold, bitter dregs. The flat was a chaotic blend of work and life, with stacks of newspapers, notebooks, and random personal effects strewn across every available surface.

She pushed a strand of hair behind her ear, tapping the pen against her lip as she considered the closing line of her piece. It was a good one—maybe one of her best. The kind that would grab her readers by the throat and refuse to let go. John Morrison had become her ticket to the big leagues, the story that could catapult her from just another crime reporter to a household name. Every new twist, every new detail she could dig up was another step up the ladder.

But something gnawed at her as she stared at the words on the screen. A sense of unease that she couldn't quite shake, like the feeling of being watched from the shadows. She had always prided herself on her instincts, her ability to sniff out a story, but this case—this man—was different. There was something about John Morrison that didn't fit neatly into the box she had created for him. Something that made her skin crawl.

Her phone buzzed, jolting her out of her thoughts. She reached for it, her fingers brushing against the cold metal of the padlocks she had been using as paperweights—a souvenir from a previous story about an old asylum. A chill ran down her spine, a reflexive reaction she quickly dismissed as she unlocked her phone.

The message flashed on the screen, simple and direct:

John Morrison will be at the Humber Bridge by nightfall. Be there if you want the scoop of a lifetime.

Cassandra's heart skipped a beat, her pulse quickening as she read the message again, and then a third time to be sure she hadn't imagined it. This was it—this was the break she'd been waiting for. An anonymous tip, right out of the blue, promising her the kind of exclusive that journalists dreamed of. And all she had to do was show up.

She didn't hesitate, didn't question the source. This was her world, after all, a world where information was currency, and the only thing that mattered was who had it first. She could practically see the headline now: *Reporter Outruns Cops to Find Fugitive at Humber Bridge.*

A smile curled on her lips as she grabbed her bag, tossing in her notepad, voice recorder, and a small camera she always kept ready. She slipped on a black leather jacket that hung by the door, its sleeves cracked and worn from countless nights spent chasing stories through the darkened streets of Hull. The jacket was like armour to her, a shield against the cold and the doubts that sometimes crept in when the world outside grew too quiet.

She paused for a moment, looking around her flat as if she were seeing it for the last time. The clutter, the disarray—it all felt oddly comforting, a reflection of the chaotic life she had chosen for herself. But that didn't matter now. What mattered was the story, the chance to capture John Morrison in the flesh, to see the man behind the headlines she had so carefully crafted.

Cassandra's thoughts raced as she slid her phone into her pocket and headed for the door. She needed to get there before anyone else—before the cops, before her competitors, before Morrison himself had a chance to slip away again. The thrill of the chase coursed through her veins, driving her forward with a single-minded focus that had served her well in the past.

But as she locked the door behind her and started down the stairs, a sliver of doubt crept into her mind, an instinctual warning she couldn't quite place. Was this too easy? Too convenient? She pushed the thought aside. This was the nature of the job—risk and reward, danger and glory. And right now, the reward was too great to ignore.

Reaching the street, she pulled her jacket tight against the evening chill, her breath visible in the cold air. The sun was beginning to dip below the horizon, casting long shadows across the pavement. She could already picture herself standing on the Humber Bridge, camera in hand, capturing the moment when John Morrison emerged from the darkness.

Cassandra's hand hovered over her phone, contemplating who to call, who to share this breakthrough with. The newsroom? A colleague? She decided on Mark, her editor and occasional drinking buddy. He'd want in on this, she was sure of it.

She dialled his number, her fingers trembling slightly with excitement. As she waited for him to pick up, she allowed herself a moment to savour the anticipation, the knowledge that she was about to scoop every other reporter in the city.

"Mark," she said, the words tumbling out in a rush

when he finally answered. "You won't believe the tip I just got. John Morrison—at the Humber Bridge. Tonight. We need to be there."

His response was laced with scepticism, but she could hear the interest in his voice. "Are you sure about this, Cass? Could be a setup."

"Of course I'm sure," she replied, her tone leaving no room for doubt. "This is the real deal. I can feel it. We can't miss this."

There was a pause on the other end, then a sigh. "Alright, I'll get a team ready. But be careful, okay? If this guy really is there, it could get messy."

"Messy is where I thrive," Cassandra said with a grin, ending the call before he could argue further. She tucked the phone away, her mind already running through the logistics of the evening.

She'd head out soon, but not just yet. She needed to prepare, to make sure everything was in place. Tonight would be the climax of the story she had been building, the moment when all the pieces came together. And she would be the one to tell it.

As she stood there, the city bustling around her, Cassandra Lane felt a strange sense of exhilaration. The kind of exhilaration that came from standing on the precipice of something big, something that could change everything. The thought of John Morrison lurking in the shadows didn't frighten her—it thrilled her.

But somewhere, buried deep beneath the layers of ambition and bravado, a quiet voice whispered that she was walking into something far more dangerous than she realized.

Chapter Thirty

Jack Palace was driving back to Hull, the grey clouds overhead mirroring his sombre mood. The countryside zipped past his window, green fields and the occasional farmhouse providing a brief respite from his thoughts. The distant sheep, grazing lazily in the misty drizzle, the rhythm of the road, the hum of the tires, it all blended into the background as he replayed the case in his mind.

John Morrison, a man unravelled by grief, had become a spectre haunting Jack's every waking moment. The connection to The Five and the cryptic notes about rituals and offerings gnawed at him. The violence, the blood, the desperate need to bring Ethan back—it all painted a chilling picture of a father driven beyond the brink of sanity. Jack couldn't shake the image of John's last entry: *The offering must be made over water.* It was like a puzzle piece that refused to fit, and it gnawed at him incessantly.

Jack's thoughts drifted to the first time he had set eyes on John, watching the CCTV playback at the hospital. He had been a shell of a man, hollow-eyed and gaunt, wearing his grief like a second skin. At the time, Jack had dismissed his oddities as the result of unimaginable loss, something he couldn't truly understand but could empathize with. Now he realized that beneath that grief had been a festering madness, one that had finally consumed him.

His phone rang, jolting him from his thoughts. The ringtone was sharp and grating, a far cry from the calm of the countryside outside. He fumbled for it on the passenger seat, his pulse quickening.

"Palace," he answered, trying to keep his voice steady.

The voice on the other end was urgent. "Detective Inspector Palace, we've got a situation in Beverley. A man was attacked after confronting another man with a sick-looking baby in his car. The attacker fits the description of John Morrison."

Jack's heart skipped a beat, a cold dread settling in the pit of his stomach. "Where exactly?"

"Industrial estate, near the building merchants."

Jack didn't hesitate. He turned on his sirens, the wail piercing through the tranquil countryside, and pressed down hard on the accelerator. The engine roared as the car surged forward, eating up the miles between him and Beverley. The urgency in his chest was palpable, a driving force propelling him faster.

As the car sped through the winding roads, Jack's thoughts raced just as quickly. The image of John, wild-eyed and desperate, flashed in his mind. He could almost see the man's hands trembling, the madness etched deep into his features. How had it come to this? How had a loving father turned into a killer? Jack's grip on the steering wheel tightened, his knuckles turning white as his thoughts spiralled.

"Any other details on the victim?" Jack asked, his voice steady but intense. He needed to focus, to drown out the gnawing fear with facts, with the cold, hard details of the case.

"The tradesman is in critical condition. Witnesses say the attacker drove off in a dark-coloured saloon. We're pulling CCTV footage now."

Jack's mind raced as he sped towards the scene. Each word from the officer felt like a punch to the gut. He had been so close, so damn close to catching John, and now another person might pay the price for his failure. The thought of John slipping through his fingers fuelled his urgency. He had to catch him before more blood was shed.

The landscape blurred past, a mix of industrial greys and green fields. The outskirts of Beverley soon came into view, the industrial estate looming ahead, a world away from the bucolic countryside he had just left. The buildings were hulking, featureless structures, each one blending into the next, creating a cold, impersonal labyrinth. The kind of place where bad things happened, hidden from the warmth of the world outside.

Jack's siren wailed, cutting through the din of machinery and the muted hustle of the industrial landscape. Workers on their smoke breaks looked up, their expressions a mix of curiosity and unease as the police car barrelled through the narrow streets. The overcast sky cast everything in shades of grey, the same dismal hue that seemed to cloud Jack's thoughts.

He arrived at the hardware store, the scene already cordoned off with police tape. Officers moved with a sense of urgency, their faces grim. The flashing lights of ambulances and squad cars bathed the scene in a harsh blue glow. Jack parked his car and stepped out, the air thick with tension.

"Detective Inspector Palace," he said, flashing his badge at the officer on duty.

The officer, a young man with a nervous energy about him, nodded quickly. "Sir, we've got the CCTV footage. The car's already been identified. We're tracking it now."

Jack nodded, his eyes scanning the scene. The area was a chaotic blend of concern and action. Paramedics hovered over a stretcher, their hands moving rapidly as they worked on the victim. Jack caught a glimpse of blood-stained clothing, a flash of pale skin, and then they were loading him into the ambulance, the doors slamming shut with a finality that made Jack's heart sink.

"How's the victim?" Jack asked, his voice tight.

"In critical condition, sir. Paramedics are with him. They're about to rush him to Hull Royal."

Jack's jaw tightened, a bitter taste filling his mouth. He watched the ambulance, its siren joining the cacophony of noise that filled the air. Another life hanging by a thread, another casualty in a case that seemed to grow darker with every passing hour.

"I need to see that footage," Jack said, his tone brooking no argument.

As they moved towards the makeshift command post, Jack couldn't shake the feeling that time was slipping through his fingers. Every second that passed was another opportunity for John to disappear, to carry out whatever twisted plan he had in mind. The ritual, the offering over water—none of it made sense, and yet it all seemed to be leading to something terrible. Something Jack wasn't sure he could stop.

The officers worked quickly, their movements a blur as they brought up the footage. Jack's eyes narrowed as he watched the grainy images play out on the screen, his mind racing to connect the dots. He had to find John, had to stop him before this nightmare claimed another victim.

And as the footage showed a dark-coloured saloon speeding away from the scene, Jack felt a cold dread settle over him. The chase was on, and he wasn't sure who would be the hunter and who would be the hunted.

The grey clouds above seemed to press down even harder, as if the sky itself was closing in on him. Jack took a deep breath, steeling himself for what lay ahead.

There was no turning back now. He had to find John Morrison before the madness consumed them all.

Chapter Thirty-One

John gripped the steering wheel tightly, the leather creaking under the pressure of his hands. The narrow, winding road to the Humber Bridge seemed to stretch on forever, the headlights of his car carving twin tunnels through the darkness. The rain had started again, a steady drizzle that blurred the world outside into a smeared canvas of grey and black.

His mind was a roiling storm of thoughts, each one crashing into the next with relentless fury. He had planned everything so perfectly, every step leading up to Cassandra Lane, the fifth and final piece in his twisted puzzle. The one who deserved it most, the one who had spread lies and painted him as a monster. She was supposed to be the last, the grand finale to the macabre symphony he had orchestrated.

But that man … that stupid man in the car park had ruined everything.

John's breath came in ragged gasps as he replayed the scene in his mind, over and over, the way it had all gone so wrong. He had just wanted to make a quick stop, just needed to pick up a few supplies, when the man had approached him. Some middle-aged nobody trying to play the hero, trying to stop him. It had all happened so fast, too fast for John to think, to adjust his plan. And then, in a blur of rage and panic, he had done it. He had killed the man.

And now … now he had crossed that line. The one he had set for himself. The five lives that were supposed to bring Ethan back, that were supposed to balance the scales and make everything right again.

John's fingers trembled as he reached for the radio,

flicking it on and off, the static a brief, harsh interruption in the silence. He couldn't focus, couldn't calm the raging thoughts that tore through his mind. Ethan was supposed to be alive. That was the deal. Five lives for one. Five people to atone for the loss of his son. But now there were five, and Ethan was still gone.

"Five …" he muttered to himself, his voice a cracked whisper in the enclosed space of the car. "Five … but it's not right … It wasn't supposed to be like this."

The man in the car park wasn't supposed to count. He wasn't part of the plan. But the blood on John's hands said otherwise. It was done, and there was no taking it back. The weight of it pressed down on him, a suffocating pressure that made it hard to breathe, to think. He could see the man's face in his mind, twisted in fear and pain, a face that wasn't supposed to be part of this.

Ethan was still dead. Still cold and lifeless. No matter how many lives John took, no matter how many people he offered up, it wouldn't change the fact that his son was gone. That realization was like a knife to the gut, twisting and tearing until there was nothing left but raw, bleeding anguish.

"Why … why isn't it working?" he hissed through clenched teeth, his vision blurring as tears of frustration and rage welled up in his eyes. "Why isn't he coming back?"

The car veered slightly as John's grip faltered, the tires skidding on the wet road. He barely noticed, his mind consumed by the chaotic whirl of thoughts and emotions. The bridge was close now, looming in the distance like a spectre, a long, dark silhouette against the night sky.

Cassandra Lane was supposed to be the last. She was supposed to be the one to make it all right. She was the one who had made him into this, who had twisted the truth and painted him as a madman. But now … now she was just another face in the nightmare, another name on the list.

John slammed his fist against the dashboard, the pain a brief, welcome distraction from the torment in his mind. The anger was growing again, that familiar, seething rage that had driven him this far. It was all her fault. Cassandra had started this with her lies, and she would pay for it. She had to.

The events of the day replayed in his mind, a relentless, torturous loop that he couldn't escape. The image of Ethan, pale and cold in the hospital bed, haunted him with every breath. The lifeless body of the priest, crumpled at his feet like a discarded rag doll, the bloodied face of the landlady, contorted in agony, the homeless man beaten and bloody, and the innocent waitress who had only showed John kindness—everything was a haze of horror and regret. Each memory felt like a knife twisting deeper into his already shredded soul.

Tears streamed down John's face, blurring his vision as he stared into the abyss ahead. He was trembling not just from the cold but from the overwhelming despair that threatened to consume him. His heart pounded in his chest, a wild, frantic beat that matched the desperation in his voice as he suddenly screamed into the emptiness, "Why is my Ethan not alive?! I did what you asked? You lied!" His voice echoed in the confines of the car, raw with despair and seething with anger, the weight of his actions crushing him from within. The words hung in the air, bitter and accusatory, as if daring the night itself to answer him.

He had done everything they asked, made every sacrifice, crossed every line he thought he would never cross. And yet Ethan remained cold and still, a haunting reminder of his failure. The thought gnawed at him, tearing at the fragile remnants of his sanity. His love for his son, once pure and unyielding, had become a twisted, desperate thing, driving him to unspeakable acts in the name of a hope that now seemed cruelly out of reach.

The silence that followed his outburst was oppressive, thick with unspoken dread. John's hands tightened on the wheel, his mind spiralling into darker and darker places. He was so lost in his thoughts that he almost didn't notice when something changed in the air around him—a subtle shift, like the world itself was holding its breath.

Suddenly, an invisible force gripped his throat with ferocious strength. John's hands flew to his neck, trying to pry away the unseen fingers that tightened like a vice. His car swerved dangerously on the narrow road, tires screeching against the asphalt as he struggled to breathe. The darkness outside seemed to close in, pressing against the windows as if it were alive, as if it were watching.

He gasped for air as panic set in. His heart pounded in his ears, loud and frantic, drowning out the sound of the engine as it sputtered in protest. The world around him began to spin, the edges of his vision darkening as his consciousness began to slip away. He clawed at his throat, his nails digging into his own flesh in a desperate attempt to fight off the unseen attacker. But there was nothing to grasp, nothing to fight against.

A growling hiss whispered into his ear, so close that he could feel the cold breath on his skin. The voice of The Five, now answering him directly, was a low, menacing murmur that sent chills down his spine.

"We do not lie, John," the voice hissed, each word dripping with malice. "You should be kinder, John. You lie, John! You owe us one more, John!"

The words wrapped around him like a noose, tightening with each syllable. The pressure around his neck intensified, and John felt himself teetering on the edge of consciousness. The world around him began to fade, the car, the road, everything slipping away into a suffocating darkness. He could feel his strength draining, his grip on reality weakening.

Then, as suddenly as it had begun, the grip loosened and disappeared entirely. John slumped forward, gasping for breath, his chest heaving with the effort. He could feel his heart racing, each beat a painful reminder that he was still alive, still trapped in this nightmare. The silence that followed was deafening, broken only by the rasp of his own laboured breathing.

His car's radio crackled to life, startling him out of his daze. The sudden noise was jarring after the suffocating silence that had filled the car moments before. "Lunchtime news," a man's voice announced cheerfully, as if oblivious to the horror that had just unfolded. "A man attacked at a hardware store is in a stable condition."

John's blood ran cold. The man he had stabbed was alive. The five were right—he still owed them one more. His mind raced as he tried to comprehend what this meant. He had thought his nightmare was nearing its end, but it was clear now that it was far from over.

John pulled the car over to the side of the road, the tires crunching on the gravel as he came to a stop. His body shook with uncontrollable sobs, his forehead resting on the steering wheel. The cold leather was a small comfort in his tumultuous world and the burning guilt and fear that consumed him. He had crossed every line, done the unthinkable, and yet he was still trapped in this hellish bargain.

"Please," he whispered, his voice breaking, barely audible in the stillness of the night. "Please let me see Ethan again."

But there was no answer, only the hum of the engine and the distant call of the night. The trees lining the road swayed gently in the breeze, their branches reaching out like skeletal hands, as if mocking his plea. The mist hung low over the fields, twisting and curling in the moonlight, creating ghostly shapes that danced just out of reach. The world around him felt unreal, like a twisted version of reality where nothing was as it seemed.

John wiped his tears and sat back, staring blankly at the road ahead. His thoughts were a swirl of fear, anger, and despair. He had no choice but to continue, to fulfil his grim obligation. The life of his son depended on it, and there was no turning back now.

With a deep, shuddering breath, John started the car again and pulled back onto the road, the weight of his actions heavy on his soul. The journey ahead was dark and uncertain, but he would see it through to the end, no matter the cost. The road stretched out before him, a long, winding path that seemed to lead deeper into the abyss. The night was far from over, and the whispers in his mind were louder than ever.

As he drove, the darkness closed in around him, the road ahead swallowed by the night. The trees seemed to lean in closer, their branches reaching out like claws, the shadows dancing just at the edge of his vision. The scent of damp earth and decaying leaves filled the car, mingling with the faint, metallic tang of blood that clung to his clothes. The wind howled outside, a mournful wail that echoed in the emptiness of his heart.

And somewhere, deep in the recesses of his mind, The Five waited, their whispers growing louder with every passing mile. They were always there, lurking in the shadows, waiting for him to fulfil his end of the bargain. There was no escape, no respite. Only the road ahead and the promise of more bloodshed to come, even if it was his own.

John's grip on the steering wheel tightened, his resolve hardening with each passing moment. He would do whatever it took, pay whatever price was demanded, to see his son's eyes open again. Even if it meant losing what little remained of his soul.

The night stretched on, endless and unforgiving, as John Morrison drove deeper into the darkness, the weight of his sins dragging him down with every mile.

Chapter Thirty-Two

Jack walked over to the yellow tape that cordoned off an area near the hardware store, the epicentre of chaos. He quickly approached the nearest officer, a tall, burly man with a stern face and a badge that read 'M. Davis'.

Constable Davis pointed towards the ambulance where paramedics were working on a man who was barely conscious, his overalls stained with blood. "Tradesman tried to stop the suspect, got stabbed multiple times. The suspect fled in a dark saloon car; witnesses say he headed south."

Jack nodded grimly and walked over to the paramedics. The ambulance was a small, cramped space filled with the scent of antiseptic and the hum of medical equipment. The victim, Trevor, lay on a stretcher, pale and breathing laboriously. His eyes were half-open, and he winced with each word as he recounted the attack.

"He ... he had this look in his eyes," Trevor gasped, each word a struggle. "Said he was helping the baby. Tried to explain ... but when I grabbed him ... he just ... snapped."

Jack leaned closer, his face a mask of concern and determination. "Did he say anything specific? Anything that might help us understand where he's going?"

Trevor shook his head weakly. "Just ... kept saying he was helping. Helping the baby."

Jack stood up, frustration gnawing at him. He needed more to go on. He turned to Davis. "Any sign of where he might have headed?"

"Nothing concrete yet, sir. We're checking CCTV from nearby businesses, but it's going to take some time," Davis replied, his expression mirroring Jack's sense of urgency.

Next to Davis, another officer, a young woman with auburn hair pulled back in a tight bun and a badge that read 'L. Price', was scribbling notes on a pad. Her eyes flicked up to meet Jack's.

"We've got units patrolling the main roads out of the industrial estate," Price said. "We'll catch him, sir."

Jack gave a tight nod, appreciating their diligence but knowing how elusive John Morrison could be. He turned back to the ambulance, looking at Trevor one last time.

"Hang in there, Trevor. You did good," Jack said, offering a small, encouraging smile before stepping away.

The scene was a chaotic mix of order and urgency. Officers moved purposefully, gathering evidence and coordinating the search. Jack knew they were doing everything they could, but the nagging fear that John was slipping further away gnawed at his insides.

Jack stood up, frustrated. He needed more to go on. He turned to the officer. "Any sign of where he might have headed yet?"

"Nothing sir. We are pursuing every possible camera in the area as well as ANPR cameras in the surrounding area."

Jack glanced at his car, the sirens still flashing. "We don't have time. I'm going to follow the route south. If he's trying to lay low, he might take back roads."

He jogged back to his car and started the engine, the roar matching the intensity of his focus. As he drove south, he kept his eyes peeled for any sign of John or his car. The road was a mix of industrial sprawl and open countryside, offering plenty of places to hide.

Jack drove away in his car, the notebook with John's manic scribblings still clutched tightly in his hand. His mind raced with possibilities, each darker than the last. As he started the engine and headed towards Beverley, he replayed Trevor's words over and over.

"Helping the baby."

What twisted version of help was John offering? The road ahead was fraught with uncertainty, but Jack's resolve was unshaken. He would find John. He had to. For Ethan's sake, and for the sake of everyone else in John's path. The siren wailed, piercing the tranquil countryside as Jack drove, the sound a grim reminder of the urgency propelling him forward.

As he drove, the radio crackled with updates from the station. Jack listened intently, hoping for any lead, any clue that would bring him closer to John. The weight of the case pressed heavily on him, but he knew he couldn't afford to falter. Lives depended on his ability to piece together the puzzle and stop John before it was too late.

Determined and focused, Jack continued down the winding roads, his eyes scanning every passing vehicle and his mind racing through the possibilities. He wouldn't rest until John was found and stopped.

Suddenly the radio came to life once more. A lane was being blocked on the Humber Bridge by an abandoned vehicle. "Fuck!" Jack thought to himself as he pushed his foot harder on the accelerator.

Chapter Thirty-Three

John's car came to a halt on the expansive Humber Bridge, its headlights slicing through the dense fog that rolled off the river below. The bridge, a colossal structure of steel and concrete, stretched out over the dark waters, deserted at this late hour. The mist from the river clung to the air, making the pathways slick and treacherous. The only sound was the distant hum of the city and the rushing water beneath, a steady, ominous whisper.

As John stepped out of the car, his breath visible in the frigid night air, he was greeted by a desolate, almost otherworldly silence. The cold bit into his skin, and the smell of damp metal and saltwater mingled in his nostrils. He moved around to the back, opening the door to where Ethan lay still and silent in his car seat. John's heart ached as he gently lifted his son, cradling him close. The smell, the lifelessness—it was almost too much to bear.

Walking to the middle of the bridge, John's footsteps echoed softly on the damp pavement. His mind was a swirl of grief, guilt, and the manic whispers of The Five. Each step felt heavy, burdened by the weight of his actions and the voices that urged him on. The fog thickened, and the bridge seemed to stretch endlessly, an abyss both literal and metaphorical.

John set Ethan down carefully on the cold, wet ground, his fingers trembling as he arranged his son with the tenderness of a father putting his child to bed. The sight of Ethan's lifeless body, small and vulnerable, was a knife to John's heart, twisting deeper with each second. He turned back to the car, his movements mechanical, driven by a grim determination. With no sign of Cassandra Lane, that lying, self-serving journalist, John knew what he now had to do.

As he retrieved the heavy chain and padlocks from the trunk, he could feel his sanity fraying at the edges. His mind was numb, the cacophony of The Five filling his thoughts, urging him on.

"It's perfect, John. No one is here. Think of Ethan. Think of your son," the voices cooed, a perverse comfort in their insistence.

Other cars began to appear through the fog, their headlights piercing the gloom. They swerved around John's stopped vehicle, horns blaring in protest, but he was oblivious to their presence. His world had narrowed to the bridge, the fog, and the voices.

John walked back to where Ethan lay, the chain clinking ominously in his hands. His face was a mask of resignation, his eyes hollow and haunted. The wind picked up, howling through the cables of the bridge, carrying with it the distant echoes of the city and the relentless rush of the river below.

He knelt beside Ethan, his fingers working with a cold efficiency as he wrapped the chain around himself. The padlocks clicked shut, their finality a bitter echo in the stillness. Tears streamed down John's face, mingling with the mist as he whispered a broken apology to Ethan.

As the fog thickened, enveloping them in its cold embrace, John's mind drifted. He was a man lost, driven to the edge by grief and desperation. The world around him seemed to fade, leaving only the bridge, the fog, and the dark water below. The whispers of The Five grew louder, a chorus of madness and sorrow, guiding him to his final act.

In that moment, John Morrison, a man once filled with love and hope, was consumed by the darkness. The bridge stood as a silent witness.

John wrapped one end of the chain around the sturdy railing of the bridge, threading it through and securing it with the padlocks. The metal clinked softly as he worked, a sound that seemed almost deafening in the stillness of the night. Each click of the padlocks echoed like a death knell in his mind. Once he was satisfied that the chain was secure, he turned back to Ethan, kneeling beside his son.

With trembling hands, John lifted Ethan again, holding him close to his chest. His tears fell freely now, mixing with the mist on his face. He whispered into Ethan's ear, his voice choked with emotion. "I'm sorry, my little man. I tried, I really tried. I want you back with me so much," John said, his voice breaking. "I'm doing this for you. For us. I don't know if it's right, but I don't know what else to do."

John's grip tightened around Ethan, his body wracked with sobs. He looked up at the dark sky, as if searching for some sign, some indication that what he was doing was not in vain. But the sky remained silent, offering no comfort or guidance. The only response was the relentless whispering of The Five urging him on.

He wrapped the remaining length of the chain around his own neck, securing it tightly. The weight of the chain was heavy, a physical manifestation of the burden he carried in his heart. He took a deep breath, feeling the cold metal pressing into his skin. His mind raced with the enormity of what he was about to do.

Then he saw her.

Standing a few feet away, partially obscured by the fog, was Sarah. She looked exactly as he remembered— beautiful, serene, and smiling. Her eyes sparkled with the love he had once found solace in. For a moment, the world seemed to stand still. John blinked, shaking his head, convinced that he was losing his mind.

"Sarah?" he whispered, his voice trembling. "Is it really you?"

Sarah's smile widened, a look of pure love and understanding on her face. She seemed to be glowing, an ethereal presence in the foggy night. John's heart ached with longing and despair. He knew this was a hallucination, a cruel trick of his tortured mind, but he couldn't look away.

"John," she said, her voice soft and soothing. "You don't have to do this. Come back to us."

John's knees buckled, the chain rattling around him. He buried his face in his hands, sobbing uncontrollably. "I don't know what to do," he cried. "I'm lost without you. I'm losing my mind."

The vision of Sarah reached out, her hand seeming to caress his face, though he felt nothing but the cold night air. "John, think of Ethan. Think of what he would want. You can't bring him back like this."

John lifted his head, his tear-streaked face contorted with anguish. "But I have nothing left. I can't live without you both."

Sarah's image began to fade, her smile bittersweet. "You have to find another way, John. Live for Ethan. Live for us."

As she disappeared into the mist, John felt a crushing sense of loneliness and despair. He knew she was right, but the whispers of The Five grew louder, more insistent. They spoke of the offering, of the ritual, of the promise that Ethan could be returned to him.

John stood there for a moment, his eyes closed, trying

to summon the courage to take the next step. The whispers in his mind were quiet now, replaced by a profound sense of sadness and resignation. He knew there was no turning back, no other path left for him to take.

"I love you, Ethan," he whispered, pressing a kiss to his son's forehead. "Always and forever."

With a final, deep breath, John turned towards the edge of the bridge. The fog swirled around him, the dark waters below calling to him like a siren's song. He stepped forward, the weight of the chain pulling him closer to the abyss, his mind a storm of conflicting emotions.

Chapter Thirty-Four

Cassandra Lane's heart pounded in her chest, a steady drumbeat that matched the roar of her car's engine as she sped down Beverley Road. The headlights of her silver Audi TT cut through the thickening fog that clung to the streets of Hull like a shroud, the sleek curves of the vehicle glistening under the dim streetlights. Her hands gripped the steering wheel with a mixture of excitement and nerves, the leather cool and smooth under her fingertips. The car, always immaculate, reflected her own meticulous nature—polished to a mirror shine, the interior spotless except for the scattered pages of her latest notes on the passenger seat.

She had the story of a lifetime within her grasp, and nothing was going to stop her from getting it. The Humber Bridge was less than twenty minutes away, and if she timed it right, she would have the exclusive that every journalist in the country would kill for—an interview with John Morrison, the man who had become a national obsession, the bogeyman of every parent's nightmare.

Her mind raced as fast as the car, thoughts tumbling over one another like children at play. She could see it all so clearly: the headline splashed across the front page, her name in bold letters just beneath it. ***Cassandra Lane: The Woman Who Faced the Monster.*** She imagined the talk shows, the book deals, the accolades. Her career, already on the rise, would skyrocket. She'd be the reporter who broke the story, who got inside the mind of the man who had terrorized the country. And all it would take was a little courage—and maybe a bit of luck.

She was halfway to the bridge when her phone rang,

vibrating against the dashboard. She snatched it up without taking her eyes off the road, her voice breathless with anticipation as she answered. "Mick, where the hell are you?"

"On my way," came the gruff reply from Mick, her trusty cameraman who had been with her through thick and thin. "Just left my flat. You really think he'll be there?"

"He'll be there," she insisted, her tone leaving no room for doubt. "This is our chance, Mick. We're going to catch him at the bridge. I need you to get there as fast as you can, set up the camera, and be ready. We're not going to have much time once he shows up."

Mick hesitated, his voice crackling with static. "Cass, you sure this is safe? I mean, this guy's dangerous. You've seen what he's done."

Cassandra's grip on the wheel tightened. "I know what he's done, Mick. And that's exactly why we need to be the ones to get this story. If we can get him on camera, if we can get him to talk … it'll be the biggest story of the decade. Trust me, Mick. We can do this."

There was a long pause on the other end of the line, then a resigned sigh. "Alright, alright. I'm on my way. Just … be careful, okay?"

Cassandra smiled, a tight, determined curve of her lips. "You too. See you at the bridge."

She hung up, tossing the phone onto the passenger seat, her eyes flicking up to the rearview mirror. The streets were empty, eerily quiet for a night like this. It was as if the city itself was holding its breath, waiting for something to happen.

Her route was clear in her mind—down Beverley Road, past the old brick buildings of the university, their dark windows staring blankly out into the night. She crossed the roundabout at Clough Road, the tires of her car hissing over the wet pavement as she sped towards the A63. The industrial sprawl of Hull faded into the background as she merged onto the dual carriageway, the river running parallel to her left, dark and glistening under the cloudy sky.

The bridge loomed ahead, a massive silhouette against the horizon, its tall towers disappearing into the fog that clung to the Humber like a ghost. Cassandra felt a shiver of excitement run down her spine as she approached, the adrenaline flooding her veins, sharpening her senses. She was so close now. So close to the story that would change everything.

But as she neared the turnoff for the bridge, her excitement soured into frustration. Blue lights flashed in the distance, the telltale signs of police presence at the bridge's entrance. Her heart sank as she saw the cordon stretched across the road, blocking any further access. The police had beaten her there.

Cassandra cursed under her breath, her foot easing off the accelerator as she approached the roadblock. She could see uniformed officers standing around, their faces lit up by the strobing lights. There was no way she was getting through—not without causing a scene. And she didn't have time for that.

As she pulled up to the cordon, her eyes narrowed, taking in the scene. The officers looked tense, alert, as if expecting something to happen. They were searching for him too, she realized. The man she had been so desperate to meet was now the most wanted person in the country. And they were just as eager to find him as she was.

Her heart skipped a beat as a familiar car pulled up

behind her with a screech of tires. She glanced in the side mirror and saw the stern face of Jack Palace as he stepped out of his vehicle, his expression as grim and determined as ever. He approached the cordon, exchanging hurried words with the officers, his gaze sweeping over the area with the practised eye of a seasoned detective.

Cassandra watched him, her mind racing. Jack Palace was here, which meant they were close—closer than she had ever been. But she had to play this smart. If she wanted her story, she couldn't afford to be sidelined by the police.

Taking a deep breath, she pushed open the door of her car and stepped out into the cold night air, pulling her coat tightly around her as she prepared to face whatever came next.

"Lane!" Jack's voice cut through the night air. "What the hell are you doing here?"

Cassandra looked up, startled but defiant. "I'm just following a lead. This is big, Palace. People deserve to know the truth."

"The truth?" Jack's eyes narrowed. "You're playing with fire. You're not just risking your own safety—you're endangering everyone involved in this case. Back off, or you'll find yourself in a world of trouble."

Jack stared at her for a moment, frustration and worry battling in his eyes. He knew he had to keep Cassandra away from the case, but he also understood that the media was a beast that couldn't be easily tamed.

Cassandra's lips twisted into a cynical smile. "You think I don't know the risks? I'm not afraid of a little danger. I'm after the truth, and nothing's going to stop me." This was her moment, and she wasn't going to let anyone, not even Jack Palace, stand in her way.

Chapter Thirty-Five

The sun was beginning to set, casting an orange glow across the sky and reflecting off the river below. The bridge loomed over the water, its cables stretching into the dusk like the strings of a giant, invisible harp. The air was cool, with a gentle breeze rustling the leaves of nearby trees, and the distant hum of traffic added a low, constant murmur to the scene.

The bridge was mostly empty, save for a few onlookers who had been kept at a distance by the police tape. Officers stood around, tense and alert, their eyes fixed on the solitary figure standing precariously on the edge.

The moonlight danced on the water, casting an eerie glow on the riverbank where Cassandra set up her equipment. Her heart was pounding with the thrill of the chase.

John's silhouette was stark against the twilight sky, his form hunched and defeated. He clutched Ethan's lifeless body tightly, the child's weight a cruel reminder of his desperation. John's clothes were dishevelled, his face gaunt and pale, eyes wide with a mixture of sorrow and madness.

The sky above was a mottled grey, heavy with the promise of rain. The clouds hung low, like a suffocating blanket, casting an oppressive gloom over the scene. Jack could feel the tension in the air, the gravel crunching under his boots as he made his way towards the chaos unfolding ahead. The wind whipped through the narrow streets, carrying with it the scent of wet asphalt and the distant tang of salt from the sea, a reminder of the unforgiving coast not far from where they stood.

Police cars, their blue and red lights flashing rhythmically, were parked haphazardly along the road leading to the bridge, forming an impromptu blockade. The vehicles themselves were streaked with dirt and rain, their polished surfaces dulled by the grimy drizzle that had begun to fall. The sirens had been cut, leaving an eerie silence that was only broken by the occasional crackle of radio static and the murmur of hushed conversations among the officers.

Jack raised his hands in a gesture of peace as he slowly approached, his breath visible in the chilly air. "John, what are you doing? It's not worth it. Come on, come back," he called out, his voice firm but laced with a compassion he barely felt. His heart pounded in his chest, the weight of the situation pressing down on him like the clouds overhead.

The barricades were makeshift but effective—metal barriers hastily pulled from the backs of police vans, now standing like sentinels at the bridge's entrance. Yellow caution tape fluttered in the wind, strung between the barriers and the cars, marking the perimeter with its garish warning. The bridge itself stood empty save for John, his silhouette stark against the leaden sky.

Jack turned to the nearest officer, a burly man with a thick moustache and a face that had seen too many long nights and hard days—Sergeant Williams. The man's eyes were sharp, but there was a weariness in them that spoke of years spent on the front lines of humanity's worst moments.

"Sergeant, increase the perimeter. No one else gets on or off until we get John back safely," Jack ordered, his voice cutting through the din.

Williams nodded, his expression grim. "Yes, sir," he

replied, immediately barking orders into his radio. The sergeant's voice was rough, a deep rumble that commanded attention. Other officers, including a young rookie with wide, nervous eyes and a senior officer whose steely gaze betrayed no emotion, moved quickly to follow the directive. The rookie's hands trembled slightly as he unrolled more caution tape, his breath coming in quick, shallow bursts. The older officer, in contrast, was a picture of controlled efficiency, his movements precise and deliberate as he helped erect additional barricades.

A small crowd of onlookers had gathered at a distance, their faces pale and drawn as they watched the drama unfold. They stood in a loose cluster, some huddling under umbrellas, others with rain-soaked coats pulled tight against the chill. The rain had begun to fall more steadily now, a fine mist that dampened everything it touched, beading on the police cars and turning the road into a slick reflective surface. The onlookers' cars, parked haphazardly along the road, were old and battered, their paint chipped and rusted in places, mirrors fogged by the moisture.

There was a low murmur among the crowd, a mix of fear and morbid curiosity. Whispers passed from person to person, speculations on what had driven John to the edge, but none of them dared to step closer. The air was thick with a sense of impending doom, the kind that made the hairs on the back of your neck stand up, the kind that told you something terrible was about to happen.

As Jack moved closer to the bridge, he could see the strain in John's eyes, the haunted look of a man pushed far beyond his limits. John's clothes were damp, clinging to his gaunt frame, and his hands trembled at his sides. The bridge beneath his feet groaned softly with the wind, a low, mournful sound that seemed to echo John's inner turmoil.

The breeze carried the faint smell of salt and dampness from the river below, mingling with the scent of car exhaust and the distant aroma of wet earth. It was a sensory assault, a reminder of the real world even as they stood on the brink of something otherworldly. Jack's pulse quickened, his mind racing with a thousand possible outcomes, none of them good.

He took a deep breath, steadying himself as he prepared to take the next step. The scene around him was a chaotic blend of urgency and dread, a tableau of human frailty laid bare under the relentless scrutiny of the cold, uncaring sky.

"John," Jack said softly, his voice carrying over the gentle rush of the wind. "I know you're hurting. I know it feels like there's no way out. But this isn't the answer. Let us help you."

John's eyes flickered with a moment of recognition and pain. "I can't. I can't do this anymore. Ethan ... he's gone, and it's my fault. I just want to be with him."

Jack took a careful step closer, his hands still raised. "I understand, John. But think about Sarah. Think about what she would want for you, for Ethan. She wouldn't want this."

John's face twisted in anguish, tears streaming down his cheeks. "I see her, Jack. I see her everywhere, and she's telling me to let go. To end this."

Jack's heart clenched, but he forced himself to stay calm. "That's not Sarah, John. That's your grief, your pain, talking. Sarah would want you to fight, to live. For Ethan's memory, for her."

John's grip on Ethan tightened, and for a moment,

Jack feared he would take the final step. But then John's shoulders slumped, a broken sob escaping his lips. "I don't know how to go on without them," he whispered.

Jack seized the moment, stepping closer until he was almost within reach.

John didn't turn to look at him. His gaze was fixed on the churning water far below, the dark depths calling to him. "I need him, but I don't know what's real anymore. Am I going crazy?" John's voice was broken, the words barely a whisper over the wind.

Jack took a cautious step closer, his eyes never leaving John. "We can get you help, John. There are people who can help you through this," he urged, his heart aching for the man before him.

John shook his head slowly, tears streaming down his cheeks. "It's gone too far. No one can help. I can't live without my family," he said, his voice cracking with despair.

Jack's mind raced, searching for something, anything, that could pull John back from the brink. "John, think about Ethan. Think about what he would want. This isn't the way," he pleaded, desperation creeping into his tone.

With a final, anguished look at Ethan, John laid him gently in a duffle bag he had brought. "I'm sorry, my little man. I tried, I really tried. I want you back with me so much," he whispered, kissing the boy's forehead.

The world seemed to slow as John's eyes met Jack's one final time, a fleeting connection that held a universe of torment. Jack opened his mouth to shout, to plead, but the words caught in his throat, strangled by the sudden rush of horror that seized him. Before he could move, before he could do anything but watch in stunned disbelief, John threw himself over the railing.

There was a sickening moment of silence, the kind that pulls the air out of your lungs, the kind that stretches into infinity. John's body arced gracefully, almost peacefully, for the briefest of instants before the chain around his neck snapped taut with a hideous, metallic clank. The sound reverberated through the bridge, a jarring contrast to the wet slap of his shoes hitting the water below, a final, mocking echo of life before it was snuffed out.

The chain bit into his flesh with brutal efficiency, carving deep, angry grooves into the pale skin of his neck as it halted his fall with a grotesque jolt. The force was enough to break his neck instantly, a loud, wet crack that seemed to shatter the frozen silence hanging in the air. His head lolled at an unnatural angle, eyes wide open but seeing nothing, the last vestiges of life snuffed out in a single violent moment.

The breeze that had been gentle only moments before now whipped around the bridge, stirring the loose ends of the yellow police tape, which flapped and twisted like dying things in the wind. The rain, which had been nothing more than a drizzle, began to pour in earnest, the drops pelting down on the scene with a relentless icy precision. The water below rippled and churned, black and unforgiving, a swirling abyss that seemed to welcome John's lifeless form as it dangled above.

A collective gasp rose from the onlookers, a sharp intake of breath that seemed to draw the colour from their faces. A woman screamed, a shrill, piercing sound that cut through the storm, her hands flying to her mouth as she stumbled backward. Others turned away, retching or covering their eyes, unable to bear the sight of the man who now hung like a broken marionette from the bridge.

The rookie officer, pale and wide-eyed, dropped to his knees, his breakfast threatening to come up as he stared, transfixed, at the swinging body.

Jack stood frozen, his mind refusing to process what had just happened. His heart pounded in his chest, each beat a painful reminder that he was still alive, still bound to the horrors of the world around him. He forced himself to move, his feet dragging as if mired in quicksand, and stumbled toward the railing. His hands gripped the cold, wet metal so tightly that his knuckles turned white, his breath coming in ragged, desperate gulps.

The chain creaked ominously under the weight, swaying slightly with each gust of wind that howled across the bridge. John's lifeless body hung there, suspended between the heavens and the depths below, a grotesque pendulum marking the seconds of a life extinguished. The cold, iron links dug deeper into his flesh, blood beginning to seep through his shirt collar, staining the fabric with spreading dark blotches.

Jack felt a deep, sickening dread settle in his stomach, a gnawing void that threatened to consume him from the inside out. His vision blurred with tears he hadn't even realized were there, tears mingling with the rain that now poured down in torrents, washing away the last remnants of hope. He had failed—failed to save a man, a father, a tortured soul who had been too far gone to reach.

Behind him, the scene unfolded in a chaotic blur. Officers scrambled to control the crowd, their shouts blending with the wail of sirens that approached from the distance. Flashing blue and red lights reflected off the wet pavement, casting eerie, distorted shadows across the bridge. The paramedics arrived, their faces set in grim lines as they rushed forward, though they already knew they were too late.

Sergeant Williams, his face ashen and grim, stepped up beside Jack, placing a heavy hand on his shoulder. "We did everything we could, Jack," he said quietly, his voice barely audible over the storm. But his words were hollow, meaningless against the backdrop of what had just transpired.

Jack didn't respond. His gaze remained fixed on John, on the life that had been snuffed out in an instant of desperation. He felt as though he were standing on the edge of the abyss himself, teetering on the brink, the weight of his own failures threatening to drag him down. He knew he would carry this moment with him forever, a scar that would never fully heal, a reminder of the darkness that lurked within even the most desperate of men.

The rain fell harder, a relentless deluge that hammered down on the bridge, washing away the blood, the tears, the traces of what had been a man driven to the brink of madness. The wind howled through the steel girders, a mournful wail that seemed to echo the despair in Jack's heart. He squeezed his eyes shut, trying to block out the image of John's broken body, but it was seared into his mind, an indelible mark that would haunt his dreams.

And Jack knew, in the deepest recesses of his mind, that he would never be the same again.

Chapter Thirty-Six

Jack Palace stood on the edge of the bridge, staring into the abyss where John had just plunged towards the murky waters below. The heavy chain John had secured to the metal rail was now taut, a lifeline to nowhere. The dark waters of the Humber churned beneath the bridge. The sky above mirrored the scene, its earlier sunset glow now replaced by a sombre, overcast gloom.

Jack's breath came in short, sharp bursts. He felt a sickening twist in his gut, a mixture of sorrow, horror, and an overwhelming sense of failure. He had been so close, so agonizingly close to saving them both. Now John was gone, swallowed by the darkness that had claimed his mind.

He forced himself to turn away from the edge, his eyes scanning the scene around him. The other officers were frozen, their expressions mirroring his own shock and disbelief. "Clear the bridge!" Jack barked, his voice cutting through the stunned silence. "Make sure no one is below!"

Sergeant Williams and the other officers sprang into action, their movements a flurry of urgency as they secured the area. Jack took a deep breath, trying to steady himself, to focus on the task at hand. He couldn't afford to lose his composure now; there was still work to be done.

Finally, after what felt like an eternity, the paramedics carefully lowered John's body to the ground. His neck hung at an unnatural angle, the chain still embedded in his flesh. The officers moved to cover him with a sheet, but not before Jack caught one last glimpse of his face—a face twisted in pain, in terror, in the final moments of a life that had spiralled out of control.

Jack turned away, unable to bear it any longer. He turned and started to walk slowly back to his car, his steps heavy, as if the weight of the world rested on his shoulders.

As he turned his attention back to the scene, something caught his eye—a movement, subtle but unmistakable, from the duffle bag John had left behind. It lay on the pavement, partially unzipped, its contents hidden in the shadows. Jack felt a chill run down his spine. Had he heard something? Had it moved?

His heart pounded harder as he approached the bag, each step feeling like a lifetime. The air around him seemed to grow colder, the sound of the river below fading into the background. He crouched down, his hand trembling as he reached for the zipper.

He hesitated, listening intently. There it was again—a faint rustling, almost imperceptible but undeniably there. His mind raced with possibilities, each one more dreadful than the last. He had to know. He had to see what was inside.

Jack approached the duffle bag with trepidation, his mind awash with dark imaginings. He braced himself for the worst, expecting to find the lifeless, decomposing remains of a young boy—a heartbreaking testament to John's descent into madness. The thought gnawed at him, threatening to undo his composure. His heart felt like a lead weight in his chest as he crouched beside the bag, each breath shallow and uncertain.

As he slowly unzipped the bag, the metallic teeth of the zipper seemed to echo loudly in the silence. Jack's hands trembled slightly, his mind racing through the possibilities of what he might see. He imagined Ethan's small body, lifeless and cold, and felt a wave of sorrow and rage. The world seemed to stand still, the surrounding darkness closing in on him as he prepared to face the grim reality within.

But as the bag opened, Jack's eyes widened in disbelief. Inside was not the rotting, decomposing corpse he had steeled himself to see. Instead, he saw a beautiful, angelic boy whose cheeks were flushed with new energy, looking back at him.

Ethan was alive.

For a moment, Jack stood there, shocked and rooted to the spot. The impossible had happened. The ritual, The Five—everything John had believed was true. Jack's mind reeled, struggling to comprehend the miraculous sight before him. Ethan's eyes, wide and bright, stared up at him, filled with innocence and confusion.

"Daddy?" the boy murmured, his voice soft and innocent, tinged with a faint hope that twisted Jack's heart.

Jack's throat tightened, his eyes misting over. "No, I'm not your daddy, Ethan. But I'm here to help you," he said gently, reaching out to lift the boy from the bag. His hands, so used to holding cold inanimate evidence, now cradled a living, breathing child.

As he held Ethan close, Jack felt a strange sense of responsibility wash over him. The child's warmth, his heartbeat against Jack's chest, was a stark contrast to the cold, harsh reality of the night. This child, brought back from the brink of death, was now in his care. Jack's mind swirled with questions and disbelief, but one thing was clear: Ethan needed him.

He turned and headed back to his car, cradling Ethan with a tenderness he hadn't known he possessed. The bridge behind him, the scene of John's final act of desperation, seemed to fade into the background.

Chapter Thirty-Seven

The hospital was a sprawling old building, its walls whispering tales of both hope and despair. As Jack Palace stood in the sterile, cold hallway outside Ethan's room, the fluorescent lights flickered sporadically, casting eerie shadows along the chipped off-white walls. The linoleum floor, dulled by years of foot traffic, squeaked faintly under his weight, adding to the uneasy silence that enveloped him.

Jack's thoughts were a tangled web of worry and confusion. The weight of responsibility pressed heavily on his shoulders, and he couldn't shake the feeling that something was terribly wrong. His mind wandered, unbidden, to the faces of the people he had failed before—cases where he had arrived too late, where his best hadn't been enough. The memory of a child's funeral flashed before him, the small coffin, the grieving parents. He swallowed hard, pushing the memory away, but it lingered, a ghost of his own making.

Inside Ethan's room, the air was unnervingly still. The bed linens were crisp and white, the walls painted a soothing pastel green—welcoming after the worn-out corridors outside. Medical equipment hummed softly, a reminder of the fragile balance between life and death. Ethan lay on the bed, his small frame almost swallowed by the blankets. The sight of him, so vulnerable, hooked up to various monitors, tugged at Jack's heart with a force he hadn't expected.

Lily, the nurse attending to Ethan, moved with the practised grace of someone who had spent years perfecting her craft. Her hands were gentle, her touch tender yet efficient as she adjusted the boy's blanket. In her late twenties, Lily had a quiet, nurturing presence that radiated calm. Her warm hazel eyes, always framed by chestnut hair neatly tied back, offered a glimmer of hope to those who needed it most. Jack noticed how she lingered for a moment, smoothing Ethan's hair, whispering something comforting that he couldn't quite hear. It was a small gesture, but one that spoke volumes of her character.

Lily had grown up in a small town, where she'd often listen to her grandmother's stories of working as a wartime nurse. Those stories had ignited a passion in her, a desire to heal and help, and it was clear in the way she moved, in the way she interacted with Ethan. Jack felt a pang of envy—how easily she could bring comfort, while all he could offer was uncertainty.

But the peace of the moment was short-lived. Jack's phone buzzed in his pocket, the vibration sharp against the quiet. The caller ID displayed *Unknown Number.* A frown creased his brow as he stepped out into the hallway to answer, leaving the tranquil room behind.

The hallway was dim, the shadows playing tricks on his eyes as the fluorescent lights continued their erratic flickering. The distant murmur of hospital staff reached his ears, blending with the occasional beep of medical devices. A porter trudged down the corridor, his cart squeaking with every push, his expression a mask of weary determination. An elderly woman in a wheelchair, a plaid blanket draped over her knees, was being pushed slowly by a younger woman—likely her daughter. They both gave Jack a polite nod as they passed, but there was a strange emptiness in their eyes, as if they too were haunted by the atmosphere of the hospital.

"Hello?" Jack answered, his voice low and cautious.

"Jack Palace." A distorted voice crackled through the receiver, sending a shiver down his spine. "You must protect the boy. They're coming for him. Keep him safe at all costs."

Jack's heart skipped a beat, his grip tightening on the phone. "Who is this? What do you mean 'they'?"

But the line went dead, the eerie silence on the other end more terrifying than any words could have been. A chill ran through him, settling deep in his bones. He shoved the phone back into his pocket, every instinct screaming at him to get back to Ethan's room.

When he pushed open the door, his breath caught in his throat. The room was empty. The bed was neatly made, as if Ethan had never been there. The monitors were turned off, their screens dark and silent, the soft hum that had once filled the room now replaced by a deafening void.

Panic surged through Jack, a cold, visceral terror that gripped him like a vice. He looked around wildly, desperate for any sign of where Ethan or Lily might have gone. He bolted back into the hallway, his heart pounding in his chest, each beat echoing in his ears like a drumbeat of doom.

His eyes scanned the corridor, seeking any hint of movement, any sign of the boy. The porter had disappeared; the elderly woman and her daughter were nowhere to be seen. The once-familiar hospital now felt like a labyrinth, each hallway stretching endlessly, each shadow concealing untold dangers.

"Lily!" he called out, his voice tinged with desperation. "Ethan!"

But there was no response, only the relentless flickering of the lights, the oppressive silence that had now taken on a life of its own. The hospital seemed to pulse with a malevolent energy, as if the very walls were closing in on him, trapping him in this nightmare.

Jack's mind raced, trying to piece together what had just happened. Who had called him? What were they warning him about? And where the hell was Ethan? He felt like he was losing his grip on reality, the line between sanity and madness blurring with every passing second.

Then, faintly, from somewhere deep within the bowels of the hospital, he heard a soft, childlike whisper. It was distant, almost inaudible but unmistakable. The whisper called his name, beckoning him deeper into the darkness.

Chapter Thirty-Eight

The Five: A Story of Power, Sacrifice, and the Impossible

By Cassandra Lane

There are tales that slither through the cracks of our collective consciousness, whispered in the dead of night, dismissed as myth and madness. But myths have a way of becoming real when we least expect it. This is one such tale, and it is not for the faint of heart.

For centuries, in the darkest corners of the world, there has been talk of a group known only as The Five. Some say they are demons, others believe them to be ancient gods. What they are doesn't matter. What they offer does.

The Five possess a power that defies comprehension, a power that can grant the deepest desires of those who are willing to pay the price. They can take your wildest dreams—your most impossible wishes—and make them reality. But nothing in this world, or the next, comes without cost.

I've seen what The Five can do. I've seen the dead brought back to life, a miracle that science can't explain and religion won't dare to touch. A young boy, Ethan Morrison, torn from the clutches of death. His father, John Morrison, gave everything to make it happen.

Everything.

John Morrison is no longer with us. He became a sacrifice, a vessel through which The Five performed their dark work. His soul was the currency, his life the payment. And now he is gone, swallowed by the darkness that The Five inhabit.

But Ethan lives. He breathes. He exists, where once there was nothing but a cold empty grave. And that, my readers, is the power of The Five.

You may ask yourself: is this a gift or a curse? The answer is both. The Five will give you what you want, but they will take what you value most in return. They are not benevolent, nor are they cruel. They are simply the balance, the ancient scales of desire and consequence.

If you seek them out, if you find the courage—or the madness—to summon The Five, know this: they will grant your wish. But they will also demand something in return. And you won't know what that is until it's too late to turn back.

The Five are not bound by the laws of man or nature. They do not care for morality, for right or wrong. They exist in a place beyond our understanding, and they offer a choice that few can resist. The chance to have the impossible. The chance to rewrite reality itself.

But ask yourself: what would you give? What would you sacrifice for that chance? Because once you've made your wish, there is no undoing it, no turning back the clock. You will pay the price, and you will live with the consequences.

Or you won't live at all.

I leave you with this warning, a whisper in the dark, a cautionary tale for those who dare to dream too big. The Five are real, and they are waiting. They can give you everything you desire, but the cost may be more than you're willing to pay.

And if you're still tempted—if you're still curious, if the allure of the impossible is too much to resist—then perhaps you, too, will find yourself standing at the

crossroads, ready to make a deal with the devil.
But remember: the devil always collects.

About The Author

Harry Minter was born in Bedfordshire but has lived in Hull for the past ten years with his wife, two small children and a dog. Harry is a producer and currently works in Leeds. His previous employment in the film industry inspired his creativity which led to screenwriting and now he has fulfilled his continuing passion for storytelling by writing a novel.

When Harry's not writing he enjoys the great outdoors with his family. He often runs and has completed several marathons.

'The Cost Of The Impossible' is his first book to be published through Blossom Spring Publishing.

www.blossomspringpublishing.com